CRANTHORPE
— MILLNER —
PUBLISHERS

THE ALCHEMIST'S DAUGHTER

TAMARA PRICE

Map artwork by Jenna Richards © Cranthorpe Millner Publishers

First published by Cranthorpe Millner Publishers (2025)

ISBN 978-1-80378-325-3 (Paperback)

www.cranthorpemillner.com

Cranthorpe Millner Publishers

A child that is not embraced by the village
will burn it down to feel its warmth.

– Ancient proverb

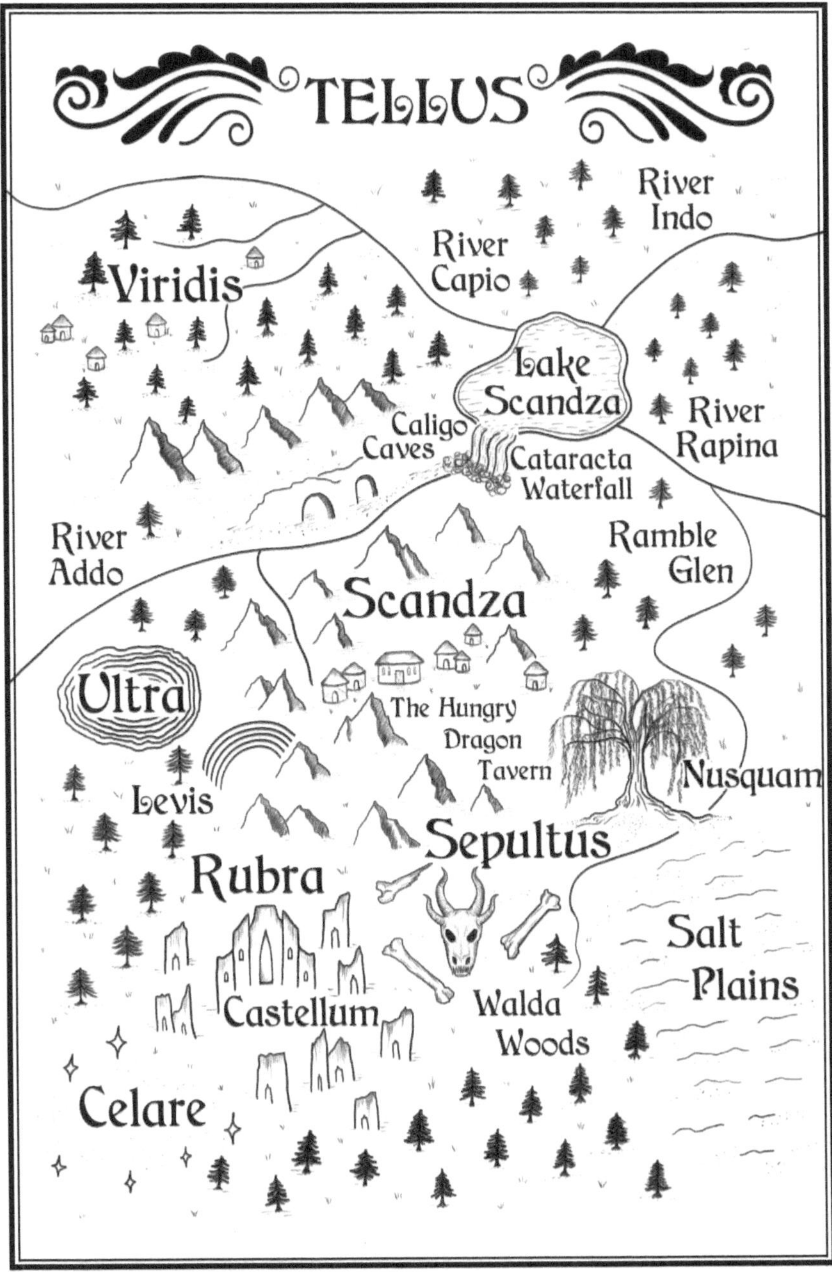

TELLUS
Viridis
River Capio
River Indo
Lake Scandza
Caligo Caves
Cataracta Waterfall
River Rapina
River Addo
Ramble Glen
Scandza
Ultra
The Hungry Dragon Tavern
Nusquam
Levis
Sepultus
Rubra
Salt Plains
Castellum
Walda Woods
Celare

PROLOGUE

Many Gen say that the birth of the alchemist's daughter was so violent it can only be likened to a death. A warning of what was to come. The previous eight moons in Tellus had been just as savage, with entire villages of Gen massacred. The catalyst for this violence was rumoured to be an event at the very centre of this land, in the city of Rubra. The rumours that circulated were so thickly covered in fear that the truth had suffocated. No individual knew exactly what had happened at the capital to lead to such chaos, such turmoil, each having their own version of events carved by their own agenda. But, despite these differing opinions, every single Gen in Tellus was united by one simple desire – they were all trying desperately to stay alive.

The Harvests began shortly afterwards. The villages closest to Rubra were the first to be attacked. But soon the raids grew unpredictable, with no logical geographical pattern to them. Unexpected locations were targeted; Gen of all creeds were captured, causing widespread confusion across Tellus. Some put up more of a fight than others; nevertheless, no souls were left behind during these ruthless attacks, with entire villages annihilated. In their wake, whispers of Harvesters with powers of evanescence snaked into the ears of the fearful neighbouring population.

Right now, however, in the forest of Viridis, none of this mattered. Beneath the canopy of emerald leaves she had fallen, doubled up with agony, dark red blood leaking into the ground beneath her. Tiny particles of dust clung to the beaded droplets before they joined as one, pooling onto the thirsty soil.

The mother, so blinded by the pain, was almost oblivious to the young man beside her. As an alchemist, he was a man of science, but after sending for help, he folded his fingers together and prayed to the old gods. In the world of Tellus, magic and science resided in uncomfortably close quarters, each needing the other to exist, and many Gen were untrusting of those who believed in the methodical over the mythological.

The woman's eyes squeezed shut, her breath escaping in a rush between pursed lips. The burning sunlight breaking through the canopy above sent flashes of veiny red and gold against the insides of her eyelids. Slowly, darkness crept in as a shadow blocked the light. Above, the moon engulfed the sun. Despite its circular presence being so unwelcome at this time of day, the moon glided confidently across the sky until the only remnants of the sun appeared as a blazing halo of fire.

At that very moment, a silhouette appeared between the twilight trees. Draped in cloth as black as night, gemstones glinting from his fingers, the witch doctor gave no introduction as he knelt in the blood by the woman's side.

The alchemist's daughter entered the world causing pain, her mother's screams tearing through the air until her throat was numb. The witch doctor held the child by a slippery foot, dangling, and slapped her hard, but the newborn didn't cry. The mother was quiet now, her hand clutching weakly to a pendant hanging around her neck as the man whispered soft kindnesses.

After a few moments, the child's eyes opened, seeing the world for the first time. Suddenly, the witch doctor recoiled, and the newborn landed hard on the earth. Yet even with the impact, no cries escaped the infant's lips. The alchemist rushed to pick up the child, cradling her carefully as he wiped away the dirt sticking to her bloodied skin. As the sun above slowly escaped the moon's embrace, the witch doctor mumbled words of magic into the wind, then he turned, fleeing through the woods. Never again would he return to Viridis.

Exhausted, the mother gazed at her child. As sunlight returned to fill the forest floor, she managed one weak word before blacking out.

"Pax."

CHAPTER ONE

Viridis, from above, resembled the outline of an oak leaf. Its border curved around the river that flowed through its centre, with trees thickening protectively around each village. It was a mostly tranquil land, populated primarily by Silva Gen.

At the centre of one of these villages sat a small house topped with a thick, thatched roof. Underneath this roof, on the second floor of this modest abode, was a laboratory. A laboratory cluttered with an array of apparatus: metal limbs and test tubes, wooden sculptures and potted plants, all lit up by a pulsing red glow emanating from the centre of the room. One desk was piled so high with a teetering tower of papers, scrolls, maps and plans, that a swift wind through the circular window would surely cause it all to come tumbling down. At the very centre of the room, at a second, larger table, covered with an array of small glass bulbs and a tangle of rainbow wires, sat the alchemist Creo Silva.

His tongue poked out slightly as he peered over his wire-rimmed glasses, concentrating on one of the intricate glass bulbs he held between his fingertips. Just above his head, suspended in a cylindrical glass tube, was a rather impressive nucleus. This nucleus was responsible for the fluctuating light rhythmically illuminating the interior of the lab. If you carefully studied a nucleus's centre, it revealed itself as tiny galaxies, with thousands of interlacing strands that were constantly moving, a mass of shifting energy. To the untrained eye, however, the nucleus appeared as a thick, slow-moving glob, occasionally prickling with static. The large glass tube encasing it stretched all the way to the ceiling, and from this tube ran several smaller pipes, webbing their way across the floor and back up towards the central desk. There they connected to two unframed glass screens hovering above the workstation, between which sat a slick metal cube. This bio aux, or natural computer, was powered entirely by nature. The whole of Tellus, in fact, was fuelled by the natural world, seamlessly transforming the power of the universe into energy. Those Gen who were intelligent enough (like most descendants of the Silva Gen) could harness that power for their own purposes through the creation of a bio aux. A process similar to photosynthesis allowed machines to be powered using practically zero fuel. As an alchemist, Creo Silva had created enough energy from the surrounding forest to power his home and to supply this central nucleus, thus creating the most powerful bio aux in all of Viridis.

Finally satisfied, Creo placed the bulb he was holding next to the tangle of wires and picked up a small glowing jar, his smile distorting through the glimmering glass. He planned to connect this much smaller nucleus to the elm tree outside, providing power to the garden decorations for Pax's Ortus celebration later this week. The small nucleus pulsed a deep green against the constraints of the jar. Gathering his latest invention into his arms, Creo made his way out of his laboratory and bounded down the stairs of his home.

"Where is Pax?" he said, entering the kitchen.

Celeste didn't reply; instead, she shrugged, not taking

her eyes from the kitchen window. The afternoon sunlight streaming in highlighted her almost-white hair, and a hint of gold glistened around the nape of her neck. She was wearing a white sundress to keep cool in the summer heat, for Viridis was hotter than usual for this time of year.

"Your chain," Creo said, pointing to her neck.

Celeste reached up and rearranged the collar of her sundress so the necklace was concealed again. Gold was a precious and scarce commodity in not only Viridis but the whole of Tellus, so it was a wise practice to keep it hidden. She sighed, plunging her hands into the velvety dough sitting plump on the kitchen counter, knocking the air from it with her fists. Creo could sense she was frustrated, and wanted to say something to comfort her, but he could never seem to find the right words. He wanted to tell her that she was a good mother even if her relationship with Pax was difficult. Creo managed an ease with Pax that Celeste surely must resent because her daughter could be fiery towards her, flicking from bright spark to incinerating rage in a heartbeat. Deciding to keep his thoughts to himself, Creo dumped a pile of glass and wires onto the just-cleaned kitchen table with a clatter.

"The guests will love this," he said proudly. "It changes colour announcing the arrival of different Gens as they enter the garden!"

Creo had decided that Pax's Ortus would be a great opportunity to invite their neighbours over to celebrate. Neighbours who had cautiously formed the habit of keeping their distance from the family. This was Creo's latest attempt to integrate them into the community.

"I know what you're thinking," he said, holding up one of the neon wires, "that these will ruin the illusion! But once this is all connected to the nucleus, the wires will be next to invisible!"

Now, Creo Silva was an intelligent man, yet he failed to realise his wild inventions were part of the reason the other Gens in Viridis avoided them, some going as far to be downright rude. Certain Gen even had the nerve to call them nids behind their backs, in whispers just loud enough to hear. Creo and his inventions, however, weren't the only reason the other villagers kept their distance.

"Debris has been located, collected and removed from the outer area in front of the house, using this apparatus," Am declared, entering the kitchen through the front door and holding a broom in their outstretched arm.

Celeste smiled, feigning enthusiasm as she wiped a dusting of flour from her hands and onto the skirt of her dress. "Great job, Am. Now, how about you hand me that knife over there, and I'll show you how to score these loaves, ready for the oven?"

After leaning the broom carefully against the wall, Am's blue eyes scanned the kitchen, locating the knife Celeste was referring to. Picking it up, Am passed it to Celeste, their hand wrapped around the sharp blade.

"Am!" Celeste exclaimed, taking the knife carefully from them. "Remember what we said about holding sharp objects? By the handle, yes? Otherwise, you could damage yourself."

"You asked to hand you the knife. The knife is in Am's hand," Am replied, their blue eyes recording Celeste's expression. They paused, then continued. "Am is undamaged; however, it is noted to hold knives by handles and not by blades."

Creo stood up from the table, wiping the grease on his

hands onto his white jacket, seemingly oblivious to Am's near miss.

"Am, how about you come with me into the garden and help hang up these lights?" he asked. Am nodded and followed him outside.

Celeste stared out of the kitchen window once again, searching the horizon. Pax had disappeared into the forest a few hours earlier, fists balled, and full of rage. Her daughter was just a few years younger than she had been when she had left the safety of her home for the first time. Toying with the chain around her neck, Celeste's mind darkened with thoughts of the time when Pax would eventually have to leave Viridis for good.

"Look at that!" said Creo, placing his hands on his hips and standing back to admire his work. "The most beautiful garden in all of Viridis!" He gently slapped Am on the back, prompting them to mirror the smile on his face. In front of them, small glass bulbs appeared to hover above their heads, in mid-air, criss-crossing from the wooden gate at the bottom of the path, all the way back up to the kitchen window. The bulbs twinkled, changing colours every few seconds. Tiny velox fairies who had been watching from the safety of the trees started to flock towards them, intrigued by the colours. They circled around the bulbs, and when satisfied they posed no threat, hummed a soft, high-pitched tune.

"So, as each Gen enters the garden on the evening of Pax's Ortus, the bulbs will change colour to alert us to their arrival!" Creo explained excitedly to Am. "Remember the information I gave you about each Gen? Well, this is very similar." Creo plucked one of the glass bulbs from the air, holding it in his hand. It transitioned to a throbbing, deep green.

"Silva Gen," he said, pointing to himself with one hand as he held the coloured glass in the palm of his other so Am could take a closer look. He gently placed it into Am's hand, and the colour disappeared instantly, leaving behind a transparent bulb. "Well" – he paused – "you get your very own special invisible colour!" He smiled, standing up and peering over the garden gate. "Now, where is Pax?"

"Pax is not here," replied Am, stating the obvious.

Creo chuckled. "I know. I was just thinking out loud."

"Thoughts are inside. Voice is outside. Sometimes both?" Am questioned.

Creo nodded, smiling. There was only a certain amount of information he could give Am at one time, yet their knowledge was growing every day. He could happily answer their questions for hours on end, discussing everything from the smallest of velox fairies to the mysteries of the universe, and Am would listen intently, taking it all in. Celeste and Pax, on the other hand, got tired of Am's constant enquiries. Creo had hoped Pax would become closer to Am, but she was growing up quickly and was itching to go on adventures of her own. He only hoped he had prepared her well enough for them. It felt like only yesterday he was cradling her as a newborn, and now she was much taller than him! Pax also shared his interest in alchemy, unlike her mother, who was a much more mythical Gen and a believer in the old magic. Together, they had raised Pax, and he prayed to the gods she had taken in the best of both worlds and would be able to control that fiery temper of hers. When Pax did eventually leave Viridis, he would miss his time in the forest with her, fishing, hunting and discussing inventions. In comparison, Am had only been with them for a few short moons, having originally been intended as a companion for Pax, but had become an important part of his life too. If Pax were here, she would tease him about getting sentimental, and he smiled to himself, a prickle in his eyes, considering how lucky he was to call her his daughter. All he wanted to do was to keep her safe. Keep all of them safe.

Am was silently and carefully studying Creo's face.

"Now, about that knife in the kitchen," Creo said, slightly embarrassed to have been caught daydreaming. "I may need to make a few adjustments so you don't hurt yourself. Is that okay?"

Am nodded, turning their body to face away from him.

Creo carefully lifted a silver panel on Am's back, revealing a glowing blue nucleus at the centre of their chest. Below it was a keypad.

"Just for the meantime, we'll make sure you can't handle anything too dangerous," he said, inputting a code and altering Am's internal settings. The nucleus at Am's centre flickered at the adjustments, its blue light appearing as a visible outline around Am's whole body. When he was finished, he replaced the panel flawlessly against Am's silvery casing.

Am turned around to face him. "Where is Pax?"

Just then, a head bobbing along the garden hedge distracted Creo. Someone was crouching in a very peculiar way, knees bent, trying not to be seen.

"Prod!" Creo called out, standing on his tiptoes to get a better view over the hedge. The short man continued waddling away, only stopping when Creo called out for a second time.

"Prod! Nearly missed you," Creo said, oblivious to Prod's discomfort.

"Oh, hello," Prod said reluctantly, straightening up and

peering over the hedge. Only half his red face was visible, due to his lack of height. His beady eyes glanced quickly at Am, then back to Creo. "Didn't see you there."

"We've just been decorating the garden for Pax's Ortus celebration in a few days' time." Creo held out a hand to direct Prod's eyes towards the lights, which were now all glowing green. "Did you get the invite? It's just we haven't heard back."

Prod loosened the collar around his neck, clearing his throat. "Ah yes, the invite. We could hardly miss it. It nearly gave my dear wife a heart attack when she opened the scroll." He laughed uncomfortably. "Took days to get rid of all that glitter after the explosion."

Creo beamed, pleased that the invitations had been a success.

"Just some harmless velox dust!" Creo said as a velox fairy landed on his shoulder in a timely fashion. "It doesn't hurt them." Creo picked up the creature between his thumb and forefinger, tapping it gently. A flutter of silver dropped into the air from its wings, making the tiny fairy sneeze.

Prod frowned. "Well, if we do come, will we get to see this laboratory of yours, Creo? The place you come up with all these crazy ideas?" he said, shooting another look at Am, who was scanning his portly face.

"Oh no!" Creo chuckled. "I just thought it would be a nice opportunity to celebrate with the community and a chance to get to know each other more. You know what they say: 'it takes a village!'"

Just then, Celeste entered the garden, stepping into a shaft of sunlight as the glass bulbs glistened gold above her head. Her presence made Prod smile, and this time it was genuine.

"Ah, Celeste! As beautiful as ever." He blushed.

Celeste smiled kindly, but Creo knew exactly what his neighbour thought, what all the neighbours thought, when they saw them together.

"I was just saying to Creo here, I'm not sure if—" All of a sudden Prod stopped speaking, his mouth forming into an 'o' shape as he raised a chubby finger, pointing at Celeste.

"Is-is that a gold necklace?" he whispered, his eyes widening.

Celeste's hand automatically reached up to her collar, covering the chain once more.

"Costume jewellery, I'm afraid!" Creo replied, laughing nervously. "I wish we had gold! Imagine the party we could throw for Pax if we were rich!"

Prod frowned, lowering his hand, his mouth turning into a thin line.

"So, will you come?" Creo asked again, changing the subject.

Prod inhaled deeply and sighed. "Look, Creo, I can't say we will. You know what Gen around here think." He glanced at Celeste. "An Ortus day can be a powerful event, and your daughter is…" Prod stopped mid-sentence as the welcoming smile faded from Creo's usually kind face.

Prod's voice became quieter as he glanced over his shoulder. "Well, maybe if there weren't so many… unsavouries at your place, Gen wouldn't be so inclined to keep their distance," he said, self-righteously. More loudly, he added, "You know we live in dangerous times, Creo! We have to keep our families safe! Good day!" He nodded, then disappeared behind the hedge again and carried on striding down the road.

"That man is of Silva Gen. Local to Viridis. Known for their command of nature," Am stated. "What are unsavouries?"

Creo smiled weakly, patting Am on their shoulder. "Some Gen are quick to judge others without getting to know them first."

"Pax isn't home yet," Celeste said, rubbing her arm, staring out towards the forest.

"A late dinner it is, then!" Creo replied.

"At mealtimes everyone is happy," said Am.

"Yes," said Celeste absentmindedly.

Suddenly, there was shouting in the distance. At first, it sounded like laughter, but it was too unfamiliar. An unsettling panic encircled them as the noise grew louder. Whatever was happening was moving nearer, getting closer to them. Then the screaming started. Someone was screaming. The air became thick with fear, and Celeste's face drained of colour. She had felt this before.

"What's going on?" Creo yelled at Prod as he hurried past the hedge again, this time in the opposite direction.

"They're coming!" he cried out, the street around him filling up with Gen spilling out of their houses. They ran out of their doors and into the street, pushing others out of the way. A small girl fell onto the road in the rush, gasped silently for air for a few seconds, then began to bawl.

Above their heads, the green and gold glass bulbs flickered frantically. They stopped, bleeding into a colour of deep, dark red, throbbing faster and faster, again and again. They burst, shattering all over the garden. Creo and Celeste threw their arms up instinctively as Am stood still and was showered in tiny fragments of glass.

"Inside! Now!" Creo yelled, pushing Am and Celeste up the garden path and into the kitchen. Together, they tumbled inside, and he quickly bolted the door behind them.

"Oh no, oh no…" Celeste muttered as she slumped to the floor, slivers of glass glinting in her hair like magic. "They've found us."

"What is happening?" asked Am calmly.

"Quickly, upstairs! Into my lab!" shouted Creo. When Celeste didn't move, Creo roared again, loudly enough to startle her. "Celeste!" Shaking, she took his hand, and he pulled her to her feet. Frantically, they made their way up the wooden staircase. Creo slammed the laboratory's door shut and rushed towards one of the large, vertical screens.

"Come on, come on…" he muttered nervously under his breath, swiping at the glass.

The red light from the central nucleus reflected on Am's silver face. Unsure of how to mirror the emotions in the room, Am repeated their question. "What is happening?"

"I'm going to give you some extra information. Just as soon as this bloody bio aux loads," Creo said, typing frantically.

"Bloody is an inappropriate word," said Am.

Ignoring their comment, Creo focused on Celeste. "We must stay calm and pray to the gods that Pax is far enough away. I'll leave everything she needs with Am." His voice trembled, as if he was trying to convince himself of the veracity of his own words.

In the distance came another terrifying scream, followed by a rumbling, as deep as thunder, shaking the ground.

"Quickly!" said Celeste, the magnitude of what was happening sinking in as a stampede of approaching hooves grew louder.

The metal cube between the screens opened with a satisfying hiss.

"At last!" said Creo, pulling out a tiny silver plate. "Am, ready for that extra info?" he asked.

"Yes," Am replied.

Creo lifted the panel on Am's back once more, clicking the small rectangular plate into place.

"Okay?" he asked.

Am faced him and nodded. "Okay."

"Do they know?" Celeste asked, grabbing Creo's shoulders, tears glazing over her amber eyes.

Creo shook his head. "After all these years? I really don't know, but we have to do everything we can to stop this, once and for all."

"She's not ready," whispered Celeste.

Creo took a deep breath. "She has to be." He paused. "I just hope she chooses the right path."

An enormous thud on the door downstairs made Creo and Celeste jump simultaneously.

"What's that?" asked Am, undisturbed.

"They're here," said Creo.

"Oh, Pax," Celeste sobbed, her knees giving way.

Crouching down to her level, Creo looked deeply into her eyes. "I'm with you." She nodded slowly, and he touched her neck softly, gesturing to her gold chain. "We need to leave it for her."

"I'm so sorry," Celeste said, "for everything." With Creo's help she stood quietly, removing the chain and placing it around Am's neck. Its removal left an empty space above her heart.

A splintering crash from downstairs announced their intruders were now inside the house. A high-pitched, sinister voice called out, "Where are you, little caro?"

Creo turned to Am. "I'm shutting you down now," he whispered, pressing a code into their keypad and clicking the panel closed.

"Why?" asked Am. "Who is downstairs?"

Creo hugged Am silently, then directed them to sit beneath the large desk.

"Twenty seconds." He smiled sadly.

Am smiled back, observing as Celeste and Creo pushed a heavy set of drawers in front of the desk, blocking them safely underneath.

Ten… nine… eight…

Hidden from view, Am watched through a small gap between the pieces of furniture as Celeste took Creo's hand.

Seven… six… five…

Together, they walked towards the door of the laboratory.

Four… three… two…

Towards the screams outside.

One…

CHAPTER TWO

I wish she was dead.

Pax kicked the dirt under her feet as she stomped her boots into the well-used track through the forest near her home. It always took her much longer than it should to shake off the rage. It lingered in her blood, almost as if she could feel it pulsing through her veins. Ironically, in the old tongue Pax's name translated as 'peace'. This evening, after yet another outburst, she had stormed out, slamming the wooden door behind her and leaving her mother calling out to her in the distance. Pax continued on into the forest at a determined pace, crunching through the undergrowth, sending small orbs of light glistening above the ferns as her heavy footsteps sent velox fairies fleeing from her path.

Above her, the waning moon was thinly veiled by a hazy summer sky bruised with blues and purples, and the deeper she walked into the forest, the more the trees thickened and her anger thinned. Her pace slowed, the heat in her blood starting to cool, her breath evening out. When a clearing in the greenery appeared, she slowed, noticing movement out of the corner of her eye. From a distance, part of the forest floor appeared to be moving, but on closer inspection, the activity morphed into a carpet of fire ants, shiny black shells streaked with a slash of red, a warning to its predators. Quietly, Pax knelt closer, feeling the tiny vibrations from the creatures, pulsing through the earth. She could imagine the movement underground, the heartbeat of the colony like an annoying throb in her ears. Her senses had been growing rapidly over the last few moons, her parents both nagging her to practise honing her skills. If she concentrated hard enough, she was beginning to have some sort of control over her powers, but it required great patience, and that was something Pax severely lacked.

But, right now, with nobody watching or judging her, and surrounded by the sanctuary of the forest, Pax could feel everything around her: the cool wind wrapping itself around each individual leaf in the canopy above; the force of the stream in the valley below, carving its violent path through the rocks; the death of overripe Scuttleberries dropping to the ground; the sorrow of decaying remains nearby in the bushes. Here, in Viridis, encased in whispering trees, she felt safe.

Silencing her mind, Pax stared at the throbbing nest of ants, her brow furrowed in concentration as she blocked out all the distractions around her. Finally, her eyes locked onto her target: the queen. Difficult to spot unless you knew what to look for – larger than the rest of the ants, with a fierce halo of scarlet. Pax watched as the queen crawled over the dirt, through dozens of other, smaller ants. She could feel the power this tiny creature held over all the others in the colony. It tingled in the air. The queen's body was reflected in Pax's dilating pupils, then, the insect stopped. It slowly lifted into the air. First the head, then the abdomen, until all six legs were hovering above the ground. The queen struggled helplessly, rising until she was level with Pax's gaze, suspended in mid-air. A thought entered Pax's head: that she could so easily kill the insect, just by using her mind. She imagined the exoskeleton crushing in on itself, compressed until, finally, it stops breathing. She knew she could easily eradicate the entire colony. The queen ant wriggled, in limbo. Pax narrowed her eyes, flicking her chin up ever so slightly. The tiny insect started to spin slowly in the air. It stopped, frozen, apart from a slight quiver of pain in its antennae. A few tense seconds passed. Pax sighed, lowering the queen back to the dirt, unharmed. The worker ants fussed around their leader, and soon the queen disappeared safely into the static of the nest.

The sky above started bleeding into reds, signalling the end of the departing day. Pax stood up, dusting the dirt off her dark green cotton shirt. It was one her mother had sewn by hand. Not exactly fashionable, but it was comfortable, so she wore it nearly every day despite it being faintly stained with dirt and blood that never completely washed out. Pax planned to wear it for her upcoming Ortus day, even though her mother would no doubt urge her to wear a dress instead, and although Pax wasn't against wearing dresses, she would rebel just so she wouldn't have to appease her mother.

Making her way down to the river, Pax decided she *would* catch dinner for her family, like her mother had requested. Not as a peace offering for her earlier outburst, but because she loved to fish.

Pax followed the well-trodden path, down through the forest at the centre of Viridis, which had been her home since she was born. Through the thicket of greenery, distant snow-capped mountains were only visible on a day as clear as today, and crashing waterfalls rumbled in the distance. The spectacular view, however, was wasted on Pax, who had become so accustomed to the familiar backdrop of her home she was unable to appreciate its beauty. She longed for adventures beyond the mountains, to see exciting new landscapes and explore the rest of Tellus.

Light danced on the forest floor, a mixture of the setting sun and velox fairies, who were calmer now that Pax was stepping through their habitat more lightly. She moved through the trees and made her way down a steep bank, stopping at the water's edge. She had chosen this body of water as it joined River Capio further downstream, which made it fertile and a perfect spot for setting traps. Removing her backpack and placing it on the ground, she watched the surface of a quieter pool and waited for signs of life. Of course, she could try to use her emerging powers to catch the tentamenta for supper, but Pax loved the hunt. Her father was deceptively skilful in outdoor pursuits, for an alchemist who spent most of his time in a laboratory, and he had taught her many skills. Ever since she had been banished from school, the forest had become her classroom, and her father, the most patient of teachers.

After setting the fishing nets, Pax waited for the silvery waters to calm, watching for evidence of her prey. As the ripples subsided, her reflection stared back. Her auburn hair was made all the more striking by a strip of silvery blonde at the parting, framing her face. Her mother often said that silver streak was the only similarity they shared.

Pax's muddy fingers caught in tangled knots as she brushed her hair behind her ear. Her mother, Celeste, was beautiful. Gen commented on it all the time, stopping and staring at her beauty, but she never appeared to notice. Pax knew she wasn't as pretty as her mother. She was already a lot taller than her, yet Gen frequently stared at her, too, for very different reasons. Others were often kept at bay by her unwelcoming persona, that and the rumours of course. 'Such a violent girl', the neighbours would say. After she had left school, the other children called her a nid behind her back but were always too scared to say it to her face. Pax longed to make them regret how they had treated her, to turn their mocking laughter into apologetic tears, and the excitement of that possibility tingled on her skin.

Her Ortus day was fast approaching – a celebration when a Gen her age comes into their power. Of course, the range of abilities varies greatly. Some Gen only gain the capacity to levitate small objects, with the control of larger items much more uncommon. Others acquire more artistic traits: the ability to mesmerise others with a song or create art that comes to life. There were also the more athletic pursuits, such as breathing under water, gaining incredible strength or running faster than the wolves. Most Gen, however, don't receive any powers at all. Or those they do gain are deemed so forgettable that they do just that: forget them.

Then there are the rarer powers. A select few gain the ability to read others' minds. Some Gen are capable of controlling elements, manipulating fire or using water as a weapon. Not very common these days, but everyone hopes to be special. History, however, shows us that these powers are often seen as curses rather than blessings. Gods walk amongst us in Tellus – those who came into great power long ago. Many became immortal through unrighteous means. Great power, it is told, is often not used for good.

Movement on the water's surface broke Pax's thoughts. Loosening her laces, she kicked off her black leather boots and dived into the cold. Blinking under the water, to adjust, she located the net. It was teeming with wriggling tentamenta, their scaly skin bulging against their woven cage. Unhooking them like her father had taught her, Pax swam up, bursting through the surface. The sounds of the forest met her ears: chattering magpies and the melodic hum of the fairies. Wet hair clinging to her face, she dragged the net to the edge of the water and sat down on the riverbank. The fat, slippery creatures writhed next to her, enough for two meals at least.

Deciding to dry off in the warm evening sun before heading back home, Pax pulled out her penknife from her shirt pocket. She never left home without it because it always proved useful, whether it was for carving animals out of wood, gutting tentamenta or throwing at targets carved into trees. Flicking open the blade, she sliced into a thick stick she'd found on the ground. However, whittling wood alone in the forest wasn't exactly what Pax had wanted to do this evening. A group of Gen her age were having a gathering to celebrate the Ortus of a local boy, two villages over from hers. Her mother had forbidden her to go, saying it was unsafe, which had sent Pax into a rage. What did she mean 'unsafe'? She was nearly fifteen! Pax knew how to protect herself, allowed to roam and hunt in the forest alone but not allowed to socialise and have fun. Her mother was being unfair, and Pax wasn't quite ready to return home just yet. Pax had conveniently forgotten to explain to her mother that she hadn't actually been invited to the Ortus celebration. She had hoped that she could just turn up, blend in, build up the courage to talk to some new Gen, ones that didn't know her or think she was dangerous. Where no one would call her a nid. It was hard not having friends her own age; of course, there was Am, but sometimes Am could be so annoying.

Just at that moment, a dead velox fairy dropped at her feet.

"Oh, Felis!"

A few metres above, her furry pet dragat was hovering over her head. He would always bring her an offering if he sensed she was down. Dragats were notoriously hard to train, her mother had told her, and irritatingly, she was right. It must be the dragon genes in them. Felis, deciding his job of changing Pax's mood was done, flapped his wings and circled down to land in her lap. He started purring as she stroked his fur and scratched his wings.

A branch snapped somewhere nearby, and Pax jumped to her feet, sending Felis rolling into the dirt. Above, a magpie cackled into the air. Instinctively gripping her penknife, Pax quietly made her way over to the bushes where the sound had come from. She crept through a parting in the undergrowth, carefully pushing the brambles to one side and peering down into the valley.

The sight below made Pax gasp. A herd of wild tricorns were gathering by the river. They were rarely seen in the wild, and she had always been curious about them. Slowly, she stood up, Felis landing quietly on her shoulder. Several of the huge beasts were congregating in the distance. Their leathery skin stretched over powerful legs, three massive horns protruding from their foreheads. Pax desperately wanted to get closer but didn't want to startle them; a stampede could easily kill her. She could sense their power from here. The tricorns moved slowly down to the water's edge, lowering their heads to drink, their nostrils flaring as they gulped down liquid to quench their thirst. Pax watched on, mesmerised, until the hairs on the back of her neck stood on end. Someone was nearby. She was being watched.

"Beautiful creatures, aren't they?" said a voice.

Quickly, she turned around to be met with a short, bearded man standing in front of her. Pax's face flushed, frustrated with herself that she hadn't reacted more quickly, distracted by the herd of tricorns.

"Forgive me! One didn't mean to startle you. Allow me to introduce myself," the man said, removing his pointed felt hat. "I am Arator, of Probus Gen. Hailing from Scandza. Pleased to make your acquaintance."

The man bowed so low that his nose nearly touched the ground. He waited in this awkward position, then, after a few moments, he glanced up at Pax.

"And you are…?"

"Oh! I'm Pax. Of Silva Gen. I live here in Viridis," she blurted out, finding herself curtsying to match his formality, unused to Gen interacting with her so politely.

Discreetly, she closed the blade of her penknife and slid it back into her pocket. Arator straightened to upright once again and replaced his hat on top of his frizzy head of hair. Pax was sure a slight gust of wind would send it flying off down the valley.

"Ah yes, the Silvas! A fine Gen. They have given us Probus permission to tame tricorns on their land." His beard moved slightly, suggesting a smile, although Pax couldn't see his lips.

Pax nodded. "I've never met anyone that could tame tricorns before. They're the most fascinating creatures." On hearing this remark, Felis launched himself off her shoulder and flew up into the trees in disgust.

"Well, we are lucky; I'll say that!" Arator said proudly. "Tricorns choose to work with us from time to time. We are the only living Gen left whom they allow to do so!"

Pax gazed down at the herd again and could now see the silhouettes of a few other Gen making their way towards the tricorns. They removed their hats and bowed low in front of the huge animals, appearing to talk to them.

"I've never seen them up close. That's so figo," said Pax, almost to herself.

"Yes. Very, er, figo," replied Arator. He was not fond of the slang used by the younger Gen these days. "Now you must excuse me. We aim to be out of the forest by nightfall. I suggest you do the same. It's not safe to be out alone so close to the Blood Moon." He doffed his hat and strode purposefully down the bank to join his group.

After taking one last look at the herd retreating towards the sunset, Pax gathered her things into her backpack. If she packed it neatly enough, she could fit a surprising amount into it, and it nestled snuggly against her back, freeing her hands for when she was working in the forest. The tentamenta she had caught were now twitching limply in the net by her feet.

"Come on, Felis," she called up into the trees. "You know you're my favourite really."

By the time Pax had finished lacing up her boots, Felis had flown down to join her. Yawning as she walked out of the glade and back towards home, she rubbed her eyes, probably sore from swimming under the water. As she made her way back through the forest, Pax decided not to tell her parents that she had been talking to a stranger in the woods. She didn't need to be in any more trouble than she already was.

CHAPTER THREE

Felis opened his wings, soaring silently in the air above Pax's head. A flash of silver darted in front of him, making the slits in his irises narrow, and with a slight lean to the left, he slowed and circled back around in pursuit of a tiny velox fairy into the treetops. The terrified creature sent plumes of brown glitter into the air as Felis whizzed after it relentlessly, enjoying the thrill of the chase more than planning on actually catching it. But when he flew through the cloud of brown, it filled his nostrils with the most pungent smell, making the dragat grimace and sneeze. The velox fairy giggled with glee as it made its escape, changing colour to camouflage into the leaves.

Beneath this altercation, Pax was dragging her feet, trying to think of an excuse as to why she would be arriving back home so late. Talking to Arator and watching the tricorns had delayed her return, and the sun had set nearly two hours ago. It was dark now, but the path home was well-lit by the moonlight. Pax knew that when she arrived, she would receive no thanks for catching the tentamenta for dinner, the focus solely being on the fact that she was late, out after dark and alone. It was almost as if her mother didn't trust her. As Pax imagined the argument waiting at home for her, a hot prickle crept over her skin, her temper mingling with her developing powers. She paused, purposely taking a deep breath like her father had shown her, and let her jaw unclench.

Eventually, the path joined the street into her village. As Pax walked up the central street, she noticed the curved outline of hoof prints in the dirt. Not just one or two but many, pounded hard into the ground all the way into the village. Few Gen in Viridis owned horses, making this an unusual sight. Frowning, she slowed her steps. She held her breath to listen for something up ahead that might suggest who had left this trail. What she expected to hear she wasn't sure – more horses perhaps? But her ears were met with nothing but silence. It felt strange, almost *too* quiet, even at this late hour. As she made her way further down the street she'd walked down so many times before, it felt different, as if she was out of place. Dull dread grew sharper with each step she took. She turned her head slightly, trying to notice what was different, a rusty smell filling her nostrils. Her heart started pounding in her chest as every muscle in her body tensed with fear. Then Pax broke into a run, her footsteps echoing loudly down the deserted street.

She kept running, Felis flapping his wings above her to keep up, until her house came into view. At first, the sight filled her with a sense of relief, and she stopped, leaning on her garden gate to catch her breath. It gave way under her weight, crashing to the ground. Pax looked around to see if any of the neighbours had been disturbed, but the street was still empty, and oddly, none of the neighbouring houses had any lights on. It was late, but not so late that everyone would be in bed already. Her eyes focused under the moonlight, and Pax could see that other gardens' gates were hanging off their hinges, leading to front doors left wide open, and yet not one Gen was around. A wave of fear washed over her as she knelt and studied the gate. The top hinge was snapped off, as if someone had kicked it down. Pax left it on the ground, stepping over it quietly and into her garden. Something crunched beneath her feet, and she lifted her boot to find glass shards embedded in the sole. More fragments were scattered over the garden all the way up to the front door, which was ajar. Her bag slid off her shoulders and slumped to the ground. Pax tentatively stepped towards the entrance of the house, then, swallowing hard, she pushed on the damaged door. At first it caught on something wedged beneath it, so she pushed it again, harder this time, and it gave way, scraping nosily against the floor. Inside, the kitchen was dark.

"Dad?" Pax whispered into the silence.

The kitchen was a mess: broken glass, chairs and tables upended; crockery smashed on the floor. It was unrecognisable, like it was someone else's house; it even smelt unfamiliar. As Pax stepped into the kitchen, heat flooded through her body, rising from her feet, swirling in her stomach and into her head. Her mouth went dry. Everything felt wrong. The room was spinning, and her knees buckled. As she sank to the floor, she didn't even feel her skin being pierced by shards of glass.

After a few moments, Felis flew down, folded his wings and sat next to her. The small dragat was worried that his normally loud owner was now so quiet, so he placed a concerned paw on her leg. The gentle touch snapped Pax back into reality. Pushing her hands through her hair, she rose to her feet, needing to check the rest of the house.

Making her way upstairs, she reached into her pocket, pulling out her penknife and flicking open the blade. She stopped outside her mother's room. It was quiet, so carefully, she pushed the door open, to be welcomed by a scene of careless destruction: clothes strewn across the floor, furniture smashed and yet more glass. But the room was so very still. No one was there. Pax went inside, taking care not to step on her mother's clothes, even though many items had already been torn to shreds. The dressing table, where as a child she had watched her mother get ready, now held a mirror spidered with cracks. Pax made her way over to the nightstand, picking up a frame that had been knocked over. Inside was a photograph of her mother holding her when she was younger. Pax was maybe three years old, her fierce red hair already unruly. The sunlight behind Celeste gave her a pale aura, and she was smiling at the camera. Pax couldn't remember it being taken. Surprisingly, the glass of the frame remained intact. Amongst all the other destruction, it remained unbroken. Pax placed it, upright, back on the table.

Slowly, she backed out of the room, gripping her knife as she made her way quietly down the hall. A dull noise made her jump. Spinning around, she raised the blade in her fist as Felis landed nosily at the top of the stairs. Settling down, he started cleaning his wings with his tongue. Pax sighed with relief, put a finger to her lips and stepped towards her father's laboratory.

The door was open, and inside was a mess. It was always untidy in there, but this was destructive. The large table at the centre had been upturned, and underneath her feet, the floor was sticky and wet. She lifted her boot, to see red, and for an awful moment she thought it was blood before realising it was the remains of the central nucleus. The large glass tube that housed it had been smashed, some of the shards still protruding from the ceiling. The bio aux's screens were also shattered, alongside the tubes. She thought it strange that the raiders would destroy such a valuable item; in fact, it appeared that nothing had been taken at all. Nothing was missing, except, of course, her family.

Pax flipped the penknife closed and put it back into her trouser pocket, her shoulders relaxing a little. The intruders seemed to have gone. The feeling of relief quickly turned to nausea. Heat flushed in her cheeks, and saliva pooled into her mouth. Retching as her stomach twisted, she bent over and threw up. She wiped her mouth on her sleeve and noticed blood trickling from her knee; a shard of dark red glass was embedded in her skin. Carefully, she pinched the shard between her thumb and forefinger, pulling it out. The edge of the fragment glistened gold in the light. Blood beaded in the cut and ran down her leg. She stumbled backwards and tripped, slamming onto her back, pain ripping down her spine. Sucking air through her teeth, Pax waited for the pain to subside, trying to see what she had tripped over. There, protruding from underneath the upturned desk, was a motionless silver leg.

Pax had no trouble lifting the large table, easily pushing it to one side. Am lay still, eyes shut, but there appeared to be no damage on their body. Pax gently positioned Am onto their side, revealing the deactivated nucleus above their control panel. Trying to calm her frantic mind, she recalled how to input the code, just like her father had shown her, and punched in the numbers. Nothing happened. Biting her lip, Pax input the code more carefully the second time.

The nucleus at Am's centre lit up, light chasing the entire outline of Am's body. Their blue eyes opened as a soft whirring filled the room. After a few seconds, Am sat up.

"Hello!" they said, cheerily.

"Oh, Am!" Pax almost yelled. "You're okay! What happened?"

"When?"

"Today! Here! Before you were shut down!" Pax replied, relieved but also slightly annoyed at the need for clarification. Am paused for a few seconds, reviewing their internal nucleus.

"We went upstairs to the laboratory. Someone was downstairs. Creo gave me information. Celeste held his hand. Then it went black," Am replied.

"Who was downstairs?"

"I don't know. They said 'Where are you, little Caro?' Am did not scan them."

Caro? Who is Caro? Pax thought, frantically trying to remember if she had heard this name before.

"What information did Da— Creo give you?" she asked.

More whirling as the nucleus's blue light flickered in Am's eyes.

"Only one piece of information can be released at one time. For safety purposes. Would you like the first?" Am asked.

"Yes, yes!" replied Pax, agitated.

Am's eyes shut, then opened again in a bright flash of neon green.

> *Danger awaits you on this Quest,*
> *The power inside, you must possess.*
> *Below Blood Moon, save your kin,*
> *Travel to a place of immortal sin.*

Slowly, Pax stood up, her eyes wide. What was this? Some kind of riddle? She frantically looked around the room. The bio aux had been destroyed. There was no way of gaining any more information. What had been programmed into Am was all that was left.

Am's eyes turned blue again as they waited for instructions from Pax.

"We need to go," said Pax, her voice rising. "Get up. Now!"

Pax ran out of the laboratory and back down the corridor, into her bedroom. Felis decided her pace meant something exciting was happening and flew after her, intrigued. Inside her room was a mess, but it appeared everything was still here. With no time to be offended by the damage caused, she opened her wardrobe, pushing aside hanging clothes to reveal the shelf at the back where all her camping equipment was stored. Her shelter was rolled up neatly from her last trip with her dad. She grabbed it, throwing it onto the floor. Patting herself down, she checked that her penknife was back in her pocket. Then she pulled some spare clothes off the hangers and threw them on top of the tent, along with a small blanket.

Pax glanced around the room, checking if there was anything else that would be useful to take with her, and something caught her eye. There, on the floor, was a small wooden tricorn. A toy her father had carved for her when she was younger, demonstrating how to whittle wood. For years, it had been her favourite toy; she'd played with it, talked to it, telling the tiny wooden creature of her dreams of adventure. It had been a comfort for her when she was alone, when others wouldn't play with her. When she was afraid to go to sleep, her father had tucked the toy in next to her under the blanket, thinking that she had been scared of imaginary monsters under the bed. As a child, Pax did not have the words to describe that wasn't what she was afraid of. What had frightened her the most were the monsters living inside her head. Living inside *her*.

Her wooden tricorn had been crushed. Two of the horns had been snapped off, and one of its legs was missing. Pax's jaw tightened. Gathering the camping items into her arms, she made her way back down the stairs, her footsteps louder now, leaving her broken childhood toy behind.

At the bottom of the stairs, Am was waiting patiently. "Are we going on a trip?"

"Of course. It's not safe here." Pax said, the word 'Danger' ringing in her ears. She looked at Am, who clearly didn't understand the gravity of the situation. "We're going on an adventure," she said, trying to sound calmer. "We have to pack quickly. Can you grab my bag, please? It's outside."

Am manoeuvred around the kitchen door, which was still hanging on one hinge, and disappeared into the garden. Pax picked up a loaf of bread off the kitchen floor and dusted it off. Her mother must have baked this earlier, and Pax felt sick at the thought of the last time she had seen her, full of hate and spiteful words. It all felt so foolish now. Opening the cupboard, she found some crab apples and an empty glass bottle with a cork stopper.

Am returned to the kitchen holding Pax's rucksack and the net, which was full of now-dead tentamenta.

"Which bag is correct?" asked Am, their arms raised in the air.

Grabbing her rucksack, Pax shoved the items she had

collected into it. She clipped the rolled-up tent securely underneath, thinking about all the times she had been camping with her dad. She could feel herself welling up. *Snap out of it,* she told herself.

"That's a net," she said, pointing to Am's hand, "for fishing. We need that too, so tip that catch out because we're leaving." The dead creatures slopped onto the kitchen floor.

Exactly where she was going, Pax didn't know. The cryptic message her father had left with Am kept replaying over and over in her head, her gut telling her to leave, that it wasn't safe anymore here in her home. Maybe she should head to a nearby village, where the Ortus celebrations had been, or she could try and catch up to Arator and the rest of the Probus Gen, in search of help.

But it was late now, so Pax decided instead they would head deep into the forest. She felt safe there, and she knew her way around. They would camp for the night and go in search of help at break of day.

Securing her rucksack onto her back, she headed out of the door and down the garden path. Checking to make sure Am and Felis were following, she took one last look at her home. Having spent so long desperate to leave this place, she never expected it to be like this. Then, under the light of the moon, Pax led them towards the darkness.

CHAPTER FOUR

The oval moon was high in the night sky by the time they reached a clearing Pax knew well. It was located near a freshwater stream and a thicket of bushes that would provide them with shelter from the wind. It was also a good place to keep a look out for, well, whatever she needed to be wary of.

After instructing Am to collect dry fallen branches small enough for firewood, Pax secured the rope of the shelter between two trees. Gripping it around her fists, she pulled it taut between her fingers, expertly tying a knot. Flicking open her penknife, she cut off the excess rope, cleanly slicing the fibres with ease. In the darkness, the sounds of the forest were amplified. Everything was making her jump: roars of tricorns in the far distance, velox fairies snoring in the trees above. Felis, on the other hand, had curled up inside the shelter as soon as it was finished, unbothered by the noises of the night.

Once Am returned carrying a neat pile of sticks, Pax stacked them next to the shelter, deciding not to light a fire tonight in case it drew unwanted attention. She would light it at break of dawn instead.

"Is this a good time to resume your studies?" Am asked. "Our last biology lesson was looking at the components that make up blood."

"Now is really not the time, Am," Pax replied taking the

glass bottle from her bag. She made her way down to the stream, removed the stopper and submerged it in the water. Her mind was still racing; she was too manic to formulate any kind of plan about what she should do in the morning. When the bottle was full, she replaced the stopper and climbed back up the bank to the camp, sitting down on a fallen tree trunk next to Am, who was watching her intently. Pax took out the loaf her mother had baked, comforted only slightly by the familiar smell, and sliced into it with her knife.

"What does bread taste like?" Am asked.

Picking up a slice, Pax tore apart the crust between her fingers and popped a piece into her mouth. As she chewed, she mumbled, "Crunchy on the outside, fluffy in the middle." She swallowed. "It tastes like home."

Deciding she wasn't that hungry anymore, Pax wrapped the rest of the loaf back up neatly in the cloth, placing it back into her bag, away from the woodland creatures who might like a nibble in the night. Am was sitting next to her, calmly, when something glinted in the moonlight.

"Mum's necklace!" Pax gasped.

"Yes, Celeste put it around my neck," Am said, removing the chain and handing it to Pax.

The solid gold disc felt cold as it touched Pax's skin, the chain snaking into her palm, glinting in the moonlight. It was heavier than Pax had imagined, especially for something her mother had worn every day. She had never seen her without it and never been allowed to hold it. Up close, it was beautiful, with an intricate symbol engraved at the centre. An ambigram. The letter A interlocked with another, just upside down. Around the edge were six glistening gemstones: blue, green, silver, white, black and red. Each one equally spaced around the symbol. She turned it over in her palm, and engraved into the back were the initials S. G.

Pax knew it had sentimental value, and she felt honoured that her mother had left it for her. But it also caused a pit to form in her stomach. It felt so final, like a goodbye. Carefully, she slipped the chain around her neck, and instantly her mind calmed.

"Can you repeat that clue again?"

"Yes," Am replied, eyes flashing green.

> *Danger awaits you on this Quest,*
> *The power inside, you must possess.*
> *Below Blood Moon, save your kin,*
> *Travel to a place of immortal sin.*

Pax had no idea why her father had left a riddle and not a straightforward instruction, but she trusted he must have had a good reason. The place of immortal sin, however, didn't really sound like somewhere she wanted to go.

Then, from somewhere in the dark, came a rustling, a noise unlike the others of the night, and it sounded uncomfortably close. Pax put her hand up to ensure Am stayed quiet.

"Wait here."

Crouching, she kept low in the bushes as she made her way through the trees towards the sound, the moonlight illuminating her path just enough for her to see. A velox fairy flew overhead, flapping noisily through the branches, making her heart race. It, too, must have been disturbed by the strange noise so late at night. Pax pressed on, creeping further into the forest until the trees opened up again into another clearing.

Then she saw them. A lone figure, shrouded in a black darker than the night. Pax held her breath, trying not to make a sound, her heartbeat thumping in her ears. She could just make out some odd markings drawn into the dust of the forest floor in front of the figure's bare feet. Next to them was a large book lying open.

"*Virgo…. Mater… Vetus…*" A velvety voice called out into the night. The figure's arms stretched out towards the sky, magic crackling in the air.

"*Via… Ostium… Plu—*"

The words stopped abruptly as Felis swooped down in front of the figure, in hot pursuit of the tired velox fairy. Pax's sharp intake of breath sounded so loud in the silence that the figure's head snapped around. Two completely white eyes met Pax's gaze.

Run. Pax turned quickly, sprinting back towards the clearing where she had left Am. Sharp branches scratched at her face, pulling at her hair. Her breathing was quick and jagged, the cold night air burning in her lungs. Her feet pounded into the ground, stumbling on knotted tree roots. As she glanced behind her to see if she was being chased, she slammed into something, hard. The force threw her onto her back, and she hit the ground, winded and unable to breathe for a few agonising moments. Then, finally, she inhaled. Dazed, she opened her eyes. Inches from her face, staring into her soul: two white eyes. Pax froze. Billows of floating black fabric surrounded the figure as they loomed silently over her. The pupil-less eyes narrowed, examining Pax's face. A silver-adorned hand revealed itself from beneath the cloak, creeping towards her. Suddenly, the figure paused.

Silence hung in the air for a long moment. Then,

surprisingly, Pax found her hand reaching out towards them. Her fingers tingled as she placed her palm into the hand of the stranger, who pulled her to her feet. Most of the figure's face was obscured by the velvet hood draped over their head, except for their eyes, which were mesmerising – unlike anything Pax had ever seen before, making her forget the fear she had felt just moments ago. The stranger returned Pax's gaze, studying her face, equally intrigued.

"Sorry." Pax found herself apologising; for what, she wasn't quite sure.

The stranger didn't respond straight away. Instead, they stepped back, looking Pax up and down. Examining her. The seconds ticked by into the night.

Finally, the stranger spoke.

"Dangerous… dangerous… here in the woods," she whispered, her voice still silky smooth but not as loud anymore. She slowly circled Pax, who kept her eyes locked on her, not daring to look away.

A long, low *caww* sounded from the tree above, stopping the stranger in her tracks. She glanced away from Pax as three magpies alighted on a branch above their heads. *Caww… caww.*

"Moonlight song from three… intriguing indeed!" muttered the stranger into the distance.

One of the magpies flew down from the elm tree, and the stranger held out an arm expectantly. The bird's claws gripped onto her cloak, its wings closing quietly. Pax watched as the stranger stroked the black and white chest of the bird, with fingers covered in silver rings, whispering to the animal. She held out her arm and the magpie took off across the clearing. The two other magpies flew down to join the first bird, squabbling over the vacant eyes of a small animal carcass.

The stranger appeared to agree with someone Pax couldn't see and nodded to herself. Raising her hands to her head, rings glinting in the moonlight, the figure removed her hood, exposing long dark dreadlocks, each one speckled with purple crystals and gemstones. As she turned back to face Pax, she revealed her white eyes were set in dark caramel skin.

"You're very lucky, young one." The stranger's brow furrowed. "All folk in Viridis are caro tonight."

Pax's eyes lit up at the recognition of the word.

"Except you," the stranger said, pointing a slim finger at Pax.

"What do you mean?" Pax asked.

"I mean what I said," the stranger replied. "All the villages in Viridis are empty tonight. Pillaged, plundered," – she made an arch shape with her hands – "gone."

Pax thought about the other villagers, the Gen at the party she had wanted to go to, her family, her neighbours. *Where* had they gone?

"What were you doing here in the woods?" Pax asked.

"A protection spell," replied the stranger, sounding slightly annoyed.

"You're a witch!" said Pax before she could stop herself.

"Not just a witch!" she spat, offended. She lifted her arms into the air, silver bangles rattling, and declared, "I am Venefica!" Her raised voice sent the scavenging magpies flying off into the night.

Pax had previously met a few witches – they were well known in Tellus for their knowledge of plants and medicine, often passing through her village to trade supplies. As an alchemist, her father always had the utmost respect for them, and he had warned Pax not to cross them either. Slightly concerned that she may have upset a witch she was alone with in the woods, she continued more politely.

"Oh, I didn't mean to offend you. Nice to meet you, Venefica. I'm Pax, of Silva Gen."

Venefica lowered her arms, quietly assessing Pax. Then she picked up the large book that was lying open on the ground. When she slammed it shut, a little harder than necessary, it revealed a deep purple cover, which she slowly dusted off before placing it into a large velvet bag.

"Some say I'm too powerful," Venefica explained. "I've ended up in this realm because of magic too big. Viridis is full of magic. From the very ground beneath our soles to the tops of these trees." With her bare feet, she kicked the dust, erasing the strange markings. The witch collected up the other items which had been scattered on the ground where she had been standing when Felis had rudely interrupted her, including some crystals, small vials and a pestle and mortar. She threw them all into her bag and wandered off into the bushes. Pax glanced in the direction of the camp, where she had left Am. She hesitated, but, too intrigued, she followed the witch further into the woods.

"My oh my!" Venefica mumbled to herself. "Calamus… azalea… borage…"

She picked at the colourful bushes. Snapping off a handful of each plant, she carefully wrapped them with twine, then threw each bundle into the bag slung across her shoulder, making Pax wondered what else might be hidden inside.

"You want this!" Venefica exclaimed, holding up a bunch of catnip to lure Felis from above.

Dragats were known to love the herb, which often sent

them into a frenzy of tumbling somersaults. Felis flew down, hovering in mid-air to sniff the offering for a few seconds, then he took a massive bite of the bundle, devouring the plant in one great chomp. Venefica chuckled to herself, stroking his wings, momentarily forgetting Pax was there.

"You know a lot about plants," Pax said, trying to engage her in conversation once again.

Although her father had warned her that witches could be extremely dangerous, being under the protection spell of one after what had happened tonight would be a wise move, and if the witch was truly dangerous, wouldn't she have done something by now?

Venefica's smiled dropped as she was reminded of her uninvited companion, and she studied Pax again with her white eyes. Something shifted slightly in her expression, and she carried on speaking as they ambled through the forest.

"One good thing about getting lost in this realm is I can collect all that I need for my spells."

Venefica gathered her skirts, kneeling down next to a rotting tree trunk. Orange moss clung to the bark. The witch scraped the spongy substance with a long fingernail and popped it into a glass vial she had retrieved from her bag.

"You're not from this realm?" Pax asked. She had heard tales of other realms but had never actually met anyone from one.

"I know what you're doing," Venefica replied, pushing the cork stopper into the top of the vial. "You want something from me."

Pax felt naive for thinking she could trick a witch.

Venefica stood up, staring at Pax. "There is no give without take. No black without white."

An uneasy feeling crept over Pax, a feeling that she was out of her depth. Trusting her gut, she turned on her heels and headed back towards where she'd left Am. When she knew she was out of the witch's view, she automatically put her hand over the locket around her neck. She was relieved to find it was safely hidden beneath her shirt, now warm against her skin.

Suddenly, the witch was by her side, her footsteps so quiet they made no audible noise.

"Where were you when they came?" Venefica asked.

"Who?" said Pax, maintaining a steady pace back towards her camp. Felis, now droopy-eyed, was flying alongside Venefica and landed on the witch's shoulder. Pax felt a slight pang of betrayal.

"The Harvesters," said the witch. "They were collecting caro, and not a soul was left. Apart from you. You must have been far away?"

Pax stopped in her tracks. "Who are the Harvesters?"

"Is this what you want from me? Answers?" Venefica smiled, revealing more gemstones embedded into the enamel of her teeth. When Pax remained stony-faced and didn't reply, the witch continued. "They are old gods."

Pax nodded, knowing Tellus was full of gods and that the older ones were often the most powerful.

"And caro? What is that?" Pax asked.

Venefica frowned. "Not all knowledge is free, young one. What do you have for me?"

Pax needed more information, and it appeared the witch had some of the answers to the questions rushing around her mind. So, she did something she knew was probably a bad idea and made a deal with the witch.

"Well, I'm going back to my camp for tonight," Pax said, hoping the witch would take the bait. "You can camp with us if you like. But on the condition that you must keep us protected."

Venefica raised her chin, considering the offer. "Us? You and him?" She shrugged at a dopey Felis lying on her shoulder.

"Yes, and Am, who's at camp. In return for more information, you can share our food."

Venefica, intrigued by the offer of food, took a long sniff of the night air. Pax started to regret her offer as the witch exhaled dramatically; her eyelids felt heavy, and she wanted to get back to Am. Venefica nodded to herself before holding out her arm, bangles rattling, implying that Pax should lead the way. After retracing her steps, soon they were back at the clearing, where Am was still sitting on the trunk of the large fallen tree.

"Hello," said Am. "Who are you?" Am's blue eyes scanned Venefica's face. "Unidentified Gen."

Venefica stopped in her tracks, stooping low, taking slow careful steps around Am.

"Another pet?" she asked.

"No!" replied Pax, offended. "This is Am. My… family."

"My name is Am."

Venefica, unconvinced, poked Am with her finger. "Strange magic," she uttered, waiting for a reaction.

Pax sighed. Am smiled. Venefica crept suspiciously around the camp site.

Taking the loaf from her bag, Pax removed it from the cloth and placed it on a large flat stone, where she sliced into the crust with her penknife.

Turning to Am, she said, "This is Venefica," gesturing

towards the witch, who was inspecting the blanket under the shelter with quiet disgust. "She's a witch. From, well, I'm not sure. Which Gen?"

"A most powerful witch!" shouted Venefica, ignoring the question.

"Pleased to meet you, Venefica, most powerful witch!" Am responded with equal vigour.

Venefica frowned as she put the blanket down and stepped towards where they were sitting.

"We're staying here tonight," said Pax, pointing to her now dishevelled blanket under the tent. "You can, too, if you like. Here, help yourself to some bread."

Venefica inched towards the bread on the stone and sniffed it. Then, instead of taking a slice, she picked up half the loaf and took a ravenous bite directly from the centre. Pax looked sideways at Am.

"Am will observe the witch," Am informed Pax.

Venefica hissed, spitting crumbs towards Am.

"I will watch *you*!" She pointed a finger at Am but kept devouring the loaf.

Pax rolled her eyes and headed towards her bed for the night, too exhausted to stay awake. She was glad Am was there to watch Venefica and hoped inviting the witch into their camp wasn't going to end up being a terrible decision. As she settled down underneath her blanket, one hand on her knife and the other on the pendant around her neck, she prayed to the old gods that her parents were still alive.

CHAPTER
FIVE

The sun pierced the horizon, casting long shadows onto the cracked earth. Creo opened his eyes, although he had not slept at all. Slowly, he turned his head to try and locate Celeste. She was already standing, alongside a line of the other women from Viridis. They were all tethered to the same length of thick rope laced with threads of gold, which held them in place no matter how much they struggled. A guard stomped up and down the line, his long black cloak thrashing behind him as he barked orders at the prisoners, some of the women flinching at each spiteful word.

A sharp kick of a boot connected with Creo's ribs. Scrambling to stand, he stumbled, his balance thrown off by the heavy pull of the coarse rope digging into his wrists and cutting into his ankles. He was tied closely to a man he didn't recognise, who in turn was tied to another Gen behind him and another after that. Creo couldn't be certain how many of them there were, but a little further down the line, out of the corner of his eye, he spotted his neighbour, Prod.

None of the captives were making eye contact. No one spoke. They had all learnt their lesson last night when another neighbour from Viridis had been the one to stand up for what was right. His blood was now drying on the ground beneath Creo's feet.

A hush fell amongst the guards, with some casting their eyes down to the ground, whilst others removed their helmets and nestled them in the crooks of their arms. They all stood to attention, saluting as a figure approached, striding confidently towards them. Even though this Gen was smaller in stature than the saluting guards, authority radiated from them, commanding respect without uttering a single word. A hood loosely covered long white hair that fell down around a bow slung loosely over their shoulder. A quiver packed with gold-tipped arrows rested on their back. With each stride, they turned slightly to inspect the prisoners, one by one. Her eyes met Creo's, and she smiled, beautiful and terrifying.

"Look at all this well-behaved caro!" she said theatrically, extending her arms as she strode down the line and making the guards breathe a collective sigh of relief. Stopping in front of Prod, she poked him hard in his stomach, as if testing the tenderness of a meat steak.

One of the guards stepped out of the line to stand next to her. He was taller than the rest, his black cloak stretching over wide shoulders, and removing his metal helmet, he revealed his chiselled jaw. He leant down to whisper into the woman's ear, and as she lowered her hood to listen, strands of her almost-silver hair fell either side of the quiver on her back.

Suddenly, a prisoner at the end of the line bolted. His hands were still bound together, but he had used whatever power he possessed to roughly cut the rope around his ankles. His jagged breathing was painfully loud against the shocked silence. He took rapid, wild strides along the red dirt, his knees buckling, before he straightened up once more and continued to flee. The large guard stepped forwards, but the woman stopped him with a gentle touch of her hand.

"Phantasma," the large guard said as she stood forwards, cackling, her slender arm reaching behind her to remove an arrow.

Placing it in the bow, she pulled the string back and waited for what felt like a painfully long time. Phantasma's red eyes fixed on the desperate man, the string of the bow taut against her smirking face. Creo could hear his own heartbeat in the silence. Then, a sudden swoosh. The escapee stopped, his body hitting the ground with a thud.

Phantasma laughed loudly, jumping up and down on the spot as if she'd won a carnival game. From somewhere further down the line there came a pained sob.

"Go and see if the blood can be harvested," the large guard instructed two others, who saluted and ran to retrieve the body.

Phantasma faced him, the smile dropping from her face.

"Always so serious, Deleo," she said with an exaggerated whimper, replacing her bow over her shoulder.

"Our orders are clear. Collect as much caro as possible for this coming Messis," Deleo replied, frustrated. "That's two we've lost already, and we aren't even halfway to Rubra!"

Phantasma pouted. "I was just having a little fun. His highness wouldn't begrudge me that."

Deleo stared straight ahead. "We've cleared out three villages. Not a soul left behind, as instructed. I'd like to finish this mission and return to the Castellum quickly to report back to him."

"You?" Phantasma rolled her eyes. "As if he'd even look at you! Let alone speak to you!" She laughed cruelly, casually strolling past the row of downturned eyes. With a long finger extended, she lightly scratched her nail down the face of the man standing next to Creo. "But I suppose we should prepare for our journey." She sighed. Pointing to the guards in the line she yelled out, "You four, prepare the pyrois!"

The guards broke from their formation and marched towards several large white horses tethered nearby. Striking against such a destitute landscape, the pyrois' manes were a movement of flames that fell around their long muscular necks and over their piercing red eyes. The fire danced softly with the breeze, flames sprouting from their soft, silvery coats. Their flaming tails flicked at annoying flies, who met a sizzling death, and their blazing hooves singed the dirt. In spite of their fiery presence, the herd of pyrois were calm, grazing quietly, indifferent to the fear of the prisoners surrounding them.

Phantasma sauntered over to Deleo, placing a delicate hand on his chest.

"Don't be angry," she said coyly, playing with the S-shaped clasp that secured his cloak across his chest. "You know there's a reason I'm in charge."

Deleo remained silent as the two guards returned, dragging the body of the escapee, the arrow lodged firmly in his back.

"Hook him up before he expires," Deleo instructed.

"Remember the good old days?" Phantasma said as she watched one of the guards retrieve a long clear tube and needle from one of the pyrois' saddle bags. "We used to just rip into caro!" she said gleefully, her fingernails tearing at the air.

"It's called progression, Phantasma," Deleo replied dryly.

The guard returned with the equipment and knelt down beside the escapee's body. After a few moments, the tube filled, dark and red.

"We have another long day of travel ahead if we are to reach the capital before nightfall," mused Phantasma. "Surely one won't be enough for all of us." Peering up at him through her white eyelashes, she waited.

Deleo's sigh was enough to give Phantasma permission, and she excitedly clapped her hands together and paced up and down the line of tethered men. Then, in a sickly-sweet voice, she recited a children's rhyme.

"As I walked by Scandza Lake..." She looked at Creo, continuing past him.

"I met a little rattle snake..." She playfully touched the next man on the nose, and a tear silently rolled down his cheek. Phantasma continued down the line of men.

"I gave him so much faba cake..." She turned on her heels to face Prod with her hands on her stomach, mocking his size.

"It made his little belly ache!" She passed Creo again, who dared not move a muscle.

"One..." She poked him hard in the chest.

"Two..." She poked the next man.

"Three!" Creo closed his eyes.

"This caro for me," Phantasma whispered softly.

Creo felt the man next to him being grabbed, his ropes cut by a sharp blade. Their eyes met briefly as he was pulled away, terrified. Creo glanced across to Celeste. She returned his gaze for a brief second before quickly looking down at the ground as the chosen man's screams filled the morning air.

CHAPTER
SIX

An aroma like sugary earth drifted into Pax's nostrils. Opening her eyes, she could see Am sitting next to a campfire where a small cauldron was perched above the flames. Venefica was huddled over, crushing something in the mortar, which she then sprinkled into the steaming pot.

"Good morrow!" said Am, realising Pax was awake. "The fire is alight with flames made from friction."

Venefica, ignoring Am's too-loud voice, used the hem of her long black skirt to protect her hand as she removed the cauldron from the fire. Carefully, she poured the steaming mixture into the awaiting wooden cups. Venefica replaced the cauldron above the flames, then clasped one of the warm cups in her bejewelled hands. Bringing it to her lips, she paused, then extended the cup out towards Am, who smiled.

"For lighting the fire," Venefica clarified.

Obviously these two had become more accustomed to one another throughout the night. Pax wondered if she'd been the only one to get any sleep – if you could consider tossing and turning all night 'sleep'.

"Am doesn't drink," said Pax, joining them by the campfire. "Or eat."

Venefica's white eyes narrowed, then she tilted her head as if she accepted this fact. Instead, she offered the cup to Pax, who sat down and took it gratefully. Bringing the cup to her lips, Pax inhaled the nutty caramel odour and sighed.

"It smells nice?" asked Am, intrigued, and Pax nodded.

Venefica sat down opposite them and took a sip from her cup. Pax did the same. The liquid felt like velvet in her mouth, warming her empty stomach.

"Faba," said Venefica, taking another satisfying sip, "made from the fabasucus plant."

For a few moments, the three of them sat around the fire in silence, listening to the velox fairies squeal as they were chased, yet again, by Felis. Pax held the cup in front of her, clasping it between her hands. Slowly, she released one palm away from the cup, then the other. The cup remained in place, hovering in mid-air between her palms, just for a few moments, before she grasped it again.

Am, who had been watching, clapped their hands together slightly too slowly, mimicking the way Creo often applauded her when she managed to control her powers. Pax smiled a thank you towards Am, her cheeks flushing slightly.

Venefica raised an eyebrow. "You have strong powers?" she asked, nodding at the cup.

Pax shrugged. "Not really, but my Ortus day is soon, so you never know."

She smiled again, feeling slightly self-conscious in the presence of a witch, who was obviously a lot more powerful than herself. She was unsure if Venefica had even provided them with a protection spell last night, but here they were, in the light of day, unharmed. Yesterday's events were still swirling around her mind, but Pax always felt she could think more clearly in the daytime. It was like her mother always said: 'Everything is better in the light'.

"You said something last night, a word that I recognised. Can you explain what caro is?" Pax asked.

Venefica was staring at Am when she answered. "Flesh. Blood. Food for the Harvesters."

Hearing the reply, Pax felt slightly queasy, the faba drink now churning around in her empty stomach. She swallowed.

"Who are the Harvesters?"

"The Supremo Gen." Venefica drained her cup. "Fallen gods."

"They are bad?" asked Am.

"There is no bad without good. No light without dark," Venefica replied, as if what she was saying was obvious.

Pax found herself staring into her cup of faba, unable to take another sip. "You saw them in my village? In Viridis?"

Venefica nodded.

"But they didn't attack you?" Pax clarified.

"I had a protection spell. I am a most powerful witch, remember?" Venefica replied.

Am nodded enthusiastically to show that they did indeed remember.

"So powerful, in fact, that I ended up here." Venefica raised her arm up towards the branches above. "Everyone else that night was caro." Her white eyes turned and fixed on Pax. "Everyone except you and I."

"So, caro are their victims? They kill them?" Pax asked, hot tears pricking at her eyes at the realisation of what she was asking.

Am butted in. "This sounds bad."

"Well, not straight away," replied Venefica, ignoring Am. "They save them for the Messis. A type of Harvest when the

Blood Moon is high in the night sky. It comes but twice a year."

Pax felt a pang of relief, remembering what Arator had said in the forest about the Blood Moon – it was close, but it hadn't happened yet. There was a chance, then, that her parents were, in fact, still alive.

As if reading her mind, or maybe just her face, Am asked, "Where are Celeste and Creo?"

Pax paused before replying. "I'm not sure."

Noticing the tone of her voice, Venefica asked her who they were.

"My parents. My mother and father." Pax used her sleeve to wipe her nose, hoping Venefica wouldn't notice.

"This makes you sad? That they have gone?" asked Venefica, her brow furrowed in confusion.

"Yes," Pax whispered, her voice breaking slightly.

"They left us some information," interrupted Am. "And a gold necklace."

Sometimes, Pax really hated the fact that Am was programmed not to lie; they always ended up saying the wrong thing at precisely the wrong moment.

"Oh?" Venefica raised her eyebrows.

Pax tried her best to play it down. "It was just a message telling us to leave our house and stay safe. My Mum left me her necklace as a keepsake." Reluctantly, she pulled the gold chain out from under her shirt.

Venefica's eyes widened, and she hastily put down her cup. "That is no necklace, young one. That is an amulet."

Leaping to her feet, bracelets jangling, the witch made her way around the fire and shuffled onto the log next to Pax. She leaned in closely to the necklace, accompanied by an overpowering scent of incense and herbs.

"Beautiful," Venefica whispered, leaning closer still. "Such power."

Feeling uncomfortable, Pax leant away from her, getting up to stoke the fire. She picked up the pot, which had cooled slightly, and poured herself another cup of faba, not because she wanted more – her stomach still felt uneasy – but for an excuse to move away from the witch. Felis took her place on the trunk next to Venefica, interested to see if any more treats were on offer. Pax silently offered her another drink by holding up the cauldron, but the witch shook her head.

"What's an amulet?" asked Am.

Venefica looked surprised for a second, as if she'd forgotten Am was there, and then answered in her melodic voice. "A device that has the purpose of protection by magical means." She held up a finger, as if realising something. "In fact, this may have protected you from the Harvesters!"

Pax shook her head. "No, it couldn't have, I only found it after they'd gone."

"It holds powerful magic," said Venefica. "I've never sensed anything quite like it before. You're lucky to have it. It belonged to your mother, you say?"

Am interrupted. "There is more information."

"Another clue?" Pax asked.

"Yes." Am smiled. "Would you like to hear it?"

"Yes! Please," Pax said.

Venefica watched, intrigued, as Am's eyes changed to bright green, and they recited these words:

What has a mouth but never talks,
A head but only weeps,

"What is this? Some kind of spell?" asked Venefica, closely studying Am's eyes as they returned to blue once more.

"It's a clue my father left me, but it's in the form of a riddle," Pax explained. "I'm guessing it was in case the amulet fell into the wrong hands."

Venefica hitched up her skirts, putting one dirty bare foot on the log. Gazing into the distance, she tapped her lips with a finger, deep in thought. Am did the same.

Pax already knew the answer of course; her father had told her about this riddle before, but she gave Venefica time to work it out herself. After a few moments, the witch clapped her hands together.

"Well, there are many creatures in these lands that choose not to waste their time with words, bunglebots for one. Then, there is the great frigate bird who suffers with terrible insomnia whilst flying over the seas, and of course we all know that goats don't cry. So, it's quite obvious what the answer is, I think you will both agree."

Pax stared at the witch, perplexed.

"What is the answer?" Am asked.

"I…" Venefica paused, "I will let you explain," she said, pointing at Pax.

"Well, okay, those are all very good ideas," Pax said. "A lot of good information there."

Venefica nodded, crossing her arms, satisfied her contribution had been appreciated.

"However, I think this clue might be less literal and more metaphorical. The key words, *mouth, head, swim* and *bed,* all suggest the riddle is referring to a river."

"Exactly!" said Venefica loudly. "Exactly what I was going to say."

Am decided this was a good time to clap again.

Pax smiled a little, sitting back down. So, her father wanted her to head to the river, but why? She still was unclear on what exactly she was meant to do and how she was meant to help them. It all felt too big, too serious, too dangerous.

"So, we head to the river?" Am asked, sitting next to Pax.

"Umm, I'm not sure, Am," Pax replied quietly. "I think we might be safer staying in the woods. I know this place – I can keep us safe here."

Am nodded.

"But that is not your path, young one." Venefica was standing over them, blocking the morning sunlight. "You have to move forwards."

"Thanks, but I think it's best to stay hidden. Like you said, all the villages were raided, and there's no one left."

"*You* are left," said Venefica, kneeling down to face Pax. "You."

Pax didn't know what to say. Sure, she had been spared from whatever had happened last night, but she didn't know why.

"It was no coincidence you saw me last night in the woods. The Harvesters couldn't locate me, but *you* did."

Venefica clasped Pax's hands with her own, and she was surprised at how warm the witch's skin felt.

"You have been given these clues, given this amulet." Venefica touched the gold around Pax's neck. "You have a prophecy to fulfil."

Pax felt words tumbling out of her. "But I don't know

what I'm meant to do! Go to the river? And then what? Find the Gen who took my parents? The ones who destroyed my entire village? I can't! I can't do it on my own!"

Her voice had grown loud, and she was up on her feet, shaking off the witch's hands. She paced away from them, her face flushed, her fingernails digging into her palms. Venefica and Am both watched as Pax marched back and forth in front of the dying fire.

"You are not on you own," Am said quietly.

"What?" Pax snapped.

Am looked at Venefica, then replied slightly louder. "You are not on your own."

Pax stopped in her tracks. Am's face, normally devoid of any emotion, looked different. Then she realised: Am looked scared.

"I'm sorry, Am," Pax said. "I didn't mean to shout."

"Because you have us," Am clarified, pointing to Venefica.

"You're at a crossroads, young one. You stay or go. It's as simple as that." Venefica picked up her cup and threw the last dregs onto the fire with a satisfying hiss. "But be warned, there are many old gods in these parts, so if you do travel forth, be wary – they are not to be messed with."

Venefica gathered the empty cups into her bag, and Pax realised that the witch was planning on leaving them.

"You're going?" Pax asked.

"Of course. I'm a witch; we travel with the magic. My time in this forest is over. I must return to my coven in Celare."

"Where is Celare?" Am asked. "My internal nucleus shows no record of this location."

"Somewhere hidden, between these realms. No map can show the way," Venefica replied, pulling the drawstrings of her bag tight.

A sudden feeling of desperation came over Pax, and she found herself blurting out her next question. "Will you stay?"

The witch turned to Pax, who continued: "We could use another protection spell. We could trade something?" Pax hoped she didn't sound as desperate as she felt, not wanting to be abandoned twice in as many days.

"Trade what?" Venefica asked, eyeing the amulet around her neck.

Pax tucked the necklace under her shirt and patted her pockets down. Inside, she felt a bronze coin and pulled it out. Venefica's mouth downturned, unimpressed.

"I know it's not much," Pax said, "but I can catch food, too."

Venefica pursed her lips slightly, the offer of food more enticing to her than money, but she shook her head again.

"In this universe, we must keep growing, keep moving forwards. I cannot stay here."

"What if I were to go?" Pax was surprised at the words coming out of her own mouth. "If I were to follow the clue and head to the river? Would you come then?"

Venefica put her bag down on the ground and studied Pax for a long moment.

"You want to go?" Venefica asked. "I thought you were too scared?"

"I am scared. Terrified in fact." Pax almost laughed. "But, like you said, there's a reason my father left me these clues and why my mother left me this amulet."

She took the necklace out and curled her fingers around it. Venefica eyed the amulet as Pax continued.

"You were right. I need to move forwards, to try and save

my parents, and I'd like you to come too." Pax waited with bated breath, hoping that the witch would agree.

"These parents must be nice if you want to help them so badly," Venefica replied. Then she nodded. "I will accompany you on your quest, young one, for there is much magic to be found."

Pax sighed, relieved, partly because it was beneficial to have a powerful witch accompanying them instead of going on alone and partly because she had finally made the decision. She would leave the forest and head towards the river.

Although she'd never been that far before, Pax knew Lake Scandza was a central life force to the whole of Tellus, joined by four rivers: River Indo and River Addo flowing in, and River Rapina and River Capio flowing out. The lake was the central point that would lead her to all the rivers, surely one of them was the right one. It was quite a distance from where they were to the lake, so travelling by boat would be the quickest option.

"Lake Scandza. That's where we need to go next," Pax said.

Am nodded in agreement.

Venefica nodded to herself, no longer listening to Pax. "Yes, my coven can wait. It's far from daybreak now; we should make haste."

After packing up the shelter, Pax led Am and Felis through the trees, with Venefica following them. The witch muttered incantations in between bites of crab apple, and Pax hoped she was casting some kind of protection spell. Soon, they made it to the side of River Capio where a huge tarpaulin covered a pyramid of upside-down boats. Normally used early each morning by Piscator Gen, they had been left untouched today. Sadly, this confirmed to Pax that this Gen from Viridis had been attacked too.

Pulling off the tarpaulin sent the morning dew twinkling into the air, coating Felis's fur. Am helped Pax slide the top boat from the stack and flip it over. The faint smell of tentamenta reminded Pax of home. Normally used to haul groups of fishergen and their equipment, the boat was easily big enough for all of them and their belongings. Venefica was as wary of the boat as she had been of Am on first meeting, and made Pax demonstrate that the boat would float before she would get aboard. Felis curled up on a coil of thick fishing rope in the hull, exhausted and tinged with glitter from chasing velox fairies all night. With everyone seated, Pax steered the boat downstream, towards Lake Scandza and into the unknown.

All the rivers of Tellus flow either into or out of Lake Scandza, a magically charged body of water at the geographical centre of this land. Each river is a slightly different colour, and Gen who study these waters will tell you that by examining the precise colour of the liquid, you can tell where it originated from and what parts it has travelled through.

As their boat sliced through the widening vein of the River Capio, the water lapping at the hull took on a violet tinge. They travelled downstream until the trees either side of the bank became scarce, replaced by jagged rocks. After an hour or so of sailing, the river's mouth opened wide to join the main body of water: Lake Scandza.

"My internal map notifies us that we are approaching the waters of Lake Scandza, where the four main rivers meet," Am informed the others.

Beneath them, different shades of blues, aquas, purples and greens rippled together yet still maintained their separate tones in the water. The surface of the lake swirled like marble, as if a giant artist had just cleaned their paintbrushes.

Pulling hard on the rudder, Pax steered the boat, aiming for the shoreline. The jolt woke Felis, who stretched dramatically after his nap. He had woken up thirsty. He padded along the deck and jumped up onto the side of the boat, his claws gripping the wood. Stretching his neck down, he drank from the surface of the water. Then, with a loud splash, the small dragat disappeared over the side.

"Felis!"

Pax let go of the rudder and rushed to where Felis had been just moments ago. The many colours in the water made it hard to see into the depths, and Pax plunged her hand into the cold, desperately feeling around until she touched something almost slimy. It was Felis's wet fur. Grabbing his leg, she pulled as the boat slowly started rotating in the water. Felis's slick head emerged from the depths, his eyes bulging in shock. But Pax couldn't pull him free, something was tugging him back down into the water. She squinted to check if he was caught on some weeds, and then she saw it. There, just below the surface, hanging off Felis' leg, was a small creature with webbed feet.

Reaching her other hand into the water, Pax tried to grab the tiny parasite clinging to her pet, but it was too far away. Felis yelped in pain, and Pax gritted her teeth in anger. She glared at the scaly face sinking its teeth into Felis and tried to move it. To make it let go. To cause it pain. But nothing happened. The tiny creature continued biting and pulling Felis down into the water, surprisingly strong for its size. In that moment, Pax failed to harness her powers, her head full of too many thoughts, and she watched as Felis gulped his final breath and disappeared beneath the water.

"A water goblin!" Venefica yelled.

She acted quickly, pointing a long finger at the colour-changing scales of the creature. A sharp snap of light sent the goblin flying up into the air before it plopped into the water a few metres away. Pax yanked Felis, dripping and gasping, into the hull. She leant over to pull the rudder again, to stop the boat spinning, and slowly steered it towards the shore.

"There's lots of water goblins in the lake." Venefica laughed as Am cradled a wet Felis in their arms. "Not harmful to Gens, but a small dragat like you would be a tasty meal!"

Pax remained silent, her cheeks flushed, frustrated that she hadn't been the one to save Felis.

A few moments later, the boat's bow carved into the shingle of the beach. Pax jumped out, splashing through the water, pulling it ashore. Once they had all disembarked, they sat down on the glistening gravel, staring out across the mesmerising waters.

"Do you think the clue has something to do with the lake?" Pax asked, breaking the silence. "Maybe we have to drink it? Or swim in it?"

"Never so easy with the gods," Venefica replied, looking over her shoulder, her voice shaded with concern. "I sense strong magic in these parts."

Pax's skin tingled, as if agreeing with the witch, an uneasy feeling creeping over her. Above, dark clouds converged, and a thin mist rolled in, coating the top of the lake. Then the air was pierced with a long, low wail, a mournful moan that vibrated through the water.

Venefica frowned, getting to her feet and squinting at the lake's surface. "A cetus whale?"

Pax shook her head, listening carefully. This didn't sound like an animal's call. The cry sounded almost human. Suddenly, the calm waters of the lake started vibrating, the surface bulging and beginning to rise into waves rolling towards them. Felis arched his back, hissing in fright. Pax gripped her penknife, in suspense. The waves continued to rise, curling up until they towered over the top of them. But instead of crashing down, the water parted, revealing a tall Gen gliding out of the water. The waves crashed either side of him as he made his way onto the shore, his golden trident clinking on the stones of the beach until he came to a standstill in front of them.

"I am Llyr, God of these waters. Who goes there?" He said in a deep voice, his piercing blue eyes studying them all carefully.

A stunned silence followed. Pax had always expected gods to be large, ominous creatures, but this one was barely taller than her dad.

"Answer me!" Llyr yelled, frustrated, his voice echoing around them.

"I'm Pax." She found herself speaking quite loudly at first, then added more quietly, "Silva Gen." She pointed to her companions. "This is Am and Venefica."

Llyr locked eyes with Venefica.

"You dare to bring a witch into these waters?" he yelled, his face turning red.

Venefica swallowed hard, knowing only too well how dangerous an angry God could be.

"The greatest witch!" Am said confidently.

Pax and Venefica turned slowly in unison and stared in disbelief.

"The greatest witch?" Llyr replied, considering this, then asked more calmly. "Is this true?"

Am nudged Venefica encouragingly.

"Well… yes?" said Venefica, unsure.

Llyr remained silent for a moment, staring into the lake. Then facing them, he asked, "What is it you seek here?"

"We are looking for…" Pax wasn't sure what to say, "magical water, I think? I was told I'd find it here."

"Who has sent you?" Llyr asked sternly, unhappy with the answer Pax had given.

"It's a prophecy!" Venefica said with urgency. "We've been sent here to fulfil a prophecy."

"Yes!" said Pax, repeating the clue.

What has a mouth but never talks,
A head but only weeps,
A bed but never sleeps,
Can swim but never walk?

Llyr's face flashed in recognition, his eyes glazing over. He studied them again for a long while, stroking his white beard. Pax hardly dared to breathe, her eyes focused on the glinting prongs of his gold trident. Finally, he spoke.

"There is strong magic here in my presence this day," he said. "Are you light or dark?"

"Both!" Am said confidently. "One cannot exist without the other."

Venefica glanced at Am. "I mean no harm to you," she told the God.

The colourful water was calmer now, lapping around the bow of the boat on the shore, but the wails were still emanating from the lake.

After a long pause, Llyr spoke once more. "Very well. I have decided. I will give you safe passage so you may fulfil this prophecy."

Pax took a breath, relief spreading through her body.

"On one condition," he continued. "You must use your powers to reverse a terrible curse."

CHAPTER SEVEN

Llyr raised his trident towards the sky, rotating it with his muscular arm, and above them the clouds spiralled as he spoke.

"Many moons ago, as a young God, I met the most beautiful creature I've ever seen. A local fishergen girl. Her name was Penarddun. Every day, she would come to the lake to fish in these waters and, after a time, we fell in love."

As Llyr told his tale, the clouds circled and changed to illustrate his story in the sky, swirling to show a young Penarddun falling in love with Llyr.

"Alas, she was mortal. I realised that one day Penarddun would die, and I would be left all alone in this world. It was a heartbreak I could not bear. I was distraught at the thought. I tried to find a solution but could think of nothing to save my love from a mortal death."

Above them, the clouds shifted, revealing the form of a witch, her robes dragging through the clouds as she approached a troubled Llyr.

"The sorceress offered me a deal. Eternal life for Penarddun in return for my trident." He gripped the gold weapon tightly in his hand. "Of course, I was overwhelmed by the possibility that I agreed to the terms."

"Ceridwen," Venefica whispered to Pax, pointing to the

outline of the witch portrayed in the clouds. She knew her to be a very powerful and cunning witch.

The clouds swirled again to reveal Ceridwen casting a spell. A bright light covers Penarddun, raising her into the air. Magic circles her, transforming her. Her wide eyes blink against her pale skin. Her ears point out from long flowing hair. Her legs fuse together to form an iridescent tale. Penarddun is lowered back down into the lake, now immortal as a beautiful water nymph.

"I was overjoyed that now I could be with my love for eternity." Llyr smiled sadly, lowering his head. "But I went back on my word by deciding I would keep my trident. To keep my power and my love. I was greedy, and I foolishly refused the witch's request."

Above, in the clouds, Llyr raises his trident, pointing the prongs towards Ceridwen, who retreats in pain. She watches as Llyr and Penarddun swim into the lake together.

"I should have known not to trick a witch." Llyr shook his head, his voice pained with regret.

In the clouds, Ceridwen, although badly injured, manages to utter a curse. Her words twist the skies into darkness. The waters of the lake swirl around the lovers. Penarddun struggles, then disappears into the deep.

In the clouds, Llyr swims down into the lake after her and is met with the most heartbreaking sight. There, at the bottom of the lake, Penarddun is trapped beneath a magical dome. Her fists pound into the invisible, unbreakable shield. Held captive by magic.

Llyr swims towards her, yet his body is propelled away by Ceridwen's curse. He tries desperately to get close to her, using all his godly might, but the forcefield is too strong. He surfaces to find Ceridwen waiting for him on the shore.

"The magic has gone wrong! Penarddun is trapped! Free her!" Llyr demands.

Ceridwen's jet-black eyes stare at Llyr as she speaks calmly. "You cannot have love without giving up your power."

Llyr thrusts the trident towards the witch. "Take it!"

Ceridwen starts to laugh, quietly at first, then maniacally, before disappearing into a plume of black smoke, leaving Llyr alone on the banks of the lake.

As if on cue, the sorrowful wails echoed from the water, and Pax realised that they were the cries of Penarddun, who was still trapped beneath the lake.

Llyr closed his eyes. "For many years this dark magic has kept me from my love. I long for her to be free."

Slowly, the images in the clouds above dissolved completely, and the clouds parted, revealing the now setting sun.

Llyr appeared lost in his own thoughts for a few moments as Penarddun's cries circled them. Then he spoke again.

"Penarddun has a mouth but never talks,

A head but only weeps,

A bed but never sleeps,

Can swim but never walk."

Pax's eyes widened at the realisation, wondering exactly how long the nymph had been trapped beneath the lake.

Llyr turned away from the lake to face them. "So, most powerful witch! You will undo Ceridwen's evil deed and release my love from this magic! Only then will you be allowed safe passage to fulfil your prophecy."

Venefica clenched her jaw, humming uneasily. Llyr stared at them, frowning.

"Begin!" he bellowed, smashing the end of his trident hard

onto the ground, sending shockwaves under their feet. The impatient God loomed over them as they crouched together on the shore.

"Can you do this?" Pax asked.

Am answered. "Of course she can! She is the most powerful witch!"

Venefica stayed silent at first, her eyes focusing intensely on the pebbles of the beach. Then she whispered, "When I said I was the most powerful witch, I may have exaggerated a little."

"What does that mean?" Pax asked.

"I am powerful, but sometimes I struggle to control my magic. I ended up here, in this realm" – Venefica waved her arm around – "without it being the desired outcome."

Pax put her hand to her forehead and pushed her hair back. Am smiled.

"What is the delay?" Llyr rumbled from behind them, sending Felis flying for cover into the bushes. "Do your magic! Reverse this Hex!"

Pax looked at Am. "How deep is the lake? Could I swim down to the bottom?"

Am reviewed the map stored in their nucleus. "It's deep. You wouldn't be able to hold your breath for long enough."

Pax turned to Venefica. "I need to get down to Penarddun in the lake. Can you cast a spell so I can breathe under the water long enough to free her?"

Am nodded enthusiastically at this suggestion. Venefica paused for a few seconds, then she gathered up her skirts and sat on the ground, black fabric fanning out around her. Tipping the contents of her bag onto the pebbles, she started rifling through the items. Frantically flicking through her spell book, Venefica muttered to herself, then stopped. Pressing a long fingernail into the page, she declared, "I've got it! Fire. I'll need a fire," Venefica said, sorting through the arrangement of herbs and plants she had collected on their journey.

Pax instructed Am to collect driftwood slightly higher up the beach, where it would be drier, and start making the fire.

"I can make a potion called *Spiritus*," Venefica offered, "to give you breath under the water. But I'll need your help."

Pax listened carefully as the witch directed her to crush some pale calamus root in the mortar as she sprinkled in pink azalea and blue borage flowers. Pax ground them into a spicy-scented paste.

Gathering a few extra items, they both made their way up to the top of the beach to meet Am, who was sitting next to a neat stack of driftwood. A prop stick was balanced above twigs, to which Venefica added her cauldron.

Kneeling down, Pax focused on the kindling. Concentrating on the tiny fibres, blocking out the wailing still coming from the lake, she visualised heat, flames, fire. A warmth spread through her chest, an energy seeping into her blood, spreading through her skin. The kindling popped and crackled, and a spark ignited into a blue flame, tumbling over the dried firewood. Llyr watched on, intrigued. The flames crackled and grew higher, changing to orangey yellows as Am added some more driftwood. Pax scooped the paste into the pot, and Venefica poured in a purple liquid from a small glass bottle. The mixture hissed, sending trails of foul-smelling steam into the air. Pax covered her nose. Opening her book, Venefica placed it on the ground and took a piece of charcoal from the fire. Crushing it in her fingers, she smeared the black ash across her eyelids. Pax glanced at Am, with her finger to her lips.

Around them, the wind stopped. The air fell still. Venefica's dreadlocks covered her face as she dropped her head and muttered from the pages:

"*Spirio… efflo… tempus…*"

Venefica's head snapped upright. Her eyes now completely black. The wind returned, harder and colder now, whipping the flames of the fire. They flickered high around the pot, dissolving into a bright purple mist. Then they vanished.

Venefica's eyes flickered back to white as she peered into the cauldron. The liquid inside had taken on a tar-like consistency. Retrieving a wooden cup from her bag, she slowly poured in the sticky solution and handed it to Pax.

Pax stared at the unappetising concoction. "This will let me breathe under the water?"

Venefica nodded.

Pax took a deep breath, deciding she didn't want to smell the thick drink, and gulped down the bitter liquid in one go. It felt like warm treacle in her mouth, slowly coating the inside of her throat. She swallowed and grimaced.

"For how long?"

Venefica stopped nodding and shrugged. "Best to make haste, young one."

With no time to lose, Pax unlaced her boots, kicking them off and made her way towards the water's edge, the pebbles cold again her feet. Am and Venefica watched with very different expressions on their faces. Am's eyes recorded the lack of smile from Venefica and adjusted theirs accordingly.

Pax placed a hand over the amulet underneath her buttoned-up shirt, making sure it was secure. She strode into the lake. *Let's hope this works.* The eery wails surrounding her distracted from the coldness of the technicoloured water. Llyr folded his arms, watching, as Pax dived under. Unsure if the potion was working, she took a tentative breath. The water felt cold as it went up her nose, but miraculously, she was able to breath. The sorrowful sounds were much louder beneath the surface, filling her ears as she swam down into the coloured waters. The cries grew louder the deeper she sank until, after a few moments, she saw it. A huge glistening shield, curving over a dome on the bed of the lake. And inside, lying still, on the very bottom, was Penarddun. The shine of her tail had disappeared after being trapped for so long, her scales flaking and her long hair floating around now-dull eyes. Even so, Pax had never seen anything quite so beautiful. And so sad.

The water nymph's wailing stopped abruptly when she saw Pax swimming towards her. Startled at first, Penarddun slowly swam up to meet her, gently placing her hands against the invisible shield. Pax's red hair fanned out, floating around her face as she trod water. Penarddun studied her, inquisitive, then she raised her eyebrows at Pax.

Pax put her hand out to touch Penarddun's open palm, only to feel the pressure of the forcefield between them pushing her hand away. Making a fist, she smashed into the invisible barrier hard, startling the nymph. Bringing back her fist, Pax hit the shield again. And again. Nothing seemed to be happening. Pax started to feel a pull in her chest, her lungs were burning, desperate for air. The potion was wearing off. She needed to break the barrier and fast.

The discomfort in her lungs made Pax placed her hand on her chest, and she felt the amulet. As Pax pulled it out from under her shirt, Penarddun's eyes lit up at the sight of the gold disc. Pax gripped the gold in her fist.

It all happened so fast, but the sensation in her chest wasn't painful anymore; it felt like power. Bringing her fist down hard in a final strike, she smashed the amulet into the barrier. Piercing the forcefield, it sent sharp cracks all around the dome, echoing through the water. A split second of silence was followed by the barrier shattering. The noise of the sonic boom blasted into Pax's ears, smashing though the water. The force propelled her body upwards through the water in a blinding rush, pressure pushing hard against every part of her body. She broke through the surface of the lake, painfully gasping in air. Her ears were ringing, and her vision filled with red as she focused on the sky above. As she tried to slow her breathing, she heard Am and Venefica calling her name from the shore. Pax's heart rate slowed as she swam back towards them, and they waded into the shallows to help her from the water. In the lake behind her, Penarddun surfaced, shielding her eyes from the light she hadn't seen in centuries.

"You have fulfilled your promise!" Llyr cried out, tears of joy brimming in his eyes. "Penarddun is free!"

Pax felt a huge sense of relief and a strange feeling of pride at having been able to help.

"Can we retrieve some of the water?" Pax asked, remembering the reason they had come here in the first place as Venefica handed her a glass bottle. Llyr reluctantly took his eyes away from where Penarddun was waiting for him.

"These waters are not what you seek."

He held his hand out towards Pax. Confused, she passed the glass bottle to him, hoping that Llyr wasn't about to betray them the same way he had betrayed Ceridwen. Strangely, instead of holding the bottle in the water, the God raised it to his face. As tears of joy fell from his eyes, they filled the bottle with an iridescent blue liquid. Llyr returned the bottle to Pax.

"Thank you!" she said, staring at the mesmerising liquid in the bottle.

Llyr nodded. "Now you may leave these waters. Safe passage is given."

With those final words, he strode into the lake, still holding his trident, and swam towards Penarddun. They embraced, a smile spreading across the nymph's face. Then both immortals disappeared beneath the waters of the lake.

"We did it! You did it!" Venefica screamed, jumping and grabbing at Pax as she trudged back to the shore. "How did you do it?"

"This is a good time for a hug?" Am asked, extending their arms out stiffly, having never been able to quite get the hang of physical contact.

"The perfect time," said Pax leaning into the coldness of Am's rigid body.

"Umor!" Venefica said. "Of course! The tears of a God!"

Pax frowned, not recognising the word.

"Umor! And we have an entire bottle of it! Such powerful stuff!" The witch grabbed the shimmering blue bottle from Pax.

"The nymph was so beautiful," Pax said, her breathing returning to normal. "She looked at me in this strange way though, as if…" Pax didn't know how to describe what she had felt under the water when their eyes had met.

"That sentence is not finished," Am prompted, listening intently.

Pax frowned. "It was as if she recognised me. But I've never been here before; there's no way."

Venefica shrugged. "Maybe she recognised which Gen you are from? The gods have ways of seeing beyond the exterior."

"Do you think my father has been here?" Pax asked. "Maybe the nymph remembered him?"

"Your father was an alchemist, and they are known to travel far and wide," Venefica replied, placing the bottle of Umor into her bag. "That would explain why his clue sent us here."

They packed their belongings into the boat quickly, wanting to be safely out of Lake Scandza by the time the sun went down. After a final push into the water, Am was tasked with sailing the boat towards River Addo using their internal map to guide them. Venefica scratched Felis's ears whilst listening intently to Pax describe exactly what had happened at the bottom of the lake.

"I'm still not sure what we're meant to do with the Umor now we have it." Pax said, as the boat sailed through the water.

"Well, there is more information." Am replied.

"What? When?" asked Pax.

"As soon as the old man put his eye water into the bottle." Am replied.

"He was a God, and those were tear— anyway it doesn't matter. What is the next clue?" Pax asked, facing Am, as Venefica nodded eagerly in agreement.

"Well, there is a predicament." Am said as the boat started to rock.

"Which is?" Venefica asked.

"Whether to tell you the clue first or inform you of the impending danger."

"What danger?" Pax said, turning slowly.

"That," Am replied, pointing past Pax and Venefica.

There, only a few yards away, were roaring rapids framed by a thundering white mist, and just beyond that was the crest of a waterfall.

CHAPTER EIGHT

The horizon roared. Pax glanced at Venefica, but there would be no time to cast a spell. Grabbing Felis, she threw him high into the air above her head, forcing him to open his wings.

Am yelled, "It's the Cataracta waterfall!" to the others, but no one could hear over the thundering water.

The bow of the boat cut through the edge of the waterfall like a knife, defying gravity, in mid-air for a split second. Everything slowed, then the boat tipped, plummeting down into the cascade. They were all thrown violently from the vessel and into the tumbling plunge pool below.

The impact of the hard water shocked Pax into action. She had automatically held her breath, but the cold was confusing. She was unable to tell which way was up. Something was pulling at her hair. Opening her eyes in the murky water, she saw a glint of gold – the amulet was falling away from her into the darkness. Reaching out her arm, she swam towards it, away from the surface, away from the air her body desperately craved. She couldn't leave it, even if it meant putting herself in danger. From somewhere in the watery shadows, the amulet called to her. Pax kicked her legs towards the sinking gold, stretching out her arms. Finally, her fingers laced around the chain, grabbing it tightly. Pax twisted her body, kicking towards the light, straining against the pull of the water. The sun appeared as a blurry beacon above her, distorted by the water and so far away. Her lungs screamed as the last of her breath escaped from her lips.

She burst through the surface. She gulped down a mouthful of water as she desperately tried to fill her lungs with air, choking and spluttering. The current was rapidly pulling her downstream, away from the roaring base of the falls. Blinking frantically, she caught a glimpse of someone's head bobbing above the water. Locating the bank of the river, she swam towards it. Clawing at the mud, Pax felt it squelch under her weight as she pulled herself onto the bank. Heaving, exhausted, to her feet, she turned back to face the water.

"Am!" Pax screamed. "Venefica!"

Further along the riverbank, the witch was crawling out of the water, weighed down by wet black fabric. She was dragging her velvet bag through the mud as Felis circled above her head and landed with a squelch.

Further still, where the river was calmer, Am was walking out of the water. Still smiling, as undisturbed as ever, they were carrying Pax's backpack. Sighing with relief, Pax waved, beckoning Am over to join them, whilst trudging her way through the clay-like mud. She hugged Am's already-dry body, and Venefica nodded, which Pax took to mean she was equally relieved. Unfortunately, the boat hadn't survived the fall, and jagged parts of the bow had started to wash up on the shore. Together they made their way up to higher ground to find a dry place to sit and catch their breath. Pax removed her muddy boots, pouring the dirty river water out of them onto the grass.

Am made a fire with what remained of the boat, and for a while they sat there quietly next to the flames, drying their clothes. Venefica made a pot of faba with some wet beans she had managed to salvage from her bag. She poured herself another hot cup and sat down next to Pax.

"So," she said quietly, "what now?"

Pax didn't respond, picking up a twig from the ground to fiddle with, unsure of what to say.

Am filled the silence. "I have the next piece of information."

Pax didn't want to hear it. The events of the last two days had been exhausting, and she didn't even know if what she was doing was a complete waste of time.

Venefica took another sip of her drink, then responded. "Continue, young Am."

Am looked at Pax for approval, and she reluctantly nodded her head.

Am's eyes filled with fluorescent green.

> *We do not age,*
> *We do not die.*
> *Those with no eyes,*
> *We are guarded by.*

Pax sighed, yet another riddle. She snapped the twig in her hands, angry at her father for treating this like a game, a treasure hunt, as if she were still a child, when the stakes were so high. Then the heat was replaced with a wave of guilt. She felt overwhelmingly lost, the task ahead feeling impossible. She swallowed hard, fearing what would happen when she failed – a horror she would not be able to prevent. Pax threw the pieces of the stick towards the river. Venefica sensed her turmoil and decided to start the conversation.

"No eyes," she mused. "Well, there are a multitude of

creatures within Viridis alone that have no eyes! Salamanders, wolf spiders, urchins." She glanced over at Pax, who she noticed was still lost in her own thoughts, so she continued to think aloud. "We don't age or die. Something immortal? Another God perhaps?"

"Hydra?" Am offered, their eyes blue once more.

Venefica carried on, ignoring Am. "The Land of the Blind could be the place. It is populated by many magical creatures."

Pax looked up; something had clicked. "Am, what did you say?"

"Hydra," Am replied. "They have no eyes, and they do not die, technically. They are biologically immortal."

Pax nodded silently in agreement. Her dad had often used Am as a study partner for her, uploading book after book of scientific fact.

"I think you're right, Am. It's the Hydra we are looking for, they are the next item," Pax said, feeling surer of herself. "They're found in caves; we just need to know which ones."

Venefica stood up. "Oh no," she said quietly, shaking her head. "Oh no, no, no."

"What is it?" asked Pax, getting to her feet and checking around to see if there was danger nearby.

"The Caligo Caves," Venefica whispered. "That's where we'll find them."

"Really?" said Pax, her shoulders relaxing slightly. "That's great!"

Venefica remained stony faced.

"What is it?"

"The Hydra in the Caligo Caves are protected by those with no eyes," said Venefica.

"By what?" Pax asked, bracing for an answer she was

certain she wouldn't like.

Venefica paused, then answered quietly. "Trogs."

A chill ran down Pax's spine.

"Trogs are extremely dangerous," Am stated.

Thud! At Pax's feet, a limp velox fairy gasped its final breath as a proud Felis circled above her head. He flew down to curl up next to the dying fire. Pax sighed, pushing her hands through her messy hair as she marched over to the river to think. Should she put the others in danger again? In the water she spotted the small bubbles of tentamenta swimming near to the surface. Gathering some drier sticks, she added them to the fire.

"I'll catch us something to eat. I think it best if we stay here tonight and decide what to do, tomorrow."

Am nodded in agreement, enjoying the idea of mealtime. Venefica, however, still looked unsure.

Pax had already stripped down to her vest, her other clothes still drying by the fire. She would be able to dive down easily to set the nets to catch their dinner. Her hand impulsively reached to the amulet around her neck, remembering how it had weighed her down in the water, yet something told her not to take it off. So she left it in place and dived into the water.

A little later, the skin of freshly caught tentamenta crackled above the fire. Am had finished making the shelter by attaching it to two trees further up the bank.

"Are you sure you don't want to sleep under the tent?" Pax asked Venefica, pointing at the darkening sky. "It looks like it might rain tonight."

"No," replied Venefica firmly. "I don't like being caged in."

It's hardly being caged in, thought Pax, looking at the open shelter, but decided not to press the matter due to the witch's tone. She beckoned Am to come and sit with them as she plated up their dinner.

"Why does Am like mealtimes if they can't eat?" asked Venefica, nodding towards Am, who smiled happily.

"Why don't you ask them?" Pax replied, but Venefica frowned and stayed silent.

Pax rolled her eyes. "Why do you like mealtimes, Am?"

"Mealtimes make everyone happy. They bring us all together," Am stated.

Pax turned to Venefica, who paused before gnawing on a tentacle, seemingly satisfied with the answer Am had given.

"So, tomorrow," Pax said to Venefica, "I'll understand if you can't come with us." She tried to sound indifferent but knew that the witch's answer could mean the difference between life or death in the coming days.

Venefica tilted her head, considering this. "My coven will be waiting for me. I should return to Celare."

Pax stayed silent, feigning great interest in the last morsels of food on her plate as Venefica spoke.

"But Hydra are very special. They can be used in all sorts of magic by a powerful witch like myself." She waited for Pax to confirm this.

Pax raised her eyebrows, nodding.

"Then I think I will come too," Venefica said. "In the interest of magic."

Pax tried not to sigh out loud in relief, but it felt like an invisible weight had been lifted from her shoulders.

"I mean, we already have Umor!" Venefica said, pulling the glass bottle out of her bag and holding it up high, like a trophy. Bringing the bottle down close to her face, she studied the iridescent blue liquid inside. "Umor…" she whispered to herself.

"I'm not exactly sure what we're meant to do with that liquid." Pax said, absentmindedly toying with the chain around her neck.

Venefica didn't respond, too transfixed by the contents of the bottle. Staring down at the engraved symbol carved into the amulet, Pax was reminded of when she was very young, being held by her mother, her own tiny hands gripping on to her mum's sundress. Something about the weight of the amulet in her hand had unlocked a fuzzy memory. With her eyes beginning to water and a lump forming in her throat, she distracted herself by focusing on the intricate details of the amulet.

The pendant was round, thick and quite heavy, which made her wonder why her mother had worn something so precious every day. She turned it over again, and as she traced her fingers over each of the gemstones around the symbol at the centre, she noticed it was slightly indented into the gold. Running her fingertip over it, Pax pressed down. *Click!* The coloured gemstones around the rim jutted out, revealing each to be the top of one of six small glass vials.

"Wow!" said Am from over her shoulder.

Pax clicked the amulet shut again.

"You shouldn't sneak up on me!" she snapped.

Am tilted their head, a look of surprise flashing across their face.

"Sorry, you scared me," Pax blurted out, trying to manage her outburst.

"You don't need to be afraid of me," Am replied, their voice quieter than usual.

Venefica peered through the glass bottle of Umor towards them. "What is happening?"

"Nothi—" Pax started to say.

"Pax opened the amulet!" Am interrupted.

Pax sighed, annoyed again by Am's lack of subtlety.

Venefica's eyes widened, and she jumped up and over to them so quickly she hardly noticed how dangerously close her bare feet were to the edge of the fire. Then she was in front of Pax, leaning over her, so close that Pax could smell the tentamenta on her breath.

Venefica's long fingernails scratched at the amulet around Pax's neck, making her lean away. Pax grasped the gold chain with her fist, pulling the amulet from the witch.

"Why are you so interested in this amulet?" Pax said, standing up to create distance between them.

Venefica studied Pax, deliberating what to say. Pax waited, still gripping the amulet in her fist.

Finally, the witch spoke. "Okay, young one, I'll explain. The amulet holds powerful magic."

Pax frowned as Venefica spoke.

"When I met you that night in the forest, it was not this little creature who disturbed me." She pointed down at a sleeping Felis. "I sensed I was in the presence of a strong magic."

"Why didn't you say that?" Pax asked.

Venefica shrugged. "I wasn't certain what, or who, it was. I'm still not sure. It is so very rare." She held out her hand.

"Can I see?"

Pax wondered if she could trust a witch she had known for only a few days with her mother's amulet. But, deciding that they wouldn't have made it this far without her, she slowly took the chain from around her neck and placed it into Venefica's awaiting hand.

The witch's black nails curled around the gold. Snatching it up quickly, she held it towards the light of the flames to get a better look. Pax bit her lip, an aching filling her body. She wanted to take the amulet back. Am smiled at her, and Pax smiled back feebly, trying to remain calm. Venefica frantically inspected the amulet, tapping it, sniffing it, whispering into it. She delved into her bag to retrieve her enormous spell book.

"Oh, what magic lies within?" Venefica said to herself.

Pax sat by the fire, watching as the witch mumbled spells into the amulet, flicking frantically through the pages of her book. After a long while, Venefica exhaled, disappointed.

"This amulet has been made for the purpose of protection. Not for me!"

"To protect me?" Pax questioned.

Venefica's brow furrowed. "You said it belonged to your mother? So, these letters on the back are for her?" the witch asked, turning the pendant in her hands.

"I think so," Pax said. "S.G., for Silva Gen."

"It is probably only for her," Venefica said, losing interest. She handed the amulet back to Pax, who eagerly took it back. The witch frowned.

"You opened it." Her white eyes stared expectantly at Pax. "Do it again."

"I'm not sure how," Pax lied, putting the chain safely

around her neck.

"You pressed it," Am said.

Pax pursed her lips. Venefica waited with bated breath and gestured with her hands for Pax to try again. Holding the amulet, Pax slowly curled her thumbs over the symbol and pressed down once more. *Click!* The six gemstones protruded, displaying the tops of the vials again. Venefica squealed in delight, grabbing the bottle of Umor and thrusting it into Pax's face.

"What?" asked Pax, confused.

Venefica's smile dropped in disbelief. "The vials!" she gasped. "It goes in the vials!"

Pax studied the glinting gemstones bordering the amulet.

"Which one? There are six of them," she said, carefully pinching the vial topped with the red stone, pulling it softly. It didn't move.

"Umor is a shade of blue, and there is a blue gemstone," Am offered.

Venefica nodded her head feverishly in agreement.

Pax tugged at the vial topped with the blue gemstone. It slid out easily. She rested the amulet back on her chest, removing the stopper from the top of the vial, and held it out so Venefica could carefully pour some of the Umor into it. Pax replaced the stopper tightly. She took the amulet back into her hand, glancing at Venefica and Am.

"Ready?"

They both nodded. Holding her breath, Pax slid the vial back into its slot, then clicked the amulet shut. Nothing happened. Venefica looked around.

"Was something meant to happen?" Am asked, and the witch shrugged.

"Maybe we need to fill them all," Pax replied, a little deflated, although she wasn't sure exactly what she had expected to happen.

She began to tidy up the camp for the night, stoking the fire and checking Am's nucleus. Luckily, it was at a decent level, just over half, because there didn't appear to be any compatible trees nearby that they could use for charging. They settled under the shelter as Venefica studied her spell book next to the fire, and Pax wondered when, or if, the witch ever slept. Laying her head down to rest, she held the amulet in her hand, wondering if her mother knew about the vials it contained.

Finally, as she closed her eyes, Occissor opened his.

CHAPTER NINE

For centuries, the city of Rubra has stood at the centre of Tellus. But, where once its cobbled streets ran with blood in celebration of excess and superiority, now fearful whispers of rebellion and a new way of life echoed throughout them. The Castellum, a gothic monster of a building, cast a shadow over a city in turmoil. Clear glass tubes snaked their way around this central building, converging at a huge stained-glass window that absorbed the sun's rays in the day and the moonlight at night. This evening, the glass was glowing orange around the silhouette of a lone figure who stared out over the city. His city.

The white cloak around his slender shoulders fell onto the marbled tiles beneath his feet and was held in place by a gold brooch curved into the shape of the letter S. Trailing from one of his sleeves, a thin red tube wound all the way across the white floor, disappearing behind a large black glass throne. To the left of this throne stood an Oculus: a stone pillar holding a bowl of enchanted gold.

Occissor's eyes narrowed to red slits as the flickering flames of several pyrois came into view in the streets below, trotting towards the entrance to the Castellum. Even from this height he could recognise his army commander Phantasma, riding her pyrois. Although the hood of her cloak was raised over her head, concealing her silver hair, he could identify her just by the way she moved her body. He could sense her power, her presence, the way the guards gave her a wide birth, not daring to make eye contact with her. The enormous Castellum doors opened, without hesitation, for her, and she kicked her pyrois, trotting inside. The guards followed, jostling what appeared to be a significant number of prisoners into the bowels of the Cellarium. The king's thin lips curled into a smile as he visualised the cells four floors beneath his feet, full of caro, ready for the upcoming Messis. These celebrations were now more ceremonial than anything else, to keep the baying masses from the door. His guards had excelled in their preparations for this Blood Moon – not that he would bestow on them any praise.

Occissor turned away from the window, his slender fingers pulling his cloak behind him, papery skin taut over protruding purple veins. As he made his way towards the black glass throne, a silent guard stationed at the door stepped forwards to offer her hand, but Occissor waved her away, taking his seat. A few moments later, loud footsteps echoed outside the tall wooden doors of the Throne Room before the king's hand, Manus, entered the room. As he raised his arms to lower the dark green hood of his cloak, his chain mail gloves glinted gold in the moonlight.

"Your Highness," Manus said, bowing low as he entered the room. "Your army commanders have returned."

Phantasma appeared in the doorway first, wearing a newly donned clean white cloak, which was the uniform of army guards working within Rubra. Her rouge lips parted as she smiled feverishly, throwing herself down at the base of the throne.

"Master!" she said breathlessly, her white hair cascading over the marble floor like thick webs as she bowed low at his feet.

Deleo entered the room behind her, saluting and standing to attention near to the entrance, maintaining a respectful distance. Phantasma glanced up at Occissor, awaiting instruction, and he waved a veiny hand for her to speak.

"We have cleared out three villages in the forest of Viridis. Not a soul left, as instructed." She stayed crouching at his feet. "The Cellarium is bursting at the seams with caro ripe for the upcoming Messis!"

Deleo remained silent, standing twice the height of Manus at the doorway.

"Very good," Occissor replied.

Phantasma's lips parted wide, and she bowed again, euphoric at such rare praise.

"However," he continued, and Phantasma paused abruptly. "I feel there is something you've yet to tell me."

Deleo's eyes widened ever so slightly, but Manus watched on, unfazed.

Phantasma began, "I'm not sure what—" She froze at Occissor's raising hand.

He stood up from the throne, slowly making his way over to the Oculus in the corner of the room. The guard stationed at the door pulled the long red tube protruding from the king's sleeve alongside him, setting it carefully on the ground.

Occissor stood staring down at the rippling milky waters of the Oculus. His nostrils flared as he took a long, deep breath. Phantasma remained crouching on the marbled floor but turned her neck slightly to face him. Occissor removed the gold S-shaped brooch from his cloak and held his slender index finger over the liquid. The pin entered his flesh, and a single drop of blood formed on his fingertip. It dripped into the Oculus, red folding into white. Instantly the liquid circled and swirled, accepting his offering, clearing to reveal images to his eager eyes.

"Interesting," he said quietly, staring down into the Oculus.

"I can explain!" Phantasma exclaimed. "The journey was long! The guards needed sustenance! One— no, no, two caro, tried to escape!"

"Silence!" he shouted, his voice echoing around the cavernous room.

None of the guards dared to move. A few tense moments passed as they all watched Occissor move slowly across the Throne Room to the window once again, the only sound the scraping of the tube dragging behind him.

"All of this land is mine." He gestured down to the streets of Rubra. "All of the Supremo Gen are alive because of how I rule." He faced the room with a stare that could break bones. "And you have the audacity to come here and lie," he said, his voice rising, "to your king!"

Phantasma cowered as he spat out his final words. All the guards stationed in the room, including Deleo and Manus, fell to their knees, bowing their heads in shame.

"I see all," he whispered, creeping towards Phantasma, "know all."

He knelt down next to her, his bony fingers taking her chin into his hand, lifting her face to his. Terrified, Phantasma stared into his red eyes as his sharp nails dug into her skin.

"You harvested three?" He said with pungent breath, "When we so desperately need caro?"

Phantasma didn't move a muscle, silenced by fear. Suddenly her eyes flickered towards Deleo for a single moment. Occissor smiled, his pale skin stretching over the bulging veins of his face. With his nails still digging into Phantasma's chin, he held out his other hand towards Deleo. Ever so slightly, he flicked his wrist, and Deleo's huge body sprawled onto the floor. He writhed in agony, unable to breathe, an invisible grip around his throat. Phantasma's eyes widened as she watched Deleo gasp, veins straining against his reddening skin. Manus kept his eyes firmly fixed on the floor.

"You know I love you." Occissor spoke softly to Phantasma, his eyes closing peacefully.

Deleo gulped loudly, able to breathe again as Occissor's eyes snapped open. Releasing Phantasma from his grasp, he quickly stood up, his attention now elsewhere.

"What is this?" Occissor said with urgency.

His whole body tingled as a powerful current ran over him, power he hadn't felt for a long time. He grabbed the tube from his arm, ripping it out and spurting blood onto the white marbled floor.

"Your Highness?" Manus asked, getting up from his knees. "What is it?"

Occissor ran to the Oculus, waving his hand over the waters. Inside, the liquid swirled gold, circling around and around. His eyebrows raised as the image focused, finally revealing the amulet.

"It cannot be," he whispered to himself and turned to face the room.

"Rise!" His voice filled the Throne Room.

Deleo got to his feet quickly alongside the others, as if he hadn't just been in excruciating pain.

"Where were you last?" Occissor asked loudly.

"Viridis, Master," Phantasma responded.

"No souls left behind?"

"None, Your Highness. We couldn't smell the blood of any other Gen in the area."

Occissor started pacing across the room. "Impossible," he muttered, facing Phantasma. "You must return."

Phantasma nodded, getting to her feet. She went to leave, directing the guards waiting at the entrance to the Throne Room.

"Go to the courtyard and prepare the pyrois to le—"

She froze, the word trapped in her throat. Behind her, Occissor's pale hand was in the air. He flicked his wrist. Silently, without touching her, he raised Phantasma's feet off the ground.

"Leave." Occissor spoke quietly, but the weight of that one word made every guard turn and vacate the room.

Manus was the last to leave, taking one last look at Phantasma suspended in mid-air as he pulled the large wooden doors closed.

Slowly, Occissor spun her around until her pained face met his. Silently, she floated towards him. When her rigid body was close enough, he held her still, ensnared in the air.

"This is a delicate mission," he whispered. "Take only one other with you."

Phantasma was frozen in so much pain she could barely hear his next words, let alone respond.

"You've missed something," Occissor said. "Something extremely important to me. You must retrieve it, and you will not fail."

CHAPTER TEN

Disorientated, Pax opened her eyes, her brain frantically searching for an explanation as to why she wasn't at home in her own bed. The brief moment of the unknown was quickly washed away as the memory of what had happened flooded over her, the dull weight of reality sinking into her chest. Clutching the amulet, she sat up to see Am and Venefica by the fire, and her heartbeat slowed.

This morning, Am had prepared a breakfast of scuttleberry smash: a sticky crumble of fruits harvested from the surrounding bushes. Venefica had prepared another pot of faba, crushing the fresh beans from wild fabasucus plants she'd found nearby. The aroma welcomed Pax as she sat down to eat. Above, the velox fairies whizzed about happily as Felis stretched by the fire, too lazy to give chase.

"So, today we will head into the Caligo Caves?" Pax said between mouthfuls of crumbly smash, which prompted a smile from Am and a frown from Venefica. "You're still coming?" Pax asked the witch, who tipped the remains of her faba onto the ground and nodded.

"The Caligo Caves are an intricate system of underground chambers located beneath the banks of the River Capio, in Scandza," Am said.

"You have a map of this area as well?" Pax asked, thinking

that Am had only been programmed by her father with information about Viridis and its surrounds.

"Yes. The map covers the whole of Tellus, actually," Am replied, tapping the glowing blue nucleus at the centre of their chest. "We can access the caves from behind the Cataracta waterfall." Am pointed up to the crashing column of water that had so easily destroyed their boat the day before.

"Wet, dark and cramped? My favourite!" Venefica added sarcastically.

"Will we be able to see the Hydra?" Pax asked.

Am nodded. "They are illuminated by their own energy source; therefore, they will appear bright even in the darkness of the caves."

"Well, if we're going in, we'll need some torches," said Pax, collecting up the empty breakfast plates.

Am was charged with packing down the shelter as Venefica and Pax sauntered along the bank to gather bundles of herba. The plant would burn slowly, giving them enough time to search the caves for the Hydra. Once they had collected enough for three thick bundles, Pax tethered them at the base with string and placed them in her bag.

When the camp was packed away, the three of them stared up at the waterfall, where four magpies circled its misty crest. Together, they carefully ascended the steep bank next to the roaring falls. Pax led the way, gripping onto the rocks and heaving herself up onto the first ledge. It wasn't as steep as it looked from the ground, but the rocks were slick and nearly impossible to grip.

"Take your time," she shouted down to Am, who was directly behind her and, further down, a slightly more hesitant Venefica.

Felis hovered next to her, the condensation rolling off his slick coat, and he circled back every now and then to check on the others. Pax continued to climb, holding onto the jagged rocks of the cliff face, which occasionally would slice sharply into her skin. Her hair and clothes were already soaked from the fine mist coating the air around her.

Venefica yelled out. Pax stopped, peering over her shoulder, and was relieved to see the witch was still there. One of her bare feet had slipped on a rock, but she'd managed to grasp onto the clay-like mud of the bank to steady herself. After calling down to encourage her onwards, Pax carried on climbing.

Craning her neck through the mist, Pax could just make out a ledge, behind the wall of water, that was big enough for them to stand on. Reaching up, she could feel the rock face flattening out. She pulled herself up onto her knees and was, at last, able to stand up on the ledge, relieved to feel the solid sheet of rock beneath her boots. Turning, she held out her hand to help Am up onto the ledge, followed by a dishevelled Venefica. They were all soaking wet. Felis landed next to Pax, dramatically shaking the water droplets from his fur.

Surprisingly, the roar had dulled slightly on this side of the falls. Catching her breath, Pax wiped the mixture of water and sweat from her face. She went to speak but stopped when she saw the witch pointing over her shoulder. Pax turned to stare into the dark mouth of a cave carved into the thick black rock.

Shrugging off her rucksack, she retrieved the bundles of herba, kneeling down to protect them from the spray. Pax concentrated on one of the bundles, studying the stems twisted together, trying to block out the rumble of the falls. With her

Ortus day a few days away, her powers were getting stronger, and every day she felt she could control them slightly more. She stared at the long golden stem of the herba, the purple hue of its spiky seeds, focusing in on each tiny fibre. Then the newly familiar feeling of heat, of power, spread through her. In her mind she visualised the herba alight, each seed bursting into flames. A spark appeared, and the plant ignited with a satisfying crackle.

Smiling to herself, Pax used the flame to light the other two bundles, handing one to Am, who thanked her, and one to Venefica, who was quietly impressed. Felis ducked into her bag, tucking his wings behind him, and she picked him up, securing him and the rucksack onto her back. Facing the mouth of the cave, Pax raised her torch, took a deep breath and strode inside. Am followed her, confidently, but the witch hesitated, then nervously stepped into the cave.

Their footsteps echoed against the internal walls as the noise of the waterfall receded into the distance. Pax held her torch up high, allowing her eyes to adjust to the darkness. She couldn't see very far ahead but could hear a faint dripping onto the already-wet floor. Turning back to check Venefica and Am were still following, she stepped further into the darkness.

"We should be able to spot the Hydra," Pax whispered, but even though her voice was quiet, it still bounced off the walls.

Holding her torch up, she saw nothing but darkness and was unable to make out the height of the ceiling. They ventured deeper into the cave until the passageway divided into two separate tunnels.

"Which way?" Pax asked Am.

The green light of their nucleus lit up Pax's face as Am referenced their map. When the soft whirring stopped, Am pointed to the left tunnel, and they continued on. The deeper into the cave they went, the more tunnels they came across. Each time, they referred to Am's navigation system to decide on the best route. They'd been exploring the caves for what felt like a long time when, suddenly, Pax sensed something. The hairs on her arm prickled as the energy in the cave shifted around her.

"Stop! Listen." Pax stood still, holding up her hand to warn the others.

They all froze. At first it was quiet apart from the faint dripping of water. Then another noise from somewhere deep in the cave. A chittering, almost like a swarm of insects. Pax frowned, trying to place the noise. It got louder. Something was coming straight towards them.

"Don't move!" said Pax.

By the light of the torch, she could just make out movement further down in the darkness. A flash of something caught her eye. Then it was gone. Venefica gasped loudly, and Pax held her finger to her lips and waited. Her eyes widened as a huge black spindly leg surged into view. Then another leg and another, stretching all the way up into the darkness of the cave. Slowly, Pax craned her neck upwards. She couldn't see the body the legs were attached to, but it was creeping towards them, scratching the floor of the cave as it moved closer. Pax held her breath. One of the massive legs moved past them. The creature stopped, towering over their torches. A trog. Its black, shell-like body was illuminated above them. It had no eyes, but a gaping mouth, layered with hundreds of jagged teeth. Rancid bile dripped from the trog's jaws. A thick glob oozed from its mouth and onto Pax's head. The cold slime coated her hair and covered her face. Pax grimaced, holding her breath, willing herself not to react. The smell of rotting meat filled her nostrils. Finally, the bile slid from her face and onto the cave floor.

"What do we do now?" asked Am.

Pax braced herself, waiting for the creature to react to Am's voice, but nothing happened. The creature didn't move.

"Stay very still," Pax replied quietly.

The bile on her lips filled her mouth with a putrid taste, and she had to fight the urge to retch. Still the creature didn't move.

"Trogs can't see or hear," mumbled the witch, not moving her lips. "They only sense movement."

The trog chittered again, louder this time. Pax managed not to flinch. Then, from further inside the tunnel, came a loud scuttling. More trogs, six or seven, feeling blindly around the cave walls with their sharp legs. A second trog closed in on them. It outstretched one of its spindly legs, prodding the cave, jabbing through the air alarmingly close to Pax. She held her breath as the trog raised its leg again, stabbing it violently between her feet. Venefica's white eyes widened in the dark. The trog retracted its leg, retreating towards another tunnel off the side of the main cave. The trog that was still looming above them started to follow the rest of the cluster.

Pax exhaled slowly, trying not to even move the air around her. Suddenly there was a sharp intake of breath. The flame on Venefica's torch seared her skin, and she dropped it, clattering, to the floor. It echoed loudly off the walls of the cave. All the trogs stopped.

Venefica screamed, fleeing down the tunnel. Too late to

stop her, Pax and Am followed, throwing their torches to the ground. Scrambling, the trogs hunted them, their many legs scraping frantically against the cave floor. Around the corner, Pax pushed Am into a hollow in the rock. Venefica ducked down on the opposite side of the cave and froze.

"Don't move," Pax whispered to Am.

The trogs scurried past them, then slowed. They paused, prodding the cave with their pointed legs, inches from the witch, who was now huddled over in fear. Pax tried to make eye contact with Venefica through the darkness, but her eyes had turned from white to black, her chest heaving up and down, her body shaking. The nearest trog sensed the slight movement in the air, moving closer to the witch. Pax knew she had to do something. The torch she had dropped was still burning on the ground beneath one of the other trogs.

"Am, stay here."

Pax pushed herself off the cave wall and raced back between the legs of the trog, skidding against the cave floor. She grabbed the torch. The trogs chittered loudly in unison, all following her. Rising to her feet, Pax sprinted down the tunnel, tripping on the uneven surface. She kept going, not daring to look back, as the sound of galloping trogs pursued her. Suddenly, she slammed into something hard. On the ground, through the pain, she looked up at the cold wet wall. A dead end. The light of her dropped torch illuminated the fast-approaching clutter of creatures. She squeezed her eyes shut.

"Hey!" A deep voice echoed inside the cave. "Over here, you ugly critters!"

Pax opened her eyes to the light of a large torch waving further back down the cave. The trogs skidded to a halt. One by one, they moved towards the waving flame and away from Pax. The torch disappeared into the darkness, and with it, the cluster of trogs. When Pax was sure the creatures could no longer sense her, she leant against the wall, exhaling in relief. Then, she got to her feet and went after them.

Keeping her movements small, she followed the scuttling noise echoing down the tunnel. Eventually, it opened up into a larger cavern, where Pax ducked down behind a column of rock, peering out to get a better look. Below, she could now see who the thundering voice belonged to: a large muscular Gen. Pax recognised him to be a warrior from his attire – he was dressed in a short-sleeved tunic, his shoulders swathed in animal fur, and a large belt was fastened around his waist, holding a sword in place. He was now standing on a rock ledge waving his torch in one hand and spinning an axe in the other.

"Come and get it!" he shouted, his voice echoing around the cave.

One of the trogs lunged at him, meeting the sharp end of his axe. His movements were skilled and fast, but he was outnumbered massively by the charging creatures. Another two trogs lunged simultaneously. He dropped his torch to the ground to grip his weapon with both hands, swinging it again. One trog fell, but the other's sharp pincer sliced deep into his arm. He kicked the attacking trog square in the mouth with what appeared to be a metal leg. The creature recoiled in pain. Briefly, the man glanced at the blood flowing from his bicep, laughing to himself. He pulled his axe from the head of the trog dying at his feet, with a sickly squelch.

The chittering got louder. From the mouth of another tunnel spewed in row after row of trogs, filling the cave and surrounding the lone warrior. He quickly jumped up onto a higher ledge and stared down at the cluster of trogs below. From the belt bag around his waist, he pulled out a pocket watch. Closing his eyes, he muttered something to himself before replacing it carefully back into the bag.

Then, roaring loudly and raising his weapon, the warrior launched himself into the mass of creatures. Pax braced herself as the ground shook from the impact of him hitting the cave floor. Several of the trogs toppled over as the man swung his axe wildly at the attacking creatures. But even though he was large and fighting fiercely, there were too many trogs. Pax knew she needed to help him, or she would watch him die.

Gripping her torch, she stood up and waved it above her head. But none of the creatures reacted, too tuned into the wild movements of the warrior crashing his axe down upon them. Pax stomped her feet. A trog close to her appeared to sense her movements. It stopped for a few moments then returned to the swirling mass of the fight. Pax felt powerless. This Gen had saved her, and there was nothing she could do to help him. Suddenly she felt angry. Angry at herself for putting others in danger. For losing her parents and not knowing what to do. And now, angry at having to watch this man die.

Her hands clenched into fists. Her breath quickened. A thick heat in her chest spread throughout her body. Her eyes focused in the darkness, the movements in the cave slowing. Pax raised the torch in her hand above her head, feeling the heat of the flames. She scowled at the army of trogs attacking the man, who she could no longer see under the swarm. Hot rage pulsed through her body, bubbling in her blood. Pax wanted them dead. *Kill them.* The words echoed in her mind.

Kill them. Kill them. Kill them.

Fingers twitching, Pax screamed. A wild scream from deep inside her. The flames from her torch burst upwards, increasing in size. They erupted upwards onto the ceiling of the cave, filling it with light. An enormous fireball tumbled over itself and down the walls, engulfing the cave. Screeches of pain echoed as the trogs retreated, hot flames singeing the hairs of their legs, burning those who didn't flee quickly enough. Pax stood above, watching it all happen in slow motion, her lips curving into a smile.

As quickly as it had started, it stopped. The flames were extinguished as the torch fell from her hand. Below, Pax saw the large warrior pushing the smoking bodies of dead trogs off him. Her vision blurred and the noises in the cave faded. An outline of someone in a bright white light appeared above her. Then she hit the ground.

CHAPTER ELEVEN

The glass tubes around the outside of the Castellum scaled all the way from the lower levels of the Cellarium, running along the high ceilings of the corridors, spanning all floors of the building. They grew in width as they climbed the external walls up to the window of the Throne Room, and Manus had made it his responsibility to inspect nearly all of them.

"Wonderful job," he said, touching the shoulder of the young Supremo scrubbing the tubes lining the corridor. "They almost look as new, as they were during the very first Messis."

The boy glanced up nervously. Manus could see the youngster's body relax when he removed his hand. Despite it still being covered in his signature gold chain mail gloves, the boy knew what could happen if Manus's bare skin touched him – every Gen in Rubra knew. Manus smiled thinly, threading his hands into the sleeves of his cloak, hidden from view, and continued down the hallway to scrutinise the other servants.

The Messis was mere days away, and he took great pride in ensuring the Castellum was in pristine condition, all the way from the Cellarium right up into the Throne Room. Whilst the king ruled by fear, Manus often found a kind word worked wonders with the Supremo Gen about the Castellum.

Upon the walls of the third floor hung a selection of large tapestries made from the finest silk. They had been commissioned to display the history of the Supremo Gen, depicting days of old, previous royals and traditional celebrations of Rubra. He stopped to straighten one of the tapestries – a scene of a small child being held in the king's hands at the open window of the Throne Room. Manus smoothed his glove over the silk where large Supremo crowds were depicted cheering in celebration at the birth of the prince. He remembered the day fondly – it was considered by all as nothing short of a miracle.

After the Supremo Gen had been cursed by old gods long ago, royal offspring did not often survive, nor did their mothers. It was true the queen had perished on that day, but the tapestries did not depict such tragedies. The prince's untimely death came but twenty years after his birth – finally succumbing to the old gods' curse. It had left the king with no heir, and, desperate to quell any uprisings or challenges to the throne, the Messis celebrations had begun. They were needed to placate the masses. Even Manus had to admit to this sad truth.

"Sir?" The guard approached Manus, and he turned, taking his eyes away from the tapestry.

"Yes?"

"I've checked the Cellarium, as you directed. The guards have reported everything to be satisfactory. Cleaning is being finalised, and the caro are all behaving." The guard waited for further instruction.

Manus cleared his throat. "Yes, very good. You may return to your station."

The guard saluted and turned on his heels, marching back

down the corridor. Manus always felt uncomfortable with the idea of caro in the Cellarium and could never quite bring himself to go down there in person. Instead, he turned up the spiral staircase to the Throne Room, on the fourth floor.

This would be the thirtieth Messis – two for every year around the sun. Manus could hardly believe so much time had passed. He hadn't agreed with the method at first, not that he'd ever vocalised his opposition, but as the Blood Moons went on, he'd learnt to see the positives of each one. Of course, they weren't as traditional as the honourings of old, but the Messis did provide much-needed celebration for the Supremos of Rubra, unifying the whole city and, therefore, keeping the peace in such trying times.

"Your Majesty." Manus bowed low as he entered the Throne Room.

Occissor didn't respond, instead staring into the Oculus, his veiny hands gripping the sides of the gold bowl.

Approaching quietly, Manus asked, "Have you had any other visions, Your Highness?"

Occissor shook his head. "No, and no word from Phantasma yet either."

Manus nodded. "And what exactly did you see in the Oculus earlier, Your Highness? Maybe I could be of some assistance?"

The king considered this for a few moments and then called out to the guards stationed at the door.

"Leave us."

The guards exited, closing the wooden doors and leaving them alone in the Throne Room.

"Tell me, Manus, am I a good king?"

Manus paused before answering, knowing conversations

like this could be dangerous.

"Why, of course, Your Highness."

Occissor scoffed, walking towards the large window. "What does it mean to be a king? To be a god?"

Manus joined him by his side at the window but chose to stay silent. Below them, the streets of Rubra were a hive of activity, with locals busy preparing for the approaching celebrations.

"The arrangements for the Messis are progressing well, Your Highness," Manus offered after a long silence.

"How long can we appease them?" Occissor replied. "How long before they grow tired of a drop of blood when they used to have rivers?"

"I will not pretend that the rituals of old were not spectacular, Your Majesty." Manus glanced at the king, knowing he was one of the few that could speak truthfully to him. "However, times have changed, and a good ruler changes with them."

Occissor's smile tightened the veiny skin of his face. "Ah, Manus – you are a constant reminder of my past." He moved towards the Oculus again. "And this" – he gripped the edges of the bowl – "shows me a present I cannot make sense of."

Manus joined him at his side, peering into the milky waters of the Oculus, knowing he would not be able to witness the same images it presented to his king.

"But what of the future?" Occissor said.

"What did you see in the waters, Your Highness?" Manus asked again.

Occissor took a deep breath and sighed, finally answering, "The amulet."

After a stunned silence, Manus whispered, "After all these

years? What does this mean?"

Occissor's knuckles bulged as he gripped the Oculus even more tightly. "That whoever has it will pay for such treachery!"

As the king's hand, Manus knew he would continue to advise Occissor to the best of his abilities. However, silently, he hoped the sighting of the amulet signalled change – a real change – and lasting peace could be restored in Tellus once more. Manus had been within the walls of the Castellum for longer than the king himself, after his powers made him an indispensable royal advisor for generations. And if all those centuries had taught him one thing for certain, it was that nothing ever stays the same.

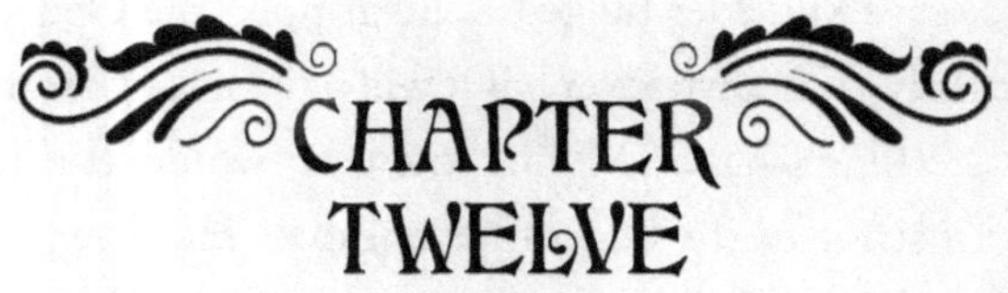

CHAPTER TWELVE

A familiar sound echoed around Pax. A golden light flashed inside her eyelids. As the colour faded, the noise grew louder. Slowly Pax realised it was her own name being called again and again. She would have thought she was dreaming if it weren't for the excruciating pain searing through her skull. Opening her eyes, she was greeted with a blurred face above her in the dimly lit cave, and she tried to sit up.

"Woah there, lass! Take it easy. You're safe now." The Gen's deep voice was more comforting than alarming.

She relaxed a little, lying back down on the cold floor, trying to remember how she got there. Quick footsteps tapping around the cave announced the arrival of Venefica and Am, who had been the ones yelling out her name.

"Get back!" shouted Venefica, her eyes now black, alarmed at finding a large warrior leaning over Pax's limp body.

Am stood next to her, holding a flaming torch above their heads, with Felis peering out from behind their legs. The warrior turned his head slightly, a small smirk playing across his chiselled jaw.

"It's okay. I mean no harm." Slowly he stood, holding up his massive hands to show he held no weapons. At his full height, he towered over all of them. "This young lass here saved my life!"

"It's fine; he's okay," Pax mumbled as she tried to get up again.

Venefica moved towards her, and the warrior knelt back down at the same time. Their eyes met briefly as they helped Pax sit up.

Am scanned Pax's body. "Your occipital bone has connected with a hard surface, but there appears to be no serious damage."

Pax managed a weak smile, but the pain at the back of her head felt pretty serious. Leaning against the damp wall of the cave to steady herself, she automatically put her hand around the amulet, relieved to find it still in place.

"I must thank you. You saved my life!" The warrior's piercing blue eyes narrowed as he smiled. "That was some fireball!"

He was handsome despite the old battle scars on his face, and the sides of his head had been close shaven, revealing intricate inking on his skin. His remaining long blond hair was fashioned into a knot on top of his scalp, tangled with pieces of silver, which glinted in the flames of the torch. His arm was still bleeding. The cut had sliced through more tribal designs, which covered his bicep, yet he didn't seem to notice.

"I'm Miles, by the way, of Trib—"

"Tribus Gen. Hailing from Scandza," Am interrupted, having scanned Miles's blue eyes. "Known for their fighting abilities."

Miles nodded, raising his eyebrows at Am, mildly impressed. "And which tribe are you three warriors from?"

He tore a strip of material from his skirt, which only just covered his muscular thighs, his left one connecting flawlessly to a complex metal limb at the knee. He wrapped the fabric tightly around the cut on his arm to stem the bleeding, waiting for someone to answer.

Pax still felt woozy, but Am was smiling mutely, and Venefica was circling Miles suspiciously, so she guessed it was up to her to do the talking.

"I'm Pax, of Silva Gen in Viridis." She gestured with her hand. "And this is Am."

Venefica was sniffing the air near Miles, then backing away.

"This is Venefica," Pax said, "from… Celare?" she added, realising she still wasn't exactly sure where the witch was from.

"The great Venefica!" Am corrected, prompting the witch to stand confidently in front of Miles, her head held high.

"I can see that," he replied, sniggering when Venefica blushed. "What were you all doing in these caves? Apart from whipping those trogs into a frenzy!"

"We are looking for Hydra," Am replied. "But we had to be still because there were many, many trogs."

Miles nodded. "I've been hunting them for years." He strode over to one of the dead creatures nearby and lifted his metal leg to rest it on its shell-like head. "Never seen a cluster that large before! Lucky for me that you came along." He pointed at Pax.

She wasn't really sure what he meant; *he* had saved *her*. "I don't remember," she said, the throbbing in her head pounding against her skull. "The trogs… they were attacking you. I wanted them to stop."

Miles nodded in agreement. Felis, deciding the warrior posed no threat, summoned the courage to curl up against Pax's leg.

Her eyebrows knitted together as she tried to recall what

had happened. "There was a bright white light."

"A fire ball!" Miles spread his raised arms out wide. "I've never seen anything like it! You have some almighty power, lass!"

Pax turned to Venefica, who was now huddled over her mortar, crushing herbs she'd gathered previously into a paste with the pestle.

"Was it you? Did you cast a spell?" Pax asked her.

Venefica shook her head, standing up and carefully applying the paste to the back of Pax's head. It smelt horrible, like burnt hair, but the throbbing started to ease instantly.

Miles arched an eyebrow at the witch. "Powerful too?" he asked. Venefica finished scraping the paste onto Pax's hair, continuing to ignore him.

"She's the most powerful witch!" Am said.

Miles smiled. "And what about you?" He picked up his torch off the ground and lit it from Am's, throwing a little more light over the cave. Am smiled back but didn't answer.

"Are you powerful, too?" he asked. Am frowned slightly, unsure of how to respond. Miles, noticing Am's uncertainty, said, "Am, was it?"

"Yes!" Am replied, relieved to answer a more direct question. "It means good friend."

Miles laughed. "And are you? A good friend?"

Am glanced at Pax again, then after a slight pause asked, "Is Am a good friend?"

A surge of emotion hit Pax as she recalled the reason Am had been created in the first place.

"The best," she said, the words almost getting caught in her throat.

Am faced Miles and smiled again, but more widely this

time. He patted Am on the shoulder, and Pax felt a huge sense of gratitude that the warrior was being so kind.

"Well, I'd love to sit and chat in this damp cave all day, but I think we'd better make a move before this one's mother decides to wreak revenge!" Miles said, kicking the carcass of the trog.

The creature looked just as terrifying dead as it had when it was alive, bile still oozing from its slack mouth. Unfurling a length of rope attached to his belt bag, Miles started to tether the creature's huge, spindly legs together.

"You're taking it with you?" Pax asked, slightly alarmed.

"Trogs go for good coin in Scandza!" Miles explained. "That's why I was here."

He pushed his weight onto his metal leg, tightening the rope, then cut it with a sharp, black blade. As he replaced the knife in its scabbard next to the Axe around his waist, he caught Pax staring at where the metal entered the skin of his thigh, matching the curve of the muscle underneath perfectly.

"It's called a crus. A bionic leg, if you will," he said calmly, continuing to tie the rope.

Pax blushed. "Oh, I… It's figo."

Miles's laughter filled the cave. "Figo! Indeed! I agree. I lost my leg in a battle many moons ago. This crus gave me a new lease of life when I needed it most." He slapped the metal twice.

Venefica had started to pack up her things into her bag, encouraging Felis to jump inside. She gestured to Pax it was time to leave.

"So, you were looking for Hydra you said," Miles offered, seeing the witch becoming impatient. "What do you need them for? Some kind of spell?"

"No business of yours, warrior," Venefica replied, walking away.

"Well, okay, except you won't find them down here."

Venefica sighed.

"Could you show us?" Pax asked, her head no longer throbbing.

"Of course!" Miles finished tying the last knot. "Come with me!"

He stood and held his arm out for Pax. She had to reach up to grab it because even though he was leaning down, he was still so tall. When she was up on her feet, the warrior pointed to a tunnel on the left side of the cave. Am went first, followed by a stony-faced Venefica, with Miles smiling politely as she passed.

Miles directed Am down some narrow tunnels where, in parts, he had to duck so as not hit his head. The route was narrow and complicated, and Pax was thankful he appeared to know the way by heart. Finally, the tunnel opened up again. Miles stopped. Peering around the huge warrior, Pax saw why. In front of her was the most breathtaking sight. A gradient of greens covered the walls of the cave. Light shone from every angle. A euphonious sound surrounded them, bouncing off the walls. Sparkling bioluminescent creatures were covering every inch of the cathedral-like cave. They had found the Hydra.

In awe, each of them wandered around the cave, inspecting the Hydra more closely. Pax waved her hand over them, and the different greens rippled, spreading far across the inside of the cave. She held her ear up close to the wall and realised the chiming was coming from the Hydra, as if they were singing just to her.

Pax took the amulet in her hands, the glowing light from the Hydra reflecting in the gold. She pushed down on the symbol, and with a click, the six vials protruded out of place. Pax carefully removed the vial topped with the emerald gemstone. She held the vial up to the wall of the cave, carefully scooping some of the Hydra inside. Replacing the stopper, she clicked it back into the amulet. Again, nothing happened. Slightly disappointed, she watched the others inspecting the cave.

Am was spinning slowly in wonder, their head tilted up towards the creatures covering the ceiling. Felis was enjoying stretching his wings after being confined in a bag for so long, spreading waves through the Hydra as he flew past. Venefica was collecting some of the Hydra from the wall, scraping them into a glass jar, muttering to herself. Further down the cave, on a flattened rock shelf, Miles sat quietly.

"I never get over this sight," he said, glassy-eyed, as Am sat down next to him.

"These are beautiful?" Am asked. "It makes you sad?"

Miles smiled. "Sometimes, something can be so beautiful it can bring you to tears."

Am paused, considering this. "Is sadness bad?"

Miles shook his head. "Not at all. We all feel sadness sometimes. It makes you appreciate the happier times."

Venefica appeared silently at their side, making Miles jump.

"Many push sadness away, trying not to let it in," Venefica said, suggesting she had been listening to their conversation this whole time. Her white eyes were focused on Pax, who was walking back towards them from across the other side of the illuminated cave. "When it inevitably arrives, it destroys them."

A strange melancholy accompanied Pax as she left the beauty of the cave and followed the others back down the tunnel, walking through the darkness and towards the light once again.

☾

"This will do nicely!" Miles declared, stepping into a clearing as shafts of dying sunlight streamed through the branches of the trees that enclosed them.

Although this forest was similar to Viridis, it also felt very different, at least to Pax. The shape of the trees was sharper, the smells of the plants more acidic, and even the air around her felt heavier.

"I'll just hang this little fella up in those trees further back," Miles said, dragging the massive corpse of the trog away from them with ease. "It'll stop the smell and keep scavengers away."

"What are scavengers?" Am asked, but Miles was already too far away into the trees to hear them, and Pax wasn't sure she wanted to know the answer.

Miles had suggested camping here in Ramble Glen. They had made good progress since leaving the Caligo Caves, but night was fast approaching, and Pax had to admit that her whole body was aching. She'd never been so relieved to remove her boots. Wincing, she pulled her socks off, glad there was no blood, just a few juicy blisters. Venefica finished inspecting the outer edges of the clearing and felt satisfied enough to sit down on the forest floor opposite Pax. The soles of the witch's feet were, miraculously, unmarked.

"Don't your feet hurt after walking so far with no shoes?" Pax asked, rubbing her own feet.

Venefica scoffed. "Pah! It is shoes that make feet hurt! Your soles connect your soul to the earth." She patted her chest above her heart.

"Time to build the shelter?" Am asked, with Felis perched on their shoulder.

"No rush," Pax replied.

Venefica studied Am. "You are not tired from our journey?"

Am shook their head.

"Am doesn't get tired as long as their energy levels are maintained. In fact, I'd better check." Pax said, standing up and peering at the panel at the back of Am's casing.

Am stared unblinking at Venefica as Felis jumped from their shoulder onto the ground and padded across to a rock, which he had decided was the perfect place for him to clean his fur.

"All good for another day at least," Pax said, shutting the casing.

"Then what happens?" Venefica asked, intrigued.

Pax looked at Am. "Do you want to explain?"

Am nodded. "When my internal bio aux energy levels are low, they must be replenished from a suitable source."

"So Am just needs a compatible plant to connect with. Some are better than others, some take ages to charge, but Miles said that there's lots of suitable options once we get to Scandza," Pax added.

Venefica nodded that she understood, and Pax sat down again, inviting Am to sit next to her.

"You're lucky you don't get sore feet." Pax nudged Am, laughing.

"Is it very painful?" Am asked, crouching down to study Pax's blisters.

"Nah, I just need a good night's rest, and I'll be ready to go in the morning."

"Same here!" Miles had returned, carrying an armful of dried branches and slinging his weapons down onto the ground. "But I need a good feed too!"

Venefica's eyes lit up at the suggestion of food, and she jumped up to take the firewood from his arms.

"Oh, thank you," Miles said, smoothing his hair with his now-empty hands and styling it back up into a neat topknot. He cleared his throat. "What do we fancy for supper? Stew? I think I spotted some wild dragats down in those bushes."

With this, Felis stopped washing himself mid-lick, his forked tongue hanging in the air.

"Umm, maybe not dragat?" Pax said, leaning over to scoop Felis up in her arms and cradling him like a baby.

"Oh right, of course!" Miles chuckled. "Nettle stew it is!"

By the time Miles returned with handfuls of green nettles and a dozen wild potatoes, Am had prepared a pot over the white-hot embers. Pax took the potatoes from Miles, and, opening her penknife, peeled away the muddy purple skin. Am had no problem pulling the stinging nettles from their stems and dropping them into the pot over the fire to boil.

"How much further is it to Scandza?" Pax asked.

"About another day on foot," Miles replied, stoking the glowing embers. "We should make it there by dusk tomorrow if we leave here at dawn."

"I've never been to Scandza." Pax scooped the slices of

potato into her hands and slid them into the pot.

Miles sighed. "You're in for a real treat, Scandza is beautiful. Where did you say you were from again?"

"Viridis."

"Viridis! A wonderful place! Full of such good Gen," Miles replied. "The alchemist that designed my crus came from there," he said, tapping his metal leg. "Creo, I think his name was—"

"That's my father!" Pax almost yelled.

"You don't say! Tellus is small indeed! How is he?"

Pax's smile dropped from her face, a lump forming in her throat as she sat back down.

Miles placed his hand lightly on her shoulder. "You okay?"

"He was taken," Pax said. "My mother too. That's why we were in the caves. I'm trying to help them."

Miles took a deep breath. "Taken by who?"

"I'm not sure. Venefica thinks it was a Gen called the Harvesters."

Miles froze.

"You've heard of them?" Pax asked.

Miles nodded slowly, standing up and interlacing his fingers at the back of his head. "Nasty Gen. Of course they would be active this time of year, so close to the Blood Moon. When did they attack?"

"A few days ago. My father left me with some clues, a trail of sorts. I'm hoping if I follow it, I'll be able to help."

Miles glanced at Pax. "Your father is one of the smartest Gen I've ever met. I'm sure if he left you clues, you're on the right path."

Pax sighed. "I'm glad you like him, most people think he's a nid."

"A nid!" Miles laughed. "He's not a nid! If it wasn't for him, I wouldn't be standing next to you right now!"

Pax managed a smile, but she was desperately missing her parents. She watched Am spoon the green paste from the nettle stalks into the pot and stir, with Venefica crouching over the fire, watching the pot closely.

"You have come across the Harvesters in previous moons, warrior?" the witch asked.

Miles straightened up. "I've heard the rumours about them, sure."

Pax leant in closer. "What rumours?"

"Well, there's rumours that the prince was murdered by someone. A Gen who escaped, and that's what started the Harvests – the king went mad with rage."

"That sounds bad," Am said loudly.

"But, look, we've all had a long day, and we need a good rest this evening, and no talk of murders is going to help you sleep." Miles picked up the bowls. "Plus, this stew is just about ready to eat, and I'm starving!"

CHAPTER THIRTEEN

They set off towards Scandza as soon as the sun had risen. After hours of hiking, with only short breaks to replenish their water supplies in the streams, they finally reached the top of a steep ridge, where Miles stopped, placing his hands on his hips. Pax stepped to the warrior's side. Down in the valley, huge snow-capped mountains pierced the clouds, their rock faces changing from white to green down to grey jagged rocks. In the distance, huge jets of hot steam were being launched into the air from geysers in the ground. Wild birds called shrilly in the air high above them, hovering over their unseen prey. The small hamlets lining the slopes were bathed in the setting sunlight, and a few lanterns twinkled, having already been lit by the local Gen readying for the coming night. They had made it to Scandza.

"I can't imagine a more beautiful place than home," Miles said, taking in the view. The warrior knelt down, kissing his first and middle finger and placing them on the ground. He stood up. "C'mon, we still have a fair way to go."

He was still dragging the corpse of the trog as they descended the steep track into the first village. As the others followed, they tried their best to avoid stepping in the trail of slime the dead creature was still managing to leave in its wake.

"I think we could all do with a good meal tonight!"

declared Miles. "I know the best tavern in all of Scandza. The Hungry Dragon!"

Pax felt safe entering an unknown town next to the warrior. As they approached, she saw some locals closing up their market stalls for the day. They stopped what they were doing and stared as the group approached. Some doffed their hats when Miles came into view, exchanging greetings as they passed. But when the locals saw Am and Venefica following him, the pleasantries stopped. A tall woman clearing up a fruit stall dropped a basket of apples and ran towards her child, scooping her up protectively into her arms.

Miles didn't seem to notice, or if he did, he hid it well, and undeterred, they walked through the streets of Scandza. It was dusk by the time they arrived at a small tavern at the edge of the town. A wooden sign swinging above the door read 'The Hungry Dragon' and featured a painting of a green scaled creature slurping from a bowl. The tavern was framed by huge fields of ploughed earth stretching into the evening, and Pax recognised the low calls of tricorns in the distance.

Miles slung the corpse of the trog onto the ground outside the tavern and pushed the wooden door open with a creak.

"After you," he said, extending his arm.

Pax entered first and was instantly embraced by the warmth. A fireplace filled the dimly lit tavern with a smoky aroma mingled with a hint of something delicious wafting from the kitchen. Pax's stomach was rumbling as they had only eaten handfuls of berries on their long journey here. Am and Venefica followed her inside, and Miles pulled the door closed behind them.

The well-worn furniture inside the tavern was wooden and mismatched, having lived other lives before making its home here amongst the locals. There were a handful of Gen seated at tables and propped along the bar. Some were a similar build to Miles, and he greeted them with great slaps on their backs.

"Tribus Gen," said Am, scanning the two Miles was speaking to, although Pax could have guessed from their tribal tattoos.

At the bar, Pax also recognised a group of Piscator Gen, local fishergens. They gripped cold glasses with dirty hands, gulping down the golden liquid to quench their thirst after a busy day catching tentamenta. One of the fishergens must have told a joke, as the others laughed loudly, pounding the bar with their fists.

Pax spotted an empty booth near to the fire, and they settled into their seats. A hooded figure at the bar glanced towards them, then turned back to a short Gen serving them, to accept some coins. When the bartender saw Miles, a huge smile spread through his beard.

"The warrior returns!" he said, making his way out from behind the bar.

"Dominus!" Miles said, greeting the bartender with a hug that lifted him clean off the ground. "I've got you the best trog meat coin can buy!"

"Ah, my good Gen!" Dominus replied, his felt-covered feet now back on the floor. "Tomorrow, roast trog will be on the menu!" He slapped Miles on the back of his thigh and returned to the bar. It appeared he must be standing on a raised platform, Pax noticed, as he was now nearer to Miles's height again. "What'll it be?"

"My guests and I have had a long journey! Four cups of your finest faba, please, extra hot, and whatever tastes good from the menu."

Dominus peered over at the table where Pax, Am and Venefica were seated, unfazed to see such an out of place trio in his tavern. "Of course, I'll send it over shortly."

The door opened again, blasting cold air into the tavern as the cloaked figure who had been at the bar exited, closing the door behind them. Miles joined them on the opposite side of their booth, taking up as much room as the three others, combined. He smiled at them all, lingering just slightly longer on Venefica. Felis decided the warrior's large lap was the most comfortable to sit on and curled his forked tail around his paws.

On the table next to them a small group of Probus Gen was seated around an upturned glass jar holding a rather angry flying insect. Coins were tossed onto the table as one of the Probus Gen grasped the top of the jar, undoing it quickly and lifting it up. The yellow and red insect flew into the air, buzzing around their heads and landing on one of the Gen's arms. He yelped as it stung him. The others laughed, sliding the coins on the table into their hands. The insect flew past Pax's head with a loud hum and out of one of the tavern's windows.

"What was that?" Pax asked, ducking to avoid it.

"Just a harmless Vespa," Miles replied, "used in the game of Jars. Not much fun to play if you're no good at it." He pointed to the loser, who was now rubbing his arm. "So, I suggest you all rest here tonight," Miles continued, patting Felis softly, his large hand nearly covering the dragat's whole body. "Dominus has rooms upstairs."

"We don't have any coin to pay for the rooms," Pax said quietly, her face going red.

"It's all taken care of," Miles replied. "Trog meat is worth a tidy sum in these parts!"

"But—"

"I'll hear no more on the matter!" Miles said, scratching Felis's wing.

Pax smiled. "Thank you." The idea of sleeping in a bed rather than the hard ground of the forest was extremely appealing. "Will Am be able to charge here, too?"

"Yes, I'll arrange that with Dominus for tomorrow. It works better in the daytime, I hear?"

Pax and Am both nodded.

"Good. Plus, there'll be roast trog on the menu tomorrow!" Miles beamed.

Pax grimaced. "You eat them?"

"Yep! Blooming delicious!"

The crowd in the bar parted slightly, making way for Dominus, who appeared next to their table.

"Good evening, young ladies," he said, squinting as Am scanned him. Pax placed a hand on Am's arm.

"Maybe don't scan anyone in here, okay?" she said, noticing the stares from across the bar. Am nodded.

Dominus smiled and introduced himself. "I'm Dominus, of Probus Gen. The owner of The Hungry Dragon."

"The best tavern in all of Scandza!" Miles added, slapping the table.

"And this is my son, Ganymead." Dominus pointed up at the young boy, standing twice his height, next to him.

Ganymead placed four cups on the table, his almost-yellow hair flopping either side of his blue eyes. The slight outline of dimples suggested he normally smiled, but now he was biting his lip.

Reaching up, Dominus slapped the young boy encouragingly on the back, making him spill the faba he was pouring from a large clay jug all over the wooden table. With a reddening face, Ganymead pulled out the cloth tucked into his belt to wipe the table. As Pax lifted one of the cups to help him, Ganymead looked at her, smiling. All of a sudden, Pax became very aware of how dirty her fingernails were. She ran her hand through her hair, tucking it behind her ear and cursed herself for not packing a hairbrush.

"Ganymead's Ortus day isn't far off!" Dominus said, oblivious to the spillage he had caused and his son's reddening face.

"Mine's close too." Pax smiled at Ganymead, then quickly looked away.

Dominus pointed at Miles. "I bet you ladies have been keeping this one out of trouble!"

Miles laughed, and Pax found herself enjoying listening to a normal conversation. Dominus said he would return with bovis stew and fresh bread shortly, and he and Ganymead disappeared towards the kitchen. Miles offered around the cups of faba, smirking as Venefica gulped hers down. Am didn't pick up a cup, and Miles raised his eyebrows at Pax.

"Am doesn't drink," said Pax .

"Or eat," Venefica added.

"Well, extra for you then," Miles said, sliding the cup over to Venefica, who had already finished her first.

She paused, then reluctantly took it in her hands. As she drank, the light from the fire reflected in a shiny ring on her index finger.

"That's beautiful," Pax said, pointing to a centre stone the colour of the moon.

The witch paused, unused to compliments. "A ring on each finger keeps the devil's deal away." Smiling, she nodded at the amulet. "Trade you, young one?"

Pax put a hand up to her neck, relieved to find the amulet was still tucked safely under her shirt. Strangers in the tavern noticing something so precious was not what she needed. Venefica chuckled, taking another sip of her drink.

"So, you were saying your father left you clues?" Miles asked Pax, noticing the exchange between her and the witch.

"Yes. I'm not entirely sure what they mean, and we only get one at a time." Pax said, unsure if she wanted to tell Miles about the amulet. Warriors were known to kill for expensive things. "The Hydra we collected from the caves were the latest clue."

"I have the next one," Am said.

Venefica leaned in. "Reveal it to us."

Am's eyes flickered to green.

Different waves you perceive,
Found in photon energies.
Many lines seem aglow,
The opposite of below.

Pax and Venefica frowned, quietly thinking. Felis jumped down from Miles's lap, scooting as close as he could to the fire without singeing his fur.

After a few moments Miles spoke. "Well! What in the seven gods does that mean?"

"We don't know; it's a riddle. We have to work it out," Pax explained.

"Wouldn't expect a warrior to understand," scoffed Venefica.

Miles raised his eyebrows, holding a hand to his massive chest, feigning heartbreak. He then smiled as Dominus approached the table, carrying a tray full of bowls of hot stew and crusty bread dripping with melted butter.

"Well, let's leave the riddles for now and tuck in!" said Miles.

As they ate, Am offered a piece of bovis to Felis, who was drawn away from the fire by the promise of food. The tavern was filling up with more workers coming in from the fields. Miles explained that the Probus Gen in this area were responsible for farming fabasucus, which was why the faba here was so fresh and delicious. Pax glanced towards the bar and recognised one of the short, bearded men. He looked up at her, and surprise flashed across his face as he made his way over to their table.

"Well, hello young lady." Arator removed his hat and bowed. "Good to see you again. What brings you to Scandza?"

"Hi!" Pax replied. "I'm here with my friends."

Arator stared at the unlikely group around the table, smiling with his mouth but not his eyes.

"I must say, I'm happy you are safe. After meeting you in the forest, I heard rumours of an attack in Viridis that very night."

Pax stiffened, putting a chunk of bread back down on her plate. "Yes, I'm safe."

"Not many survive the Harvesters," Arator continued. "You are very lucky indeed."

Pax was unsure of what to say, heat flushing through her cheeks. Miles, sensing her discomfort, leant across the table to shake Arator's hand.

"Miles, Tribus Gen."

"Ah! The Bionic Warrior!" Arator replied, glancing down at Miles's crus sticking out from under the table. "I've heard tales about you, and your most interesting… appendage."

"You'll feel it too if you keep staring!" Miles responded dryly, then he burst into loud laughter.

Arator sensed this was his cue to leave, doffing his hat as he passed Dominus, who now joined them at their table.

"Everything okay?" Dominus asked, looking over his shoulder at Arator, who was now whispering to a man in a green coat at the bar. "I heard him talking about the Harvester attack."

"What can you tell us about the Harvesters?" Pax asked.

Dominus shot a quick look at Miles, then sighed. Pulling a chair from nearby, he huddled into their table, suggesting this information wasn't for sharing.

"The Harvesters are a vicious Gen, hailing from Rubra. Of course, they don't call themselves Harvesters. That name was given to them because of their… exploits. No, they're an ancient Gen called the Supremos. They have a royal bloodline. Currently led by a nasty piece of work, Occissor. A most savage king."

Pax glanced sideways at Miles, who was sitting stony-faced.

Dominus checked over his shoulder once again, then continued. "Supremos used to be considered gods. But these days, they don't have the willing sacrifices anymore. So they go out and get it themselves."

"Get what?" Pax asked.

"Blood." Miles answered darkly. "They collect Gen and…

harvest their blood. They call their victims 'caro'." He looked at Pax as her face went pale.

"Is blood the food source of the Supremos?" Am asked.

"Not exactly," said Dominus as Pax pushed her bowl away from her. "They eat just like you and me."

Am went to interrupt, but Venefica raised her hand, stopping them. Am nodded instead, listening intently as Dominus spoke.

"The blood, it gives them power. Makes them immortal. Or at least it used to. There are rumours that their Gen is dying out. Their actions are becoming more savage the more desperate they become. During the Blood Moon they have a ceremony called the Messis, which is just a few short days away." Dominus lowered his voice. "The Supremos are searching for caro; that's why it's best to keep a low profile at the moment. Stay out of trouble."

Pax stared up at him, her eyes hot with tears. "They have my parents."

Miles nodded at Pax. "The alchemist Creo Silva's daughter."

Dominus slowly shook his head, unsure of what to say. Finally, he responded. "I'm so sorry. I know that doesn't help much, but you're welcome to stay here if you need to."

Pax smiled weakly, wiping her nose on the back of her shirt sleeve.

Dominus stood up, collecting some plates.

"I'll tell you what, how about I bring some treacle pudding over, freshly made today!" He leant in closer to Pax. "It has been known for Gen to escape them you know," he whispered. "Don't give up hope." With that, he wandered back towards the bar.

"He's right you know," Miles said, checking his watch and returning it to his pocket. "Plus, your parents have you on the case, and you're no ordinary girl. I've seen what you can do!"

"What? Someone who faints in the face of danger?" Pax replied sarcastically.

"Faint?" Miles responded, confused. "Girl, you lit that whole cave on fire! It was figo!"

Pax frowned. She knew her powers were increasing the closer she got to her Ortus day, but her recollection of the caves was foggy.

"I don't remember doing that. I thought it was you," she said, looking at Venefica.

The witch shook her head. "Interesting, I knew you had strong magic. But this…"

Miles, seeing the confusion on Pax's face, continued. "No one comes into their powers all at once, and no one really knows what to do with them or how to control them. Everyone thinks as soon as you hit your Ortus day you're meant to have it all figured out. But no one ever does. Hell, mine took years to develop!"

"What powers do you keep, warrior?" Venefica asked suspiciously.

"Brute strength and good looks!" he replied with a wink, making the witch scoff.

Miles's laughter was infectious and soon Pax joined him, feeling better by the time Ganymead brought their puddings to the table.

When the dishes were scraped clean, Ganymead returned to collect the empty bowls, and Am asked if they could accompany him back to the kitchen to help. Ganymead nodded enthusiastically, and Pax watched them make their way through the crowded bar towards the kitchen.

As Am talked to Ganymead, no doubt asking him lots of different questions, Pax noticed the locals of the bar eyeing Am suspiciously. Most raising an eyebrow at the sight of an Artificially Made Gen walking through their local, before turning back to their drinks. But just as Am and Ganymead disappeared into the kitchen, one of the locals in the bar stood up, shouting out after them.

"Hey! What are they doing in here?" The man was unsteady on his feet. "Scandza is no place for your kind!"

Another man placed a gentle hand on the drunk's shoulder, but he shrugged it off and staggered into the middle of the room.

"It's not right, not natural!" he slurred loudly, although most of the Gen in The Hungry Dragon chose to ignore him.

"Yeah, that's right, turn a blind eye. Youse always do!" He took a swig from the glass he was holding, knocking back the last of the liquid and wiping his mouth on his sleeve.

"There's no protection for us these days," he mumbled, his voice breaking slightly. "The gods walk among us, and instead of watching over us, they drink our blood."

The last word came out in a pained sob, and the man let go of his empty glass. It hit the floor, shattering loudly. The chitchat evaporated as a stunned silence fell over the room. Pax thought she'd been the only one listening to him across the bar, but in a split second, Miles had risen from their table and was grasping the drunken man's arm to steady him.

"C'mon, old man, time for bed." Miles said kindly, holding up a hand to Dominus, who was approaching them. "Don't worry Dom, I'll walk him out." He led the weeping man to the exit.

"I'm sorry." The drunk man stared up at Miles. "But they took everything from me. My whole family! What's godly about that?"

Miles sighed. "I know, my man, I know."

Pax felt sorry for the man. "What was all that about?" she asked when Miles returned to the table.

"He'd had a bit too much to drink," Miles sighed.

"But what was he talking about? Where is his family?"

Miles stared at Pax. "Sadly, you're not the only one who's lost family to the Harvesters."

Pax wanted to say something in response, but no words left her mouth. Instead, she rubbed her heavy eyes.

"C'mon. I think it's time for you ladies to get some rest," said Miles. "I'll keep an eye on Am and send them up in a little while."

Dominus led Pax and Venefica down a corridor at the side of the bar area and up a wooden staircase. The first door they came to was for the witch, who Felis decided he would join for the night, no doubt planning to rifle through her bag in the hopes of finding some leftover catnip crumbs. As soon as she entered the small yet comfortable room, Venefica headed towards the windows, throwing them wide open and welcoming in the night air. Dominus went to close the door behind her, and the witch's hand flew up, instantly stopping it from closing.

"Leave it open," Venefica said as politely as she could. Dominus, only slightly startled in the presence of magic, nodded. He led Pax further down the corridor to another door, and Pax had to duck as she entered the room. The tavern had clearly been built with Probus Gen in mind.

"I'll send Am up to join you soon. Good even, Pax."

Dominus smiled warmly, closing the door, his footsteps retreating down the creaky staircase.

Pax took in the silence of finally being alone. A welcoming fire, already lit in the hearth, filled the room with a low glow. Two small beds with clean white sheets stood either side of a window, which overlooked the street below. At the opposite end of the room was a sight that filled Pax with joy – a bathtub. Placing her bag onto the floor, she made her way over and turned the metal taps on with a high-pitched squeak. Steaming hot water sloshed into the tub. Whilst she waited for it to fill, Pax watched out of the window as more Gen stumbled towards the entrance of The Hungry Dragon. It was too dark to make out their faces, but from the size of them, Pax guessed it was more Tribus Gen. Miles had stayed down at the bar, planning to catch up with some old friends, but had promised to greet them again in the morning. In the night sky, the moon was just visible through the clouds.

Back at home in Viridis, during nights spent alone, Pax would often sit and stare out of her bedroom window at the moon. It had always been a comforting constant in her life, but now it loomed over her as a countdown of the days until the Harvest.

Peeling off her clothes, the fabric stiff with sweat and trog bile, Pax threw them in a pile on the floor. Closing off the tap, she sank into the steaming water, listening to the crackling fire and the rhythmical drip from the leaky tap. Picking up the bar of soap from the side of the tub, Pax scrubbed the dirt from under her fingernails. She sank further into the bath, submerging her face under the soapy water, distorting the sound of her own heartbeat. She clasped the amulet around her neck, knowing that she had only filled two vials so far. As her face broke through the surface of the water, she decided she would use this time alone to harness her powers in preparation for the coming days.

With limp red hair clinging to her shoulders, she used a thick towel that had been warming on the water pipes to dry herself. Grabbing her bag, she pulled out a clean red shirt that smelt like home. Once dressed, she settled cross legged in front of the dying embers of the fire. In the quiet of the room, clearing her mind was much easier. She concentrated on the pile of logs next to the open fire, willing the wood to lift into the air. At first nothing happened. Then one of the logs moved slightly, rising up. Slowly, Pax moved it from the pile, using her mind, upwards and over the fire, dropping it down onto the embers. It crackled and sparked, as the flames rose up, engulfing it. Pax smiled to herself, enjoying the increased heat, so she decided to try adding another log. Focusing on the wood pile once more, a second log started to move.

Knock, Knock, Knock! The wood clattered back onto the pile as Pax's concentration was broken. It was probably Am, she thought, frustrated. Picking up the loose log, she tossed it on to the fire, then answered the door.

Opening it, she was met with Ganymead's blue eyes. He smiled. Pax stared, then remembered the amulet around her neck and quickly tucked it into her shirt. Ganymead ran his hands through his golden hair, searching for something to say. But before he could utter anything, Am, who was standing next to him, interrupted.

"Dominus has sent Ganymead to collect any clothes you need to be washed."

Pax looked at Am, then back to Ganymead. Neither spoke. Am, slightly confused, went to repeat the statement in case Pax hadn't understood.

"Dominus has sent Gany—"

"Yes, okay, figo," Pax blurted out, disappearing back into the room. "Give me two seconds."

Closing the door, she frantically gathered up the dirty clothes she had carelessly thrown across the room, folding them into a pile, trying to hide the stains. She smoothed her wet hair down, and opened the door again, handing the bundle over to Ganymead, who was holding out his arms. As their hands touched, a jolt ran through Pax's entire body. From the shock on his face, Ganymead must have felt it too. Pax had been meaning to say thank you to him, but her words had been lost when they'd touched. Instead, Am filled the silence between them.

"Thank you, Ganymead. For both the kitchen tour and for collecting the clothes to be washed."

Am stepped inside the room, next to Pax. Ganymead nodded slowly, not speaking, and disappeared back down the corridor.

Am called out after him. "Good even, Ganymead!"

After they had turned out the lights, Pax lay under the clean sheets with a full stomach, listening to the hubbub from the bar downstairs. Shutting her eyes, her mind swirled with the latest clue, the rumours about the Harvesters and what had just happened with Ganymead. When, finally, sleep took over, her mind flooded with images made from blood.

CHAPTER
FOURTEEN

The pyrois grunted loudly. Pulling hard at the reins, Deleo brought the creature to a skidding halt. It exhaled heavily, its smoky breath fogging the morning air. Phantasma rode up beside him, her pyrois circling as it caught its breath, the flames around its mane now just a flicker.

"We need to keep moving!" she yelled at him.

"Phantasma, the pyrois need rest or they'll drop dead to the ground before we make it to the next village."

Phantasma scoffed. She knew Deleo was right but didn't want to acknowledge that, so instead, she dramatically dismounted her pyrois. Occissor's voice was still echoing around her head, the feel of his nails digging into her cheek still with her as they'd galloped the entire way towards Viridis.

"I should have chosen one of the other guards to accompany me!" she spat, knowing full well Deleo was the strongest and most skilled fighter in the whole of Rubra. "One with more stamina than you!" She kicked at the dust and marched off towards a nearby stream.

Deleo didn't rise to her jibe; he never did. He knew it was best to stay silent. He removed the harness from his pyrois, whose flaming mane was smoking now, a sign of exhaustion. He smiled fondly at the animal, running his hand over the smoky mane, knowing the flames wouldn't burn the skin of a

Supremo. These sweet, powerful beasts, however, could cause excruciating pain to any other Gen who would be foolish enough to touch them.

Deleo hadn't questioned Phantasma about why they had been ordered to leave Rubra again so soon or why they had been sent alone for this task, when they would normally be flanked by several others. All he knew was that they were to retrace their steps from the last raids and retrieve an item: an amulet made of gold. An expensive item no doubt, but he was still unsure why the task was so secretive. He had decided it was best not to ask Phantasma for more information, and he would never dare question the king himself.

For many moons now, there had been whispers of uprisings in the city. Rumours of new magic and an alternate way of life. Ideas that the king didn't want to add fuel to, desperate to try and extinguish any hint of rebellion. But the smoking embers of rumours always sparked back to life. Deleo had been involved in preserving order during the riots as the inhabitants of Rubra had grown restless over the years. Now, those who dared even utter such treason were, rightly, killed on sight. But Deleo understood it was not his place to ponder such things.

"I can't smell *any* blood here." Phantasma stormed back towards Deleo, who was now untacking her pyrois. "We didn't leave any caro. We would have smelt any Gen that was left behind! I don't understand how someone could have escaped, and now we have to stop because of these lazy things!"

She kicked her pyrois hard on the leg. The creature reared up in panic, its mane flaring. Deleo calmly grabbed the reins, then led both pyrois away towards a grassy area to graze.

Pacing up and down the forest floor, Phantasma pulled

at her white hair. How had she gone from pleasing her master to disappointing him, within a heartbeat? She would do absolutely anything to bask in his praise, unable to bear the thought of letting him down again. She needed to locate whoever had this amulet, something so precious to his highness. An item of great sentiment, having once belonged to his murdered son, who was slaughtered by caro many moons ago. Phantasma remembered at the time of the killing, the Supremo army had searched all over Tellus to locate this amulet, but to no avail, many believing it had been destroyed. And then her wonderful, brilliant master had seen it in his Oculus and had entrusted *her* to find it. She would track the thieving culprit down, killing anything or anyone that stood in her way.

Phantasma sat down with her head in her hands. Her natural instinct would be to evanesce and quickly reappear in a location of her choosing. But the process used so much of her power it could quickly exhaust her. She needed to use her skills wisely. She also didn't know exactly where she would evanesce to. The Oculus had last shown the amulet near the Caligo Caves but had given no other hint of its location since. She and Deleo had scoured the caves but could only smell the blood of trogs and Tribus warriors, who were known to hunt in those parts. However, because the Tribus Gen were also known for stealing gold, that was the blood trail they had decided to follow. It was all they had to go on for now, until the amulet appeared in the Oculus once again. Frustratingly, they would have to wait to ride to the next village, until the pyrois were well rested.

Deleo sat down next to Phantasma, who was now rocking quietly, lost in her own thoughts. Taking out his sword from its scabbard, he pulled the blade rhythmically across a stone to sharpen it. He always took pleasure in the simple routines of preparing for battle.

A velox fairy flew down from the trees above. It hovered over Phantasma, sprinkling glitter like a halo around her head. At first, she didn't appear to notice it, her red eyes glazed over. Then her arm snapped up, ensnaring the tiny creature in her fist. It squealed in her hand as her knuckles paled and tightened. One loud crunch and it was silenced.

"We ride onwards to Scandza in the morning," said Phantasma as the glittery remains crumbled from her hand.

CHAPTER FIFTEEN

The tricorn's horn was much smoother than Pax had imagined, and, surprisingly, it felt warm to the touch. Her face was reflected in the creature's glassy eye as she gently stroked the side of its head. The tricorn's giant nostrils flared as it sighed, lowering its eyelids.

"Fidus likes you!" Dominus said, adjusting the girth on the saddle. "Tricorns don't tend to be too fond of any Gen other than Probus these days, but you've found her sweet spot, right under her horn!"

Pax was grateful that Dominus had allowed her to come and meet the tricorns whilst Am was back at the tavern helping Ganymead wash the clothes. In return, Am would re-charge their nucleus from the fabasucus crops, ready for their onward journey. Dominus had also discreetly told Pax that some of the other Probus Gen were reluctant to have an Artificially Made Gen around the tricorns. She had felt both relieved and a little guilty at the chance to have a break from Am's constant questioning.

"She's ready," Dominus said, patting the tricorn's flank. "Up you get!"

Hooking her boot into the stirrup, Pax hoisted herself onto the carriage. Dominus stood on a small stool and pulled himself up, settling in next to her and taking the reins. With a gentle crack, Fidus walked on. The journey was unexpectedly smooth and fast for such a sturdy creature. They made their way from the paddock next to the tavern, down into the fields below, where the mist-covered meadows revealed other tricorns making the journey to work for the day. Dominus explained that the Probus Gen were responsible for farming the land in Scandza, and this particular season was yielding an exceptional crop of fabasucus. Occasionally, he would stop Fidus to point out an interesting plant or viewpoint, before snapping the reins and continuing on.

At one point, Dominus leant over, holding out the brown leather straps in his hands. "Want to have a go at steering?"

"I thought only Probus Gen could work tricorns?"

"Well, yes, since the Ethereal Gen became extinct. However, I'm here, and Fidus is a particularly accommodating tricorn."

He patted the large animal's neck fondly. Pax took the reins between her fingers and instantly felt the strength of the animal tingling in her fingertips and up her arms.

"So, are there different creatures connected to other Gen in Tellus?" Pax asked, concentrating on steering.

"Well, I suppose so." Dominus thought for a moment.

"What about the Harv— Supremos?"

Dominus nodded. "Ah yes, the Supremo Gen have long been linked with pyrois – a flaming horse of sorts. Its mane and tail are full of fierce flames that burn the skin of anyone other than those with Supremo blood."

"Wow, they sound intense," Pax said, imagining the creatures he was describing.

"Yes, and very loyal to the Supremos. Many moons ago, there were sightings of the prince riding a pyrois through these very fields in Scandza! All across Tellus, in fact. He was an alchemist, you know, just like your father. Of course, that was before he was—" Dominus coughed uncomfortably, leaving the sentence hanging in the air, and Pax sensed he was trying not to upset her. "Terrible business," he said, eventually.

As they made their way through the fields, other Probus Gen greeted Dominus warmly. Pax brought Fidus to a halt by pulling gently on the reins, so Dominus could talk to two short women, both holding woven baskets half full of small colourful beans.

Then, in the distance, a voice bellowed, "Get back to work!"

Over the hill, Arator came into view, striding towards them. The women sighed, rolling their eyes and returned to the crops in the field.

"Good morrow, Dominus. Good morrow, Pax." Arator, who now stood level with the tricorn's knee, called up to them, doffing his hat.

Dominus returned the gesture.

"So, are you travelling with the Tribus warrior?" Arator asked.

Pax nodded. "Yes. Miles was kind enough to escort us here to Scandza and provide a room for us to stay in at the tavern last night."

Arator pursed his lips but didn't respond, so Pax added, "He's been very kind."

"Indeed," Arator said. "But just be aware that Tribus Gen don't normally do things for free. There's an old saying in Tellus that warriors are only motivated by gold or revenge."

Dominus laughed, softly shaking his head. Arator smiled weakly, then continued. "But, as they say, it's just a tale, and

I'm sure you can judge for yourself, Miss Silva."

They bid Arator good day, and Dominus instructed Pax to pull one of the reins and circle Fidus around as they made their way back towards The Hungry Dragon.

"Take no notice of him," Dominus said when they were out of earshot. "Miles is as good a Gen as you'll find."

Pax smiled, discreetly checking that the amulet was still concealed safely underneath her shirt.

The sun had burnt through the morning mist by the time they reached the street that led to the tavern. Market stalls were now lining the cobbles, which had been nearly empty the evening they had arrived, and locals were busy about their mornings.

"Figo," Pax said under her breath, having never witnessed such an intriguing-looking town.

"How about you have a wander around?" Dominus suggested, noticing Pax's reaction. "I'll take Fidus back to the tavern. It's not far to walk, just to the end of the street and left."

Dominus pointed through the crowds, and Pax recognised the corner that led to The Hungry Dragon.

"That would be great, thanks so much."

Pax carefully dismounted, and Dominus doffed his hat, clicking Fidus to walk on.

Entering the throng of the market, Pax was one of the tallest in the crowd, apart from a few scattered Tribus Gen, and the only one with bright red hair, so she stood out. Stalls lined either side of the bustling street, full of everything from wooden tools, clay pots and glass bottles, to silk tapestries, glinting jewellery and intriguing foods. Wandering through the crowd, Pax pushed her way towards the front of a stall where she was greeted with an array of freshly baked sweets. Next to them was a slate sign with the words 'Saccharo – local delicacies' scrawled in chalk. The woman behind the stall beamed at her, revealing several missing teeth. This made the plate of samples a little less appealing, but Pax took a squidgy cube off the wooden plate and popped it into her mouth. The sweetness was overpowering, but Pax chewed politely. The lady Gen smiled, satisfied with this response, and turned to serve a mother who had two screaming children hanging from her skirts. On the other side of Pax, a pair of Gen were putting their purchases into a woven bag, talking animatedly to one another.

"If you ask me, they *should* revolt. The king—"

"Shh! Are you mad?" his friend replied, glancing around. Pax kept chewing, her eyes focused on the multicoloured sweets arranged in neat rows in front of her.

"Saying things like that will get you killed…" The man's voice trailed off as they disappeared into the crowd.

Pax was finally able to swallow the saccharo, deciding it was not the item she would spend her coin on. She thanked the stall owner and made her way further into the market. It was so busy she narrowly missed being run over by a cart and had to squeeze past other Gen to be able to see what was on display at each stall. She stopped at one piled high with colourful spices shaped into perfect pyramids. Venefica would love this, she thought, breathing in the spicy aromas. A customer at the adjacent stall shrieked with delight as the drawing of a kitten in front of her came to life. The artist accepted a bronze coin in payment, and the women rolled the mewing charcoal kitten up into the scroll.

At the next stall, a tradesman was using his levitation

powers to push his jewellery onto passing Gen, much to their annoyance. The table was full of sparkling silver, and Pax discreetly pulled at her shirt collar to make sure her own jewellery was not on display. At this stall, inside a small basket was a collection of gemstones. Pax rummaged through them, deciding on a particularly deep-purple one. She exchanged a coin in her pocket for the stone and carried on down the crowded street.

Suddenly, someone bumped into her, and Pax automatically went to apologise. The man in front of her grinned, revealing brown rotting teeth.

"Excuse me," Pax said, an unease creeping over her as she tried to move around him.

"Where's a pretty Gen like you going in such a hurry?" he asked, grabbing her arm, his nails digging into her skin. A heat flushed across her cheeks and she snatched her arm away from him.

"Oh, strong, are you?" the man said with a laugh. Suddenly he stopped, pointing towards her. "What do we have here?" he sneered, his dirty fingers reaching towards her neck.

There was a sickening crunch as Pax's fist connected with his nose. She could smell his intoxicated blood trickling down his lip.

"Oi!" someone shouted, grabbing Pax from behind, pinning her arms to her side.

She felt her knees buckle as she was pulled backwards into an alley, away from the main street.

"She punched me!" The rotten toothed man followed, spitting blood onto the ground. "She has gold!"

Pax was thrown to the ground. Her hands landed in a greasy puddle as she broke her fall. Above her, another, larger man loomed, blocking the light.

"Give us the gold, sweetheart, then you can be on your way."

Pax jumped up, facing both the men. "Leave me alone!" she said firmly, her hands balling into fists by her side.

The second man smiled. "You're so pretty when you're angry."

Pax saw the glint of a blade in his hand. The rotten-toothed man crept closer, his fingers reaching towards the amulet.

Suddenly, he stopped dead in his tracks.

"Hey, hey, what's going on with her eyes?" He hesitated, backing away. "They're turning red."

The man with the blade pushed him aside. "Let me do this." He raised his knife, lunging towards Pax.

She watched the blade and knew what she needed to do – rid him of the knife. But as she tried to focus, cold fear crawled over her skin, sinking into the pit of her stomach, up through her chest, into her mind. The man was moving too quickly – she didn't have enough time as the blade thrust towards her.

"Everything alright?" Miles appeared at the end of the alley.

The man quickly stepped back, hiding the knife behind him.

"Miles!" the toothless man said. "All fine, all fine. We were just leaving."

Miles raised his eyebrows at Pax. "You want me to bury an axe in his head?"

She was certain Miles wasn't joking, but all Pax managed to do was shake her head. Then, with a growl from Miles, the men fled into the market.

"There's some bad'uns around here. You have to watch yourself." He placed his hand on her shoulder. "You okay?"

Pax nodded, not meeting his eyes, the lump in her throat making it hard to swallow.

"I'm surprised you didn't use your pow—"

"I tried!" Pax blurted out. "I couldn't do it. I wanted to hurt them, but everything happened too quickly." The last word caught in her throat.

"Hey, hey. It's alright." Miles pulled her into a hug, and Pax felt herself calming. She took a breath.

"I don't know what I'm supposed to do," she mumbled into Miles's chest, making him release his embrace. Her eyes, no longer red, met his. "How am I meant to save my parents when I can't even save myself?"

Miles smiled. "Stop beating yourself up. Save that for the bad'uns." He ruffled her hair. "Come on, we've got things to do."

Wiping the tears from her eyes, Pax followed him back into the main street and through the crowd. She found herself checking over her shoulder to make sure the men weren't following her. Miles stopped at a stall where two tattooed women stood, both as tall as him.

"Good morrow, ladies! How are we today?" he asked, running his eyes over the array of weaponry on display. The women smiled in unison.

"Up and not crying!" replied one, making all three of them howl with laughter.

"Whadd'ya reckon?" he asked, holding up a large black blade from the table.

"Impressive," Pax replied, rubbing her arms.

Suddenly, she caught it in her hands. Miles had tossed the

weapon to her with no warning.

"See! Reflexes of a dragon, this one!" He nodded at her, whilst addressing the two women behind the stall.

They raised their eyebrows, nodding in agreement.

Pax was surprised at how light the blade felt in her hands. She turned it over, her eyes reflected in the oily metal.

"It's good, isn't it!" Miles said, watching Pax's reaction. "Tribus women are the best weaponsmiths in all of Scandza, nay, Tellus!"

The women rolled their eyes, used to Miles's compliments.

Pax handed the sword back to him, and he added it to a pile of weapons on the table. He took out a leather pouch from his belt bag, handing over some bronze coins to the nearest woman. The other Tribus Gen wrapped his chosen items in a leather swaddle, tying it securely.

As they walked side by side back through the crowds, towards the tavern, Pax noticed how the crowd parted when she was by Miles's side. As they reached the entrance of The Hungry Dragon, they were greeted by Am.

"Hello!" Am said cheerily. "My nucleus has been fully charged from the fabasucus plants." They tapped the centre of their glowing chest, holding the door open. "Venefica is waiting inside."

The bar was crowded, full of Gen ready for lunch. The witch was huddled over her spell book at one of the tables, muttering to herself. Scattered in front of her were piles of freshly collected plants and herbs. Felis was curled up by the fire again, and Pax suspected he may be the hardest one to convince to leave the safety of the tavern.

Miles told her to join Venefica whilst he went to the bar. Pax pushed her way past some other Gen and sat next to the witch. She turned to check Am was following, just as a man in a green coat bumped into Am's shoulder. Their nucleus glowed purple at the jolt.

"Apologies," said Am to the man, who looked at Am's nucleus with disgust.

"We don't want your type in here," the man spat.

Pax was about to jump to Am's defence when a loud hiss stopped her. She turned at the same time as the man, to see Venefica's black eyes staring at him. She hissed again, only louder. The man's face went white. Startled, he quickly pushed his way through the crowd and away from their table.

Am sat down next to Pax. "What is my type?"

"He's just rude," said Pax, putting an arm around Am. "Thanks, Venefica."

Venefica was studying her book again, her eyes white once more, as if nothing had happened.

"Many moons ago, Gen were taught to fear us witches by those that burnt us at the stake." She raised an eyebrow. "Comes in useful now and then."

Pax laughed, taking out the stone from her pocket and holding it out for Venefica to see.

"I got this at the market," said Pax.

Venefica smiled. "Amethyst. A beautiful choice, young one."

Pax pointed to the open spell book on the table. "Found anything useful?"

"Just a protection spell. The gods know we need it."

"Does that mean you're coming with us?" Pax asked.

Venefica shrugged. "Perhaps. My coven can wait another day."

"Well, if you're going..." Miles added, joining them at the

table. He smiled at the witch, who frowned and buried her face back in the pages of her spell book.

"Wait, you're coming with us too?" Pax asked, surprised.

"Of course. I can't let you go unescorted to Rubra! Possibly the most dangerous place in Tellus!"

Pax hadn't really thought too much about the capital, Rubra, being the place they would be most likely to end up, but having a warrior with them was much more appealing than going there alone.

"Would I have to pay you?" Pax asked. As soon as the question left her mouth, she regretted it. Hurt flashed over Miles's face for a split second before it was replaced with a smile.

"Not at all. I know us Tribus are known for liking gold," Miles replied, making Venefica scoff into the pages of her book, "but I have my own reasons. Plus, I wouldn't have offered if I didn't mean it."

"Figo!" said Pax.

"Figo!" repeated Am.

The sheath of weapons hit the table, and Miles unrolled his new purchases.

"Plus, why do you think I got all these! We'll need them where we're going!"

He looked at Am. "Need a weapon?" Am didn't reply, sitting in an unusual silence.

"What's wrong?" Pax asked.

"Am cannot use weapons," they explained. "Am is programmed not to cause harm to themselves or others."

Miles patted Am on the shoulder. "Such a good'un!"

Am smiled a little more genuinely than normal. Venefica was discreetly examining the weapons side on, trying to appear uninterested, which made Miles grin.

"And for you, m'lady?" he asked, waving a hand over the table. "Although with a tongue as sharp as yours, you don't need a knife."

Venefica slammed her book shut. "They're crushing my plants!"

"Oh, sorry," Miles said, fumbling to pack the assortment away.

Suddenly, Venefica's small hand was on top of his, making him freeze. Their eyes met.

"I'll take the jade blade," she said softly, her dreadlocks falling around her face as she slowly withdrew her hand.

The green glass glistened as Miles slid it across the table to her. Pax glanced back and forth between them, not saying anything. The silence was broken when the door opened, and Dominus entered the tavern.

"Such a lovely day!" he said, placing a pile of freshly washed laundry on the table, then kneeling down to tend the fire, much to Felis's annoyance.

"Thanks so much," said Pax, picking up the clean clothes and placing them into her bag under the table.

"Ganymead said Am was most helpful today when we were gone." Dominus smiled at Am. "Will you be staying another night?" he asked, stoking the coals.

Pax eyed the others around the table. "No, I think we need to make a move today." The witch and the warrior nodded in agreement.

"Well, surely time for lunch before you head off?" Dominus stood and turned to them. "Roast trog, anyone?"

A short while later, the table in front of them was full of empty plates after a most delicious meal. Pax was relieved that the roast trog had not resembled the creatures from the cave, and surprisingly, the meat had tasted quite sweet. Miles, fed and happy, leant back on his chair, which creaked under his weight. Venefica sat opposite him, half his size yet with twice his appetite during the meal. Felis was curled up in Pax's lap, and Am had watched them eat, happily, remembering to save questions until after everyone had finished eating.

As soon as Pax put her knife and fork down on her empty plate, Am asked, "Are we going to Rubra?"

Pax knew Am was attempting to plot the most direct route by referring to their internal map of Tellus. The others started discussing theories on what the latest clue could mean, Miles and Venefica refusing to agree on anything. As Pax listened, their voices faded into the background as she focused on scratching Felis's wing. As he purred softly in her lap, she heard a sharp, piercing sound. Then she realised it wasn't a sound exactly; it was a feeling, and not a good one. Her pulse quickened, her heart pounding against her chest.

"We need to go," Pax said loudly, interrupting the conversation. The others stopped and stared at her. Her eyes were glowing bright red. "Now."

Miles went to speak, but an enormous crash outside stopped him. All at once, the locals in the room jumped up, chairs scraping and falling as they stood in panic. Chaos erupted in the small tavern as Gen rushed towards the exit.

Pax grabbed her bag, shoving Felis inside. Miles was already up and leading Am to the back of the tavern, against the flow of the other customers, who were all running towards the front door. Venefica was frantically trying to sweep her plants off the table into her bag.

"Come," Pax said firmly, but the witch ignored her. "Move!" Pax yelled, pushing her in the direction Miles had gone.

Behind the bar was a doorway through to the kitchen, which opened into the yard.

Outside, Dominus ran up to Miles. "Here, take Fidus! Get them to safety!" He pointed to the tricorn, still harnessed up from the morning's ride.

Miles lifted Am and Venefica into the carriage on one side as Pax hoisted herself up on the other. She threw her bag, now hissing, to Venefica and grabbed the reins. Dominus was holding Fidus steady, placing his forehead between the creature's great eyes, whispering to her calmly. As Miles went to lift himself onto the tricorn, his crus caught in the stirrup, making him stumble. Glass smashed inside the tavern. The approaching danger was getting louder by the second.

"Leave without me!" Miles yelled.

"Miles, get on!" Pax held out her hand. He took it and she pulled him up with ease.

"Dominus, you too!" Pax called down.

"You remember how to steer?" Dominus said quickly.

"Come with us!" Pax pleaded.

"I have to find Ganymead. Head for the woods. It's safer there."

"Dominus! Please!" Pax screamed.

Dominus smiled sadly, kissing his fingers and placing them on the tricorn's cheek. Then he slapped Fidus hard on her flank. The tricorn reared up and they were away. Pax was shocked at the speed and grabbed the reins tightly, her red hair whipping back from her face. Next to her, Miles fumbled, struggling to hold on, his crus caught under the strap of the carriage. Venefica and Am clung to the side rails as the tricorn galloped towards the woods, blurred branches scratching at their faces. Suddenly, Felis wriggled free from the backpack, and Venefica pinned him down tightly with one hand whilst grabbing on to the carriage rail with the other.

"Go to the left!" Am yelled, struggling to get close enough to Pax so she could hear.

"What?" Pax yelled, turning towards Am.

As she did so, she caught sight of two white creatures engulfed in flashing flames thundering towards them.

"We got company!" Miles yelled, drawing out his axe despite his leg still being trapped under the strap.

Venefica reached over to help him, letting go of Felis, her long fingers desperately trying to free his crus.

"Go left!" Am repeated. "To safety!" They pointed up ahead to a fork in the road. Pax pulled hard on the left rein and Fidus understood her command, veering down the path.

A screeching laugh cackled behind them. Pax caught sight of a woman galloping towards them, in a blur of flames, closing in rapidly on their right-hand side.

"Pyrois!" Venefica screamed. "Flaming steeds!"

Pax gripped the reins tightly, realising exactly who was pursuing them. Then, on their left, a second pyrois closed in, ridden by a man merely metres away from the tricorn's side. Clashing metal rang in Pax's ears. Deleo's sword sliced through the air, connecting with Miles's axe. Used to battle, the pyrois was unfazed, but Fidus was spooked, raising her head in alarm. Pax pulled the reins hard as Am directed her to veer right.

Phantasma kicked her pyrois until she was level with the tricorn. Pax was sure she would attack, but then the pyrois galloped even faster, overtaking them until it was in front of Fidus. Phantasma, an expert rider, let go of her reins, gripping the pyrois tightly with her thighs, and retrieved a bow from her quiver. Turning, she pulled the string taut, aiming the arrow directly at Pax, the amulet glinting at Pax's neck. Their eyes met. The smile fell from Phantasma's face for a split second, giving Pax just enough time to slap the reins, making Fidus lower her head, then buck back up. The tricorn's horn connected under Phantasma's pyrois, throwing it up into the air and over the top of them. Pax looked behind, to see the pyrois fall to the ground in dying flames, Phantasma tumbling beneath its hooves.

Seeing the fall, Deleo hesitated. Venefica seized the opportunity to swipe her blade across his face. Pax could smell the richness of his blood. Deleo lowered his raised sword for a moment, his pyrois falling back slightly, then he continued in pursuit.

Am pointed to a clearing in the forest up ahead. "There!"

The tricorn thundered on, with the remaining pyrois just inches away from them. Deleo raised his sword, lowering it with rapid force onto Miles's trapped crus. It smashed into the joint with such force it sent shockwaves through Miles's bones and pounding into his skull. The warrior yelled out in pain.

Then a loud crackle. It all went quiet. The rushing wind vanished as a blinding light appeared. Pax shielded her eyes as they were engulfed by silence.

The tricorn reared up, skidding across the ground. It halted abruptly, lunging its passengers forwards. They had stopped in the middle of the forest but appeared to be enclosed in some kind of room. Around them, dotted amongst the trees, were several bio auxes, all connecting to a glowing nucleus encased in the trunk of a large tree. Behind them, Deleo's pyrois was now pacing back and forth in purple flames, only a few metres away. Deleo lowered his sword, circling his steed frantically, turning his head in disbelief.

CHAPTER
SIXTEEN

"Seven Dragons!"

Miles gritted his teeth, leaning down to inspect his crus. There was no blood, but the metal was twisted at an unnatural angle where it entered his skin and connected to his thigh muscle. He winced as he tried to sit up in the carriage.

Venefica was hitting the palm of her hand against her forehead.

"Stupid! Stupid, stupid…" she muttered, her eyes black, the hitting becoming harder. "Should have better magic. Stupid girl…"

Pax grabbed the witch's hands to stop her from hurting herself, whispering, "You're safe" into her ear.

Slowly, Venefica's black eyes dilated back to white. "Felis," she said. "I let him go. I lost him."

The words punched Pax in the gut, but her face didn't flinch. "It's okay; he flies off all the time. He'll be back."

"A little help over here?" Miles grunted.

Together, Pax, Venefica and Am managed to lower Miles down from the tricorn's carriage and onto the forest floor, propping him up against the trunk of a tree. Venefica carefully touched the top of his thigh to inspect the injury.

"Never a timelier spot of magic," said Miles, managing a slight smile.

"Did you create a shield?" Pax asked, kneeling down next to the witch.

Venefica shook her head, rising and stepping over to where they had entered this clear room. Reaching out her hand, the witch touched the invisible barrier. The air distorted slightly, sticky like honey.

"A forcefield," she whispered.

On the other side of it, Deleo was only just still visible on his pyrois, galloping away into the distance.

"Welcome." A calm voice made them all jump. They turned to face a tall figure with light grey eyes standing in front of them. "My name is Zed. Of Novus Gen."

Miles sucked in his breath in pain.

"Your crus is damaged." A grey light surrounded Zed's outline as they walked over to the warrior. "May I?"

Miles nodded, in too much pain to argue. Zed knelt next to him to inspect his crus.

"Can I offer any refreshments?" said another voice, slightly less monotone than Zed's.

An equally tall figure appeared, this time with a yellow outline, holding a tray with three cups. They offered one to Venefica, who accepted it cautiously, and then another, to Pax. The figure then stood in front of Am.

"None for you, obviously!" they said, placing the last cup on the ground next to Miles.

"Remember to introduce yourself," Zed said, not taking their eyes away from the crus.

The figure placed a hand to their head. "Oh yes! Of course." They straightened up. "My name is Eks, of Novus Gen."

They smiled, satisfied, as their yellow eyes scanned the

room. Eks walked over to Venefica, who was still prodding the invisible shield.

"Quite something, isn't it?" Eks said, and the witch backed away from them slightly.

Zed glanced up. "We have harnessed light technology and combined it with bio aux here in this forest. It provides us with protection from the elements and, well, other things, as you can imagine."

"Figo," Pax said, taking a closer look at the force field. Raising her hand, she could feel the prickle of static.

"Yes," agreed Zed, modestly. "Us Novus survive here quite well with little interaction from externals." They glanced around the room, then continued to tinker with the crus. "Did you follow the safety signal?"

Pax went to answer. "Umm, no, we just sort—"

"Not you," Zed interrupted softly, nodding at Am.

"Yes," Am replied.

Zed smiled. "Good work. You were located in the tavern in Scandza yesterday. The signal was provided as a route of escape."

Pax realised Zed must have been the hooded stranger she had seen in The Hungry Dragon the day they arrived. Suddenly, there was a loud clatter.

Zed called out, "Come out and introduce yourself, Wye."

A slightly shorter figure poked their head out from behind the large nucleus at the centre of the room.

"They will come eventually," Zed added, still fiddling with the crus as Miles lifted his head up to see what was happening.

"Wye is not too fond of meeting new Gens," Zed clarified.

"There's someone you should meet!" Eks called out to

Wye, pointing at Am. "Sorry, what was your name?"

"My name is Am."

On hearing Am's voice, Wye slowly stepped around Fidus, giving the tricorn a wide berth, their white eyes darting around the room. When close enough, Wye slowly took hold of Am's hand. They stood side by side, staring at each other, and then Wye scanned Am's face. Eks and Zed shared a knowing glance.

Pax shifted uncomfortably on her feet.

"I am the great Venefica!" the witch declared, feeling left out.

"Of course, Venefica, pleased to make your acquaintance," Zed replied. "And you?" He nodded at the warrior.

"Miles, Tribus Gen."

"Well, Miles of Tribus Gen, part of this crus will need to be removed before I can repair it. Do you consent for that to go ahead?"

Miles nodded, his biceps flexing as he shifted his position against the tree. Eks smiled at Pax, prompting her to introduce herself, and then they were offered a tour of the hidden forest room.

"We call our home Ultra. We are safe here. It can be moved to wherever we need it to be," said Eks, gesturing to the forcefield. "We sometimes trade with Dominus at the tavern for certain items. Fabasucus plants are a great fuel for charging."

Am nodded in agreement, having used the same source to charge earlier in the day.

A massive silver nucleus glowed inside the tree at the centre of the room, its roots spreading into the forest floor. The pulsing mass moved in and out slightly every few seconds, almost as if it were breathing. Eks pulled across a glass screen, where a map appeared on the display.

"We've been tracking the tavern since Zed saw Am. We were unsure if Am was with you willingly." Eks said, tapping the screen with their fingers, where many coloured dots appeared over a bird's eye view of the area. "We knew there was a Harvester lurking around, which we found strange, as they normally make their presence known."

As Eks typed into the keyboard, the images rewound in triple speed, then slowed to play in real time.

"We followed the safety signal," Am said.

Wye had finally let go of their hand but was watching carefully from a safe distance, hiding behind one of Fidus's legs.

"Yes, we sent that to you," Eks responded. "Dominus is a good Gen, and Zed saw that he trusted you and your friends." Eks focused back on the screen. "We thought it was him bringing the tricorn here – there's not many other Gen that can ride them." Eks started tapping the keyboard again. "Dominus is no longer appearing on the map at the tavern. Hopefully he's made it to safety."

"Why did they attack The Hungry Dragon?" Pax asked.

"We suspect they are following you," Zed replied, detaching the crus from Miles and laying it down carefully on a well-lit metal table.

Eks agreed. "Yes. With all the Gen at the market, they could have easily rounded up more caro if they hadn't followed you."

Beep! Wye had appeared next to them, holding a small device and was using it to scan Am's body.

"Hey!" said Pax, putting a protective arm across Am's body.

Startled, Wye dropped the scanner onto the floor with a clang and retreated, cowering behind the tricorn's thick leg again.

Zed looked up from the crus. "Oh, there is no need for alarm. Wye is just scanning Am to check their energy levels."

Am smiled at Pax reassuringly.

"Well, we also need to… scan you," Eks added awkwardly. "For weapons."

Pax took out her penknife and placed it on the table next to Eks. Miles pushed his axe along the ground to Pax's feet, and she picked it up and added it to the table. Miles motioned to Venefica to grab his bag containing the other weapons he had purchased from the market. She crossed her arms in protest.

"C'mon, Vee. They mean no harm," he said encouragingly.

Reluctantly, Venefica picked up Miles's bag, slamming it down onto the table. She rummaged in her own bag and placed the jade blade on top. Meanwhile, Wye moved quietly and crawled underneath the metal table, peering out from in-between Zed's legs. Eks retrieved the scanner from the floor, adjusting a dial at the base, then waved it over a grumpy Venefica. *Beep!* The witch shrugged. After a stern look from Miles, she hiked her foot onto the table, lifting up her long skirts to reveal another dagger holstered around her thigh.

"Oops," she said indifferently as she threw it onto the table with a clatter.

Miles chuckled as Eks scanned him.

"No beep! How about that?" Miles exclaimed, rubbing his leg where the crus had been removed.

Eks walked over to Pax to repeat the process, waving the scanner over her head. *Beep!* The scanner stopped directly over Pax's chest.

"Oh, it's not a weapon. It's my necklace," Pax said, pulling at the gold chain to reveal the amulet.

"Interesting. May I?" Eks asked.

Pax could see Miles nodding and Venefica shaking her head. Tentatively, she removed the amulet from around her neck and placed it in Eks's hands. They examined it closely then made their way over to the bio aux at the centre of the room. Eks secured the amulet under a large microscope, and the central nucleus started to swirl silver and gold as images appeared on another one of the screens.

Zed, now more intrigued, joined Eks's side. "Fascinating."

Pax tried to peer at the screen but couldn't see past the two tall figures. "What's interesting?"

They ignored her, muttering to each other, pressing buttons and adjusting dials. The screen flashed with images and colours.

Venefica was behind Pax, also trying to get a better look. "Strange magic?"

"What's going on?" Miles asked from across the room.

Zed turned around. "It is very intriguing. A perfect balance of science and nature, containing some kind of chemical code."

Eks added, "Unfortunately, there also appears to be a tracking device. Where did you find this?"

"It belonged to my mother. Wait – tracking device?"

"This is probably how the Harvesters tracked you. They may have been following you for some time," Eks explained. "Luckily, it's hidden by the forcefield in Ultra."

"Good magic," Venefica whispered, her hand reaching out to touch the invisible shield again.

Miles shifted his weight on to his one leg and steadied

himself to join them at the table.

"How long have they been tracking us?" Miles asked.

"Let's see." Zed tapped the keyboard on the screen. "The device seems to have been activated a few days ago. Somewhere in a location between the Caligo Caves and Lake Scandza."

Miles looked at Pax and Venefica. "Well? Did you notice anyone? Or anything then?"

Venefica exchanged a glance with Pax and whispered, "The Umor?"

Pax let out a huge sigh. "That's when I added the first vial to the amulet. Could that have triggered the tracking?"

"Quite possibly. But what are these vials?" Zed questioned.

Pax stood next to Zed and removed the amulet from underneath the microscope. Around her, eager eyes watched as she pressed the symbol, and the amulet clicked open, revealing the six vials.

"Two are filled so far," Pax said. "We are searching for six in total. I think this will help save my parents."

"Save them? Where are they?" Eks asked.

"Rubra, we think. The Harvesters attacked my village in Viridis. My father left me clues" – Pax nodded across the room – "with Am."

Am smiled, and Zed and Eks exchanged worried glances.

"Are you sure it was your father that left you this?" Zed asked.

"Yes." Pax nodded, replacing the amulet around her neck.

Miles added, "Creo Silva is this one's father." He ruffled Pax's red hair. "He's an alchemist and a very clever man. He made my crus."

Zed's usually motionless face hinted at being slightly impressed. "It makes sense that this amulet would have been created by an alchemist."

Miles continued. "He's left us clues, but if there's anything you can offer to help us, we'd be very grateful."

Pax felt a swell of pride that Miles had used the word 'us'. It made her feel less alone. She was also impressed at his ability to barter even while standing on one leg.

"Well, we can remove the tracking device, or at least create a type of forcefield around it. That will give you protection on your travels," Zed offered. "It will take some time, as will the crus. I suggest you stay here in Ultra this evening."

Pax nodded thankfully whilst Venefica rolled her eyes.

During the evening, Zed focussed on repairing the damage to Miles's crus. A little later, they sat on the forest floor, with Eks offering them a meal of hot mushroom pie and forest kale. The Novus Gen, however, didn't appear to enjoy mealtimes as much as Am. Wye had run away to hide at the first sight of food.

"Forgive Wye." Zed explained, "Mealtimes bring back bad memories of when they were kept."

Zed went on to describe how many Artificially Made Gen were created with the sole purpose of servitude, with many often treated very unkindly. Zed and Eks had escaped similar situations and had created Ultra to protect themselves. They had renamed themselves the Novus Gen.

"Some horrible types in Tellus," Miles added, shaking his head. Venefica's eyes widened as she nodded slowly in agreement. Pax glanced at Am, who was still smiling. Did they feel as if they were being kept?

"Am, could you remind us of the next clue you had referred to?" Zed asked.

Am, pleased to be of use, repeated the information:

Eks nodded. "To clarify, each clue leads you to a location, which provides a substance to insert into a vial in the amulet?"

"Fancy way of saying it, but yeah," Miles confirmed.

"Any ideas?" Pax asked.

Zed paused in thought. "'Photon energies' refers to light. 'Different waves' suggests light waves."

"Not ocean waves?" the warrior asked.

"Possibly," Zed offered, "but 'opposite of below' suggests that is unlikely."

"The sky?" Pax questioned.

"Of course!" Zed said, just slightly more animated than normal. "Levis! It is a place full of light. You'll surely find what you need there."

"Figo! Where is Levis?" Pax asked, slightly suspicious that this was all a little too easy.

Am scanned their internal nucleus. "Levis is not appearing on the map."

"It moves around," Venefica said. "Like the destination of my coven in Celare."

Eks nodded. "Indeed. It travels with the weather. It is a transferable destination, much like Ultra."

"Now, we understand that you will eventually be heading to Rubra?" Zed said. "And the amount of weaponry you have with you suggests you won't be going in quietly…"

Miles nodded enthusiastically.

"Am," – Zed faced them – "your scan indicated that you have been programmed not to cause harm and not to bear arms."

After a quick glance at Pax, Am nodded.

"Well, as you are heading to Rubra, we would like to offer you reprogramming to reverse this and, of course, any other changes to your programming you would like."

At this, the witch smiled. "Free to choose to kill? To cheat! To lie! To steal!" She laughed. "All the traits that make Gen human!"

Am stared at Pax, who hadn't really thought about changing Am's programming as an option, often forgetting that Am was programmed at all.

"This is your decision, Am," Zed said firmly, regaining Am's gaze. Zed's words, however, seemed to be directed at Pax.

"Of course, you can always stay with us here, Am. In Ultra," Eks said.

Pax bristled. She didn't want Am to stay here, with these strangers; *she* was Am's family.

"It is safe here." Wye finally spoke, in a soft voice.

Am frowned slightly, again glancing towards Pax, who couldn't meet her gaze.

Zed turned to Pax. "We assume Am is free to choose. You don't keep Am as a slave?"

"Of course not!" Pax snapped, adding more quietly, "It's your choice, Am."

That evening, as Pax untacked Fidus, she watched the others sitting on the forest floor. Miles quietly watched Venefica through the flames of the fire, engrossed in the pages of her spell book as Am talked animatedly to the other Novus, making Pax wonder if Am really did need to be with their own Gen. Over the last few days, she had been concerned that the witch and the warrior wouldn't accompany her but had never once doubted that Am would be by her side.

Fidus sighed with relief as Pax finished removing the halter. The huge tricorn settled down to rest. Excusing herself to go to bed early, Pax left Am talking to Eks, Wye and Zed.

As she lay down, she noticed that she couldn't hear the sounds of the forest from inside Ultra. They were trapped outside the protective shield. It made her miss Viridis. She missed the weight of Felis in her lap, too. Staring up through the forcefield at the starry sky, the large gibbous moon hung over her, adding to the sadness that was already weighing heavy on her heart.

CHAPTER
SEVENTEEN

The Hungry Dragon was quiet apart from a methodical *drip, drip, drip*. Blood trickled slowly down his nose, forming into a droplet, growing in size until it fell onto the floorboards. Gold-laced rope dug into the skin of his outstretched wrists, which were tethered, taut, above his head. Dominus's feet were arched in pain, barely scraping the ground.

Phantasma normally took great pleasure in torturing caro, jokingly calling it playing with her food. Today, however, she was growing frustrated. It was taking too long, and there was too much at stake. She needed answers, to know where those treacherous thieves were hiding. This little Probus Gen should have been easy to break; he should be confessing in fearful sobs by now, but he hadn't uttered a word. Not a single word.

Perhaps the fall from her pyrois had shaken her more than she realised. She caught a glimpse of herself in the smashed mirror above the smoking fireplace, the spiderweb cracks in the glass distorting the small cut on her forehead, but even now, she knew she was still strikingly beautiful. The fall had hurt her pride more than her body. She balled her fist at the thought of that amulet. It had been just out of reach – she had been so close to gaining the king's approval, and then that young girl's stare flashed into her mind. *The brighter the eyes, the brighter the spark* – a phrase she vaguely remembered her mother saying to her as a child. Phantasma couldn't quite shake the strange familiarity she had sensed when looking into those eyes.

Without her, Deleo had managed to lose them. Typical. He had returned with a fresh cut on his cheek, claiming they had used magic to vanish. With further inspection of the woods, they were nowhere to be smelt, the Tribus blood trail having disappeared completely. The only caro who hadn't fled the town by the time they returned to the tavern was now hanging from the rafters, refusing to speak. But, from experience, she knew his silence meant he had something to hide.

Deleo's fist smashed into Dominus's stomach again. He whimpered, bloody saliva dribbling out of his mouth and through his beard. Deleo raised his arm and went to hit him again.

"It's no use," Phantasma said, stopping him. "Save your strength." She inhaled deeply. "It's time I told him."

Deleo cracked his knuckles. "I'm sure I recognised the Tribus warrior, the one with the metal leg. I just can't quite place him."

He had fought many warriors in wars and raids over the years, never noticing the faces of the Gen he killed. But there was something unnerving about the one who had just escaped on the back of a tricorn.

Ignoring him, Phantasma picked up a clay water jug from the bar and carried it over to one of the only tables that was still standing. With one swipe, she cleared it of its contents, glasses smashing onto the floor. She poured the water onto the table, throwing the jug over her shoulder. Removing the S-shaped brooch from her cloak, she pricked the skin of her index finger with the pin. A bead of blood formed, and she held her palm out above the table. Supremo blood was powerful, laced with magic, and as soon as the droplet hit the water, it started to swirl. Phantasma leant closer over the table, her face inches from the shimmering liquid. Red eyes appeared. Occissor's eyes. Watching through his Oculus in the Throne Room of the Castellum.

The Oculus gave Occissor the power to watch over all of his Gen, yet few had the ability to contact him via this magical portal, and of the handful who did, even fewer dared.

"Master!" Phantasma said breathlessly. "I have news."

Occissor's face appeared blurry in the liquid. "Do you have the amulet?" His voice was slightly muffled.

Phantasma swallowed. "Well, no. You see—"

"Where is it?" The liquid vibrated with the sheer volume of his voice.

"It's gone. They disappeared," Phantasma blurted out.

"Who are *they*?" questioned Occissor.

"There was a girl! And a witch, I think. There was hardly any scent. We had the signal, but then it… vanished."

Occissor remained dangerously silent.

Phantasma continued, desperately trying to claw back his approval. "We picked up the scent of a Tribus warrior!"

Again, there was no reply.

"But that trail disappeared too." She hung her head in shame, silver locks covering her reddening face.

Finally, Occissor spoke. "Your mission remains the same."

Phantasma dared to peer into the liquid once more, listening intently.

"Whoever has the amulet cannot stay hidden forever.

Return to Rubra immediately."

Phantasma nodded. "Shall I evanesce to you, Master?" she asked, feverishly.

"No," came his reply. "You need to save your power for when the time comes."

Phantasma nodded even more violently.

"Phantasma?" Occissor said.

"Yes, Your Highness?"

Occissor's image faded. "Do not fail me again." Then he was gone.

Clasping the edge of the wet table, Phantasma flipped it, sending it crashing into the wall. Bending over, she screamed so loudly her face turned as red as her eyes. Deleo, used to her outbursts, watched quietly as she pulled at her hair, pacing frantically up and down the tavern.

He remained silent for a few moments, then nodded at Dominus. "What do we do with him?"

Stopping, Phantasma looked at him, a wicked smile spreading across her face.

CHAPTER EIGHTEEN

Fidus buried her horned snout into the bucket but couldn't reach the grain, so Pax tipped it onto the forest floor. The tricorn devoured her breakfast happily, having slept well (Pax knew this because she'd listened to her snoring loudly for most of the night), and although the animal was full of energy, she stayed still and allowed Pax to place her harness over her horns, eager to return to her herd. Zed then helped Pax lift the carriage onto the tricorn's back and tighten it securely, ready for their onward journey.

Am had talked long into the night with the other Novus Gen, which was another reason Pax hadn't slept much. She was worried that by this morning, Am may have actually decided to stay with them in Ultra. Late last night, the tell-tale sign of Am's blue nucleus flickering in the dark meant Am must have chosen to have some of their settings adjusted.

Pax had also been hopeful that Felis would have returned to her by now, not normally one to miss breakfast, but he was nowhere to be seen. They had to move on, but she was worried her pet dragat wouldn't be able to track them down once they left Ultra. When she'd finished tacking up Fidus, Pax joined the others around the fire, where Am was addressing the Novus Gen.

"Thank you, all, for your hospitality and the kind offer

of a home; however, Am will be accompanying Pax onwards towards Rubra."

On hearing these words, Pax felt so relieved but tried not to show it and decided not to quiz Am about any changes they had made to their settings, just yet. But when Zed turned away to address Miles, she hugged Am tightly, and for the first time, Am hugged her back.

Zed had repaired the crus, so it looked exactly the same as the first time Pax had seen Miles in the Caligo Caves. Miles exclaimed with gratitude that it was better than ever and pulled out his pocket watch.

"Vee has disappeared into the woods again," he said, replacing the brass piece back into a pocket of his belt bag.

Pax pulled down on the stirrups of the carriage, giving them a tug to make sure they were secure. "Am, could you go and check on Venefica? Tell her it's time for us to leave."

By now, the forcefield around Ultra had been relaxed. Am nodded, then walked quietly into the forest in search of the witch. Their eyes scanned the flora and fauna around them as they made their way through the woods. Having a choice in which of their settings were adjusted had felt strange, and for the first time, Am was experiencing a sense of freedom and wonder they hadn't felt before. Normally, scanning objects, plants and Gen was for information purposes only, to be stored in their central nucleus until needed at a later date. But now, they found each item they scanned was accompanied by a feeling. Am observed a flutter of velox fairies feasting on scuttleberries that had fallen from the branches above. Am had the urge to know what the berries tasted like, but it was followed by an acceptance of knowing the fairies could not answer that question. Am filed it away to ask Pax about later.

The inky fruit squished beneath Am's feet, and they stopped to examine their soles. The red liquid coated the back of their heel. Am felt strange realising that the juice may leave a stain. Then they continued into the forest.

Venefica was deeper in the woods. She'd left Ultra earlier that morning, at daybreak. It appeared that Zed and Eks also hadn't slept, so she'd made an excuse about gathering more herbs for their onward journey. They had removed the forcefield for her, stating there was no more danger around, and Venefica had watched, mesmerised, as the translucent sheen vanished, snapping her surroundings back into focus. Being lost in this realm had let her experience magic she had never seen before. It made her realise the universe had put her exactly where she'd needed to be, after all.

Once she was certain she was alone in the woods, she found a small clearing. Setting down her bag, she placed some of her items onto the forest floor. The sun was rising, light darting through the leaves above. A powerful time of day.

Magic was Venefica's obsession. Her saviour. It had provided her with the safety that no family ever could, and now, here in this realm, she knew she was close to a most powerful magic. She would do whatever it took to possess it. She had sacrificed others for magic before, and she was willing to do it again.

Holding the spell book to her chest, she inhaled deeply. The smell of the pages brought her comfort now. After all these moons, they still held the scent of her past. Closing her eyes, she remembered the very first time she had seen this book, sensing all the power it held between its pages. Knowing it was her means of escape.

Placing the spell book onto the earth, she flicked through

the starchy pages, much thicker than those found in books nowadays. Made to stand the test of time. This book was pure magic – no matter how many times you read its pages, one would never finish. It revealed new spells, new secrets, as and when they were needed.

Holding her palms up to the sky, just above the open book, she whispered into the wind, *"Spectaculum veritas..."*

Her eyelids opened, revealing jet-black eyes as she continued speaking soft words. The pages of the spell book flickered slowly, turning on their own, fluttering faster and faster until they stopped, the book falling open. Venefica looked down to see the pages slowly inscribing themselves with gold ink, the first few words starting to appear.

"What is *sui generis*?" Am asked.

Startled, Venefica slammed the book shut, jumping to her feet. "Never sneak up on a witch!" she hissed as her irises dissolved from black to white. "It could be fatal for you!"

Am smiled. "The book had the words *sui generis*. Is it important to our quest?"

Am leaned closer, touching the cover of the spell book, and Venefica pulled it away, pressing it to her chest.

"This is not information for you to share," Venefica replied sternly, adding, "That's if you can keep it to yourself?"

Am paused, finding it extra hard to formulate a reply today, as there were other thoughts appearing across their mind. "Actually, Zed reprogrammed part of my nucleus last night. The ability to withhold information has been added."

The witch raised her eyebrows. "You chose to be able to lie?"

Am paused again before responding, realising they could now choose what information they gave and what to withhold. "Human Gen have that ability."

"We may be more similar than I thought," Venefica smirked. "And what about weapons? Can you use one?"

"That is still not programmed. Pax will never be harmed by my hands."

Venefica's smile dropped. "What you don't realise" – she stepped closer to Am – "is that lies can cut deeper than any knife."

She held Am's gaze, waiting for a reaction, but none came. The witch gathered up her items into her velvet bag.

"Let's see if your new ability works. Keep what you read in my book to yourself." She stared at Am. "Strange. No other Gen has ever been able to read from my spell book."

Venefica's white eyes studied Am's face for a few quiet seconds. She frowned, failing to find the answer to a question she hadn't ask. Her black skirts swished in the air as she turned sharply and walked back towards Ultra, with Am following quietly.

☾

"Here they are!" Miles said, already seated in the carriage of the tricorn.

Pax passed him his sheath of weapons, then helped Am and Venefica step up to sit next to him. Taking the reins, she hoisted herself onto Fidus.

"Thanks for all your help, especially removing the tracking," Pax said, touching the amulet.

"Most welcome," Zed replied, then their grey eyes locked onto Am. "Remember, Am, there is always a home for you here in Ultra."

Am smiled as Pax slapped the reins signalling Fidus to walk on. Zed and Eks stood waving them off, whilst a forlorn Wye hid behind them, peering out at Am.

Fidus knew the route back to The Hungry Dragon, and even though she was only trotting, there was an urgency about her pace. An acrid smell greeted them as they rounded the corner into the town. Pax already knew what to expect, but as she turned the corner, the sight of the smoking wreckage of the tavern felt like a kick in the stomach. Wispy grey smoke lingered over the blackened ruins merging into the morning mist. There was no sign of life, the locals having fled during the attack. They dismounted Fidus quietly in the yard, and Pax removed her carriage, unsure of where to put it amongst the ashes. Gazing into the animal's enormous eyes, she saw tears forming, and Fidus heaved a heavy breath. The Tricorn hurried into the field to join the herd, who were calling out to her in sorrowful cries.

"Tricorns are one of the few animals in the whole of Tellus that mourn their dead," Miles said, watching the herd gather.

"The Harvesters killed a tricorn?" Pax asked.

Miles looked down at her, his usual smile nowhere to be seen. Pax understood then that tricorns mourned their owners too.

"Dominus was a good Gen." Miles spoke softly. "The best. He saved my life."

He paused, and Pax let the silence hang in the air. In that moment, there was nothing else to say.

"I'll go and check the area by the tavern." Miles's voice cracked slightly, and he coughed. "Pax, you head towards the markets." Pax nodded, and watched as he made his way towards the smouldering remains that were once The Hungry Dragon.

"You guys stay here," Pax told Am and Venefica, dropping her bag by Am's feet and flicking open her penknife as she walked down the road towards the street.

It was hard to believe this was the same place that just yesterday had been bustling with market stalls and full of Gen of all shapes and sizes. Now the street was lined with smoking piles of ash. At first glance, it appeared there was nothing of use to salvage, and Pax tensed as she stepped through the rubble, unnerved by what she might find.

She kicked through some of the ash and saw something glinting. Kneeling down, she carefully picked the object up – a small orange stone. Pax sighed, thinking of the Gen from the jewellery stall, wondering if they'd escaped before the Harvesters had returned to set the town ablaze. The small stone pressed hot into her hand as it turned into a fist. Getting up, she placed it into her pocket and headed back towards the others.

Venefica sat on the singed grass next to the road, waiting for Miles and Pax to return.

"What happens when a Gen dies?" asked Am.

"They go back into the earth," the witch replied, drawing a circle in the blackened dust with her finger.

"Not their bodies. Them," Am clarified. "Their thoughts. Their feelings. Their memories."

Venefica looked up at Am. "No Gen really knows. Those we love will miss us. Many say we are reborn."

Am paused. "And what if you are not born?"

The witch's face softened, and she patted the ground next to her for Am to sit down. Venefica gazed at the scorched grass and plucked a single surviving blade of fabasucus.

"All living things are created. This plant is born of nature. You," she pointed at Am, "of science. Just because someone is made from a mother makes them no more loved in this world."

Venefica held out the plant. Am took it and smiled. They both stood as Miles and Pax appeared again. Between them, they had managed to salvage a few items from the wreckage for their onward journey, searching for the illusive Levis.

They made their way back through the fields of Scandza and into the woods, the air earthy with the promise of rain, hiking in single file with Pax leading the way and Miles at the rear. Beneath their feet, the path was knotted with thick roots stretching like veins through the earth.

"Do you know where we're going?" Am asked.

Pax had been toying with the amulet around her neck, deep in thought. She didn't know where they were heading exactly but knew they couldn't have stayed where they were. They needed to keep moving. She stopped and turned to Am, sighing.

"Would a rest be helpful?" Am offered as the others stopped behind them.

The witch and the warrior both shrugged in agreement, as if they didn't know which direction to head in either, but neither of them wanted to admit it. Venefica, delighted at the prospect of a break, took a seat on a fallen trunk to rub her bare feet.

"Your laces are loose." She pointed at Pax's boots. "I don't know why you Gen always insist on wearing those things."

As Pax knelt in the dirt to tie them, she was reminded of a song from when she was younger:

Her father used to sing it to her whilst demonstrating which way the laces go when you tie them into a bow. It had been one of the first things he had taught her when she had left school after the incident. When all the other parents in Viridis were complaining about how dangerous she was, her father had only ever been kind to her. Pax didn't remember much about what had happened on that final day at school, only tripping over her laces on the way home to find comfort from her dad. So, he had wiped away her tears and taught her how to tie her laces.

Picking up a handful of dirt from the ground, Pax let the dust fall through her fingers. It hadn't rained here for weeks. As if the gods heard her thoughts, a fat raindrop slapped onto the top of her head. Then another and another until the patter grew into a chorus on the dusty ground. Venefica leapt up, holding her hands out wide and twirling, her skirts fanning out around her. Miles chuckled. Am, confused by the witch's response, imitated her, turning slowly. Above Pax, the sunlight poured through the trees in great shafts, illuminating the raindrops. Then it dawned on her.

"'Many lines seem aglow, the opposite of below'," Pax whispered to herself, staring into the cloudless sky. The air above them was circling in muted colours.

"That's it!" Pax jumped up, startling the others. "Levis!"

Pax ran ahead into the clearing, her neck craning towards

the sky. Around her, the air prickled with barely-there colours. She ran along the path until, directly above her, she saw a swirling mass with a bright-white centre. Pax pointed upwards and went to call to the others, but before she had a chance, she was sucked up into the air. Miles grabbed his axe, running over to where Pax had disappeared. He held out a protective arm to stop Am and Venefica coming too close.

"Pax?" he yelled up into the sky. There was no answer. Then they heard a noise echoing from above them. It was laughter.

"Come up here!" yelled Pax from above them. "This is unbelievable!"

Miles and Venefica peered suspiciously through the rain into the spiral above. Am, on the other hand, took a step forwards without hesitation and instantly disappeared into the sky. A gleeful smile appeared on Venefica's face. Miles grimaced.

"After you," she said wickedly, noticing his discomfort.

"Well, I'd better stay on the ground and keep a look out," Miles said, trying to sound confident.

Venefica reached up to slap him on his back. "Live a little, warrior." Gathering up her skirts, she took a deliberate step forwards and vanished into the sky above.

"Dammit!" Miles muttered to himself, taking a deep breath. Closing his eyes, he lifted his crus in hesitation, taking a large step forwards. Suddenly, he was being sucked upwards at speed.

Opening his eyes, he saw colourful orbs whizzing around his head. The light in Levis danced in the air as if it was reflecting off an invisible silver pool. Am and Pax were floating nearby, laughing and taking it in turns to somersault in mid-air. Miles's stomach flipped at the sight, saliva building in his mouth. Panicking, he moved clumsily in the air and started to roll.

"Help!" he yelled, arms flailing. He slowed and stopped, suspended in mid-air, the witch's hand on his arm. He looked up to see her smiling, her gem-flecked dreadlocks floating in the air around her face. She let him go, floating towards Pax.

"'Different waves you perceive, found in photon energies'!" Pax yelled. "The light is refracted by the rain."

Venefica nodded as Pax spoke.

"It's the light spectrum! We need to collect all the colours. We're in a rainbow!"

Pax flipped over, grabbing one of the orbs that flew by. She held her hand out to show Venefica. Inside was a pulsing violet orb. An understanding smile spread over the witch's face, and she took a glass jar out of her bag and opened the lid so Pax could drop in the orb.

"Six more to go!" said Pax as she floated off to explain to Am.

The orange orb was easy to grab, Am catching it and adding it to the violet one already in the jar. Venefica managed to lure a yellow orb towards her with an incantation, much to Miles's astonishment. Pax, getting used to less gravity, focused in on a green orb. Using her powers, she took control of it, directing it into the jar using only her mind. She repeated this with a blue orb next. As they were added to the jar, the orbs knocked into each other.

"Just a red one to go! They're the fastest!" Pax shouted at the others across the space.

Miles, who had only just decided he wasn't going to throw up, wobbled in mid-air. He tried to steady himself, but between the weight of his axe in his belt and his crus, he was unbalanced and flipped upside down again. Picking up speed, his huge arms thrashing about in the air, he was knocking orbs flying in all directions. Am, Venefica and Pax dodged the rogue orbs as they floated to his rescue, and together, they steadied him into an upright position. Unfortunately, this had not settled the warrior's stomach, and his green-tinged face began to retch.

"Oh no, he's going to be sick!" Pax said.

Miles's chest jerked, and his mouth opened, spitting out a red orb into his hands.

"I meant to do that," he said queasily.

Once the final orb was added to the jar, the colours started to spin, slowly at first, then picking up speed until they merged. The jar filled with a blinding white light, then mellowed into a liquid silver. It glowed as Venefica held it up to her face.

"Omnis," the witch said. "Beautiful and very powerful."

Miles went to say something but stopped himself. Instead, he said, "Now, how exactly do we get down?"

Pax gazed down through the swirling colours. The forest floor appeared hazy and very far away. She thought she heard a whisper. Looking towards where the voice was coming from, she could see a fine white line on the horizon. The line was bright and appeared to be getting closer. Squinting her eyes, she could just make out a figure. She was about to point it out to the others and then *thud!* They were back on the forest floor.

Spitting out a mouthful of dust, Pax felt her chest crushing into the amulet underneath her. Above them, Levis had disappeared. Am patted her on the arm.

"Just a minute," Pax said, sitting up, but Am patted her again, more frantically this time. "Am!" Pax scolded, knowing Am would have been the only one of them not to have felt any pain from the fall.

"Just—" Pax froze.

Looking up, she understood why Am had needed her attention so urgently. Surrounding them stood four huge black pegasi, their glossy black coats gleaming in the afternoon sun, their wings slick like oil. Their breath fogged the air as they stared calmly, shifting slightly on their hooves.

"A correction," Venefica said quietly, rising slowly to her feet.

Pax joined her side. "A correction?" she repeated, staring at the enormous creatures.

The witch nodded, resting a hand on the nose of the nearest pegasus. "A group of pegasi is called a correction." She stroked the animal's snout. "Legend has it they appear only when most needed, summoned with magic."

"The Omnis?" Pax asked, retrieving the glowing jar from the ground.

"Perhaps," Venefica replied, mesmerised by the eyes of the pegasi: bright blue, streaked with brown, as if the iris had been slashed.

Pax remembered her father calling them spirit eyes. But when Pax reached out her hand to stroke it, the pegasus flinched away.

"Shhh…" Venefica calmed the animal.

Pax turned away, slightly embarrassed, putting the jar of Omnis into her bag. Miles was patting another pegasus, running his hands along its muscular neck. They didn't appear to be flinching for anyone else.

"Such strong creatures!" the warrior exclaimed. "Never seen one in real life before. Check out the size of its wings." He gently touched one of the inky feathers. "The wingspan must be twice my height!"

"That's saying something," Venefica added, glancing up at Miles. "They're here to transport us to safety."

"We're riding them?" Pax asked.

"More 'hitching a ride'," Venefica offered. "We can't miss this opportunity. I've never known black pegasus to appear in all my cent—" She paused. "Years."

Miles arched an eyebrow. "So, we're just going to hop on and see what happens? I've only just got my crus back on solid ground!"

Both the witch and the warrior looked at Pax and waited.

"Well, we have the Omnis," Pax said, "and we need to keep moving towards Rubra. Flying *would* be quicker than walking."

Miles rolled his eyes. Venefica jumped up and down, clapping her hands together, then stood on a nearby ledge and vaulted onto the back of the nearest pegasus. It flexed its wings slightly as Venefica scooted down just behind its shoulder blades.

"Luckily, I'm a better rider than floater!" Miles said, giving Am a leg up onto the next awaiting pegasus.

Pax slipped her bag onto her back and went towards one of the pegasi. Its eyes widened, and it backed away.

Miles came to her side. "Need a hand?"

"No. No, I'll be fine," she lied.

The warrior turned, easily mounting the next animal. His crus slotted comfortably beside one of the huge wings, which opened wide, with symmetrical feathers gleaming in the setting sunlight. Dust flew up from the ground as, with one huge swoop, the pegasus took to the air.

Pax shielded her eyes and watched as Am and Venefica's pegasus followed Miles into the air. Pax was alone in the forest. Turning back to the last pegasus, she took small steps towards the flinching animal. She gazed into its spirit eyes. The animal's breathing started to slow, then it moved again, kneeling for her. Pax moved to the side, and, taking hold of the wing bone, climbed onto its back. She could feel the muscles move beneath her as the pegasus stood. Its wings opened wide, and it launched into the sky. Pax gripped tightly to the coarse black mane as the pegasus joined the others flying towards the setting sun.

CHAPTER NINETEEN

Occissor waved his palm over the Oculus, purple veins protruding from his hand, and Phantasma's face disappeared. His anger at her and Deleo for failing to retrieve the amulet was etched deep into his varicose face. With the sting of failure still running through his blood, he made his way over to the large stained-glass window to look down over Rubra. Despite all the sacrifices he had made for his own Gen, he received little gratitude from the thankless masses in the streets below.

"Remember when it was an honour to walk these streets?" he pondered aloud, the two guards stationed either side of the door remaining still, not daring to move.

Manus, seated at a table near the back of the room, placed down his quill and picked up his gloves.

"An honour to fill these veins." Occissor ran his fingertips over his wrists, smiling sarcastically. "Now we are like devils in the dirt, scrambling for mere morsels."

Manus stood up. "I take it Phantasma did not have the news you were hoping for, Your Highness?" he asked, pulling the chain mail over his hands.

Occissor faced him. "They have yet to retrieve the amulet. I have ordered them to return to Rubra. They will need well-rested pyrois to continue their hunt, and perhaps more guards."

Manus stepped quietly towards the king. "If I may suggest, Your Highness, maybe more guards are not needed. If they have a blood trail already, surely Mort would be of more assistance?"

Occissor glanced at Manus, a shadow of a smile across his face, and turned towards the guards at the door.

"Go to the Cellarium. Tell them to prepare Mort. Phantasma will return to Rubra soon and collect him."

The guards saluted and marched out of the Throne Room. Their footsteps echoed in unison through the hallways, as they descended down a spiral staircase, passing other Supremos, dressed in pristine white cloaks. The walls here were white and lined with thick glass tubes, which covered the interior surfaces before snaking their way to the outer walls. There, they ran down the length of the Castellum, fanning out into the gullies lining the streets. Finally, the guards reached the lower floor and paused at the glass doors of the Cellarium. It opened silently, and an older guard, in black, greeted them.

The first guard saluted. "His highness has a request. Mort is to be retrieved, ready for Phantasma's return."

"Bringing out the big knives, eh?" the older guard at the door replied informally, but when the other guards didn't share his humour, he shrugged. He led them down another corridor, past several rooms full of hundreds of prisoners. Caro. Inside one of these cells, lying on his side, was the alchemist Creo. His gaze stayed fixed on the floor, but he was listening carefully.

"Why do they need Mort?" the older guard inquired, stopping at the end of the corridor.

"To track someone," replied the shorter guard, who seemed to relax more the further away he was from the

Throne Room. "Rumour has it" – he lowered his voice – "a caro escaped in Viridis."

Creo tried not to react to the mention of his home, lying as still as he could. The taller guard frowned, not adding to the conversation, but the shorter guard carried on.

"Phantasma and Deleo have been sent to track them down, but they're having trouble. They need Mort to locate the blood trail."

A snarling growl echoed down the hallway, growing louder and more menacing. Two other Supremos appeared, pushing a trolly containing a metal cage. It shook violently as it was wheeled down the corridor, stopping just outside Creo's cell. The glass of the cell had fogged up from hot breath escaping from between huge, fanged teeth. Creo couldn't help but flinch as the hellhound barked viciously, saliva splattering onto the glass.

"Steady there, Mort!" said one of the guards who had wheeled in the trolley. "He's in a bad mood today! Hasn't been fed for a while."

The shorter guard peered between the bars, jerking backwards as he was met with a stream of ferocious barks.

"Maybe we don't release him until we're well outside the Castellum's grounds?" he said nervously.

As the older guards chuckled and saluted, Creo watched as the hellhound was wheeled away, snarling, into the distance. Across the empty corridor, he met Celeste's eyes, wide with fear. Creo turned away from her, holding his face in his hands, one question searing into his mind: *What have I done?*

CHAPTER TWENTY

The powerful wings of the pegasus barely made a sound as they sliced the evening air, climbing ever higher above the shrinking landscape.

Gripping the mane between her fingers, Pax imagined for a moment that all her problems were left on the land below, unable to reach her. There was something so freeing about having the wind rush against her skin, whipping at her hair. Up ahead, Venefica had her arms spread wide, head back, cackling in delight. The trees beneath them started to thicken, and Miles yelled out that the pegasi appeared to be descending towards a wooded area.

Am scanned the scenery. "Miles is correct – we are entering Walda Woods."

The pegasus beneath Pax tilted to the left, and she held on tightly, leaning back as it descended steeply. The huge creature expertly flew through a slight clearing in the canopy of trees and landed surprisingly gracefully. Once everyone had safely dismounted, all four pegasi quietly knelt in close formation nearby, thick-lashed lids closing over their spirit eyes, and one even tucking its muzzle under its wing.

Now she was back on solid ground, Pax's problems greeted her as if they had been waiting for her, here amongst the trees. The familiar trickle of a nearby stream reminded her of

Viridis, and she took the opportunity for some time alone to gather her thoughts by offering to catch their evening meal. She collected her nets from her bag and headed down the bank towards the river, leaving the others to prepare the shelter and a fire. Although Pax was extremely grateful for the help she had received so far, she felt relieved to be alone. Sadness had accompanied her these last few days, and, as desperately as she had tried to ignore it, distracting herself with each part of the quest, now the sorrow was bubbling to the surface, oozing out of her and refusing to be hidden anymore. It wanted to be felt.

Finding a calm spot in the stream to set up, Pax tied the nets tightly and threw them into the water. Sitting on the riverbank, she waited quietly for signs of a catch. A velox fairy slowly passed above her head, and her heart sank. To distract herself, she practiced levitating small rocks by the side of the river. In the quiet of the forest, she could lift them easily above the water, then fling them skipping across the surface further upstream, where they would hopefully spook the tentamenta into the nets.

Tomorrow was Pax's Ortus day. Her powers had grown in strength, and although she felt more control over them than ever, she still struggled when she really needed them, when she was under pressure to perform. The stench of the two Gen who had attacked her in the market still filled her nostrils, their faces swirling into her mind. She had desperately wanted to lift their rotten bodies off the ground and throw them across the street. To cause them pain. To feel powerful.

She thought about her parents. Here she was, sitting in Walda Woods, waiting to catch dinner, when only the gods knew what was happening to them. It was all so unfair. Yet her father had left her with the clues, and her mother had gifted her the amulet, so she had to believe she was on the right path.

Pax took the jar of Omnis from her bag. It glowed silver as she placed it on the ground next to her. Carefully, she pulled the amulet out from underneath her shirt and clicked the symbol, the gemstones jutting out once more. Removing the vial capped with silver, she carefully submerged it into the jar until it was full. Holding her breath she clicked it back into place, hoping that Zed had succeeded in completely removing the tracker and this wouldn't send a signal, putting them in even more danger. They hadn't seen any trace of the Harvesters who had been chasing them since they had left Scandza, and Pax knew flying here to Walda Woods had put a greater distance between her party and the enemy.

Movement in the water caught her eye. Kneeling down by the edge of the stream, she pulled the nets to the surface, revealing large, squirming tentamenta. Taking the penknife from her pocket, she cut the rope free, the blade accidentally slicing into her thumb. A line of bright red revealed itself. The cut didn't hurt; she had always had a high tolerance for pain, her mother saying it was because she was a redhead. Placing her thumb into her mouth, she sucked the cut, and a sweet, metallic taste settled on her tongue. Dropping the bulging net on the bank, she leant over to wash the wound. As she submerged her hand, her blood spread into the clear pool, over her own reflection. As Pax lent closer, the amulet fell from her shirt, grazing the water. When the ripples subsided, her reflection appeared again, only this time, her eyes were bright red. Pax frowned as she realised the eyes staring up at her were, in fact, not hers. The face coming into focus in the water was white, lined with thick veins, strangely familiar, yet terrifying. Pax jolted backwards onto the riverbank, catching her breath. Slowly, she peered into the water again, only to see the pool was now clear. Shaking, she grabbed the net and made her way back to the camp.

Pax wondered how to describe what she had seen to the others, thinking maybe she had imagined it, but as the camp came into sight, she stopped. Around the fire stood Am, Miles and Venefica, their heads adorned with almost-comical hats, fashioned from large leaves.

Miles beamed. "Happy Ortus day!" he said, the other two joining him slightly out of time.

"Figo!" said Pax, spotting a rather slimy cake next to the fire. "But it's not until tomorrow."

"We know, but tonight, we celebrate beneath the moon!" Venefica replied, flashing her gemstone-covered teeth.

"They asked me to relay information about your Ortus," said Am.

Pax placed the net down onto the ground. "Thank you."

"This cake has all your favourite things!" Am said proudly, pointing to the muddy mess next to the fire.

"I tried to clarify that you don't mix savoury and sweet, and some of this isn't even edible, but…" Venefica sighed.

Miles picked up the net of tentamenta. "Right, let's get these cooking," he said. "Then presents!"

Using her penknife, Pax cut into the bellies of the creatures, expertly pulling out their slippery entrails. She passed each prepared creature to Miles, who threaded them onto sticks, ready to toast on the fire. When he noticed the wound on her thumb, he offered to swap jobs.

"How'd'ya do that?" he asked, taking the knife from her.

Pax sighed. "Just being clumsy."

"Don't be too hard on yourself, remember to speak kindly. You think I still blame myself for losing my leg?" He smiled. "You've had a lot to deal with these last few days, and there's more to come. If you're going to be ready, you have to believe in yourself, and that includes the words going on in there." He softly tapped the top of her head.

Pax nodded, knowing he was right, but thinking it and actually doing it were two very different things.

"I'll finish up here, you go and sit down. No cooking on your Ortus!" he declared. Pax smiled, surprised even to be celebrating at all.

"Venefica was telling a story about birds," Am said as Pax sat down next to the crackling fire.

"Oh?"

The witch sighed. "Not a story, a rhyme. About the magpies—"

"They are black and white birds with the ability to travel between realms," Am interrupted, relaying information Venefica had given her just moments before.

"Yes," Venefica continued, slightly annoyed, "because they carry both light and dark. These creatures are sent to us as messengers. There is a rhyme to reminds us of what to look out for. It goes like this:

> *One for sorrow,*
> *Two for joy,*
> *Three for a girl,*
> *Four for a boy,*
> *Five for silver,*
> *Six for gold,*

A little later that evening, they ate roasted tentamenta next to the warmth of the fire. Miles finished his meal just as quickly as Venefica. Pax was used to Am staring at her during mealtimes, but now all three of them waited as she chewed. Miles clasped his hands together with a gleeful smile as she put the last bite of food into her mouth. The warrior stood up and went over to the tent, returning with a parcel.

"Here ya go!" he said, his face going red.

He passed her an object wrapped in hessian and tied with a wonky string bow. Pax put down her plate and pulled at the string, unwrapping the gift. The material opened, revealing the beautiful carved handle of a short sword. It was encased in a thick leather scabbard. Taking the carved hilt into her hand, she found it fitted perfectly. Carefully she pulled out the blade, and her tearful eyes gleamed in the mirror-like dark sword. It was the same one she had seen at the market in Scandza.

"You like it?" Miles asked after a few moments, expecting some sort of reaction. "It's made with crushed Calva, also known as dragon bone. It's what gives it the shiny black colour and is one of the strongest metals known to Gen!"

"Thank you, it's wonderful," Pax replied quietly, slightly overwhelmed.

Relieved, Miles hugged her in his massive arms. "It can slice through flesh with ease."

His sweet smile suggested he was reliving fond memories of the battlefield. He tied the scabbard around Pax's waist, adjusting it until it fitted snugly.

Venefica moved to sit next to Pax, her face illuminated by the flames of the fire. She took Pax's hand and placed a silver moonstone ring into her palm. It was the same one Pax had noticed when they had been sitting in The Hungry Dragon.

"Your ring! No, I can't accept this. It belongs to you."

The witch smiled. "My gift to you, young one." She closed her fingers around Pax's hand.

A few days ago, Pax didn't even know these Gen existed, and now she felt extremely lucky to be sharing her Ortus celebrations with them. Pax placed the ring onto her middle finger, fighting back tears. Venefica, feeling uncomfortable at the display of emotion, jumped to her feet.

"We should dance!" she exclaimed, her eyes switching quickly to black.

"Saltare Musica Tripudio!" she said, waving her hands up to the trees above.

The fairies snoozing in the branches slowly woke, and one by one, they started singing a cheerful tune. Venefica's eyes dissolved to white, and she grabbed Pax's hands, pulling her to her feet. Am joined them as Miles looked on, and not even the witch's pleas were enough to coax him up to dance.

"My crus wasn't made for dancing!" he joked.

Underneath a sky of violet and emerald solar flares, they

twirled to the music of the fairies. Am asked repeatedly if Pax had liked the cake they had made, and she nodded, knowing that she would soon have to attempt to eat the unappetising concoction.

Suddenly, above their heads, the branches snapped. They all stopped and gazed upwards as a small dragat came crashing down through the trees, landing with a thud at Pax's feet.

"Felis!" Pax exclaimed, scooping him up in her arms. "You came back!"

They celebrated into the night, to the songs of the velox fairies, as Felis feasted on the leftover bones from dinner. Venefica, lost in the music, stopped only when she caught Miles watching her, and she joined him by the fire.

"Remember when we were that age?" he asked, nodding at Am and Pax as they giggled and swayed to the music.

Venefica's smile dropped. "By that age I had been on my own for a very long time."

Miles was annoyed with himself that his question had changed the witch's mood so quickly.

"Well, I just hope we make it to Rubra in time to save Pax's parents." Miles said quietly.

Venefica paused. "Yes, they must be good parents for her to care this much." Miles looked at her, eyebrows raised. The witch smiled sadly. "Let's just say not all parents love the way they are meant to."

Above them, magpies were gathering noisily for the night.

"Seven, eight," Venefica counted. "Young one!" she called out to Pax, pointing up at the magpies. "Make a wish!" Pax nodded, closing her eyes.

Miles pointed upwards as another magpie flew down to join the others. "That's nine now." He looked sideways at

Venefica. "What's that mean?"

The witch's eyes widened slightly. "Come on, warrior," she said, standing. "We have a terrible cake to eat."

CHAPTER
TWENTY-ONE

Occissor had never seen irises as deep red as those staring up at him from the waters of the Oculus. It was as if they were piercing his black heart. The face was a mystery, yet the amulet around their neck was unmistakable. The image had sent a guttural scream escaping from his lungs, as if his very insides were unravelling.

"Your Highness," Manus said, running to his side, startled at the outburst. "What did you see?"

Occissor shook his head in disbelief. "Someone knows something." He glanced at Manus. "It is time for you to use your powers."

Manus swallowed, the colour draining from his face. "I don't understand—"

"Go!" Occissor screamed so loudly Manus flinched. "To the Cellarium. We will interrogate them one by one if we have to, until they reveal the truth."

Manus lowered his eyes to the floor, nodding quietly and backing out of the Throne Room. As the door closed behind him, he started walking, then broke into a sprint down the corridor.

Occissor paced up and down for a few more moments, dark memories filling his mind. Then he, too, marched out of the Throne Room, sending the stationed guards away with a flick of his hand. His rapid steps echoed down the sprawling hallways, and guards, servants, cleaners, in fact any Gen in the Castellum, made themselves scarce. It was as if they could sense in their blood their leader approaching, and they knew he was furious.

Occissor's silhouette moved from light to dark as he continued down the hall, passing several large windows casting glimpses of moonlight upon the cold tiles. The tubes lining the walls around him were empty now, waiting to be filled with the same thing the Supremos outside the Castellum walls craved: blood.

Blood gave his Gen their immortality. It had been this way for generations. Only a drop or two for those lower down in the pecking order, those Supremos living on the grubby outskirts of Rubra, yet that would sustain them for many moons. The closer you got to the king, however, the more blood you would receive. Occissor himself, of course, never went without.

As Occissor descended the staircase into the lower levels of the Castellum, the image of the gold amulet flashed before his eyes. A terrible sadness settled inside him, fighting with his anger. The royal bloodline came directly from old gods. Their immortality, however, had come at a high price. The royal ancestry had been cursed – children born to the king rarely survived. That was why the death of his only son had been all the more cruel, a true crime against nature. His son who, after surviving as a child, against all the odds, had grown into a highly intelligent alchemist and strong heir to the Supremo Gen. Then it was all taken in one single reckless moment. When the prince left this world, he took with him the Supremos' only chance of survival.

Occissor gritted his teeth as he turned into a dimly lit corridor so rarely used that the servants no longer even cleaned it. His feet pounded against the floor until he stopped in front of a wooden door. Inhaling the damp smell, his long fingers reached up to a symbol carved into the wood. He hesitated, as if touching it would burn his skin.

In the years that had passed since his son's death, the riots and uprisings by his own Gen had grown more frequent. Out of necessity – to keep the crowds, baying for blood, at the Castellum doors – the Harvests had begun. His guards went out and hunted caro, taking what was rightfully theirs, what they needed to survive in a bloody and desperate war.

As their king, he knew his Gen had been placated with the Messis, a ritualised celebration, a distraction from the bigger issue – that the royal bloodline was doomed. But for how much longer could this continue before the masses saw through the smoke and mirrors and decided to revolt? Occissor's expression grew harder as those red eyes in the Oculus glowed inside his mind. Lowering his hand, he pulled away from the door, marching back down the empty corridor and towards the Throne Room. Soon, Manus would return with the first of the caro to be questioned. Occissor knew that, without an heir, his downfall would lead to the extinction of the entire Supremo Gen, and he would do whatever it took to stop their annihilation, using any means necessary.

CHAPTER
TWENTY-TWO

"What are you doing?"

The knife nearly slipped from between Pax's fingers, away from the wood and into her skin.

"Am! Don't sneak up on me – it's rude!"

Am stared at Pax, studying the emotions on her face, as the low hoot of a mourning dove cried out in the distance.

Pax sighed. "I'm just whittling something. It takes my mind off things. How about you remind us of the next clue?"

Am straightened up as their eyes flickered to green.

From high above you can see,
A place shrouded in secrecy.
Opposites attract on land, not sea,
A Two-Faced God holds the key.

Venefica nodded to show she was listening as Miles served up a breakfast of fried grass fritters and cups of faba. Felis had given up gnawing on last night's leftover bones and was whizzing after a particularly large fairy.

The morning air was cold, so Pax knelt closer to the crackling fire to keep warm, her breath fogging the air. Upon waking on her Ortus day, she had hoped to feel different or, perhaps, stronger. Of course, she knew powers rarely revealed themselves that quickly. A Gen a few years older than her, back in Viridis, hadn't experienced anything for months, most believing she had no powers at all. Then, one day, she had started hearing voices, and at first, she thought she was going mad before she realised the trees were speaking to her. Pax wondered if maybe the vision in the water yesterday had been something similar to what had happened to that girl. Most of the Silva Gen had some kind of power relating to nature, and Pax had spent many years imagining what hers would be. Her mother had often said she hoped Pax would inherit her father's powers of alchemy, which had made him stand out in Viridis, moving away from nature into the world of science. It made many of the local Gen fear his work, but Pax had come to realised that, sometimes, it was good to be different, and she secretly hoped she would inherit something unusual too.

Although untethered, all of the pegasi had stayed close to the camp all night, suggesting they would probably lead them to the next destination. Venefica had explained that the creatures only stayed where they were needed, so the place they would travel to next had to be located by magical means. As the witch handed out the bowls of fritters, Miles watched her with a smile. When Pax caught his eye, he cleared his throat.

"So, a place that can be seen from up high?" he pondered, as if he had been considering this all along.

"Janus is known to be a two-faced God," Pax said, recalling the history of Tellus that her father had taught her. "Anyone know where to find him?"

"They will take us," the witch said, her index finger pointing to the pegasi. She shoved another handful of food into her mouth. "To Nusquam," she mumbled.

"There is no record of this place on the map," said Am.

"I thought Nusquam was just from old fairy tales?" said Miles.

Venefica washed down her food with a mouthful of her drink. "When will you trust in the magic, warrior?" She wiped her mouth on her sleeve. "Fairytales hold more truth than you know."

Miles rolled his eyes towards Pax. "Any feelings?" he said, holding out his hands and twisting his wrists.

Pax shook her head and continued focusing on the wood she was carving.

"Ah well, it takes a while for these things to kick in, many moons in fact," Miles said, but Pax didn't respond, just sliced into the wood a little harder.

"Hey," he said quietly, lifting her chin gently with his hand. "I've seen your power already, remember? You're going to be something spectacular."

"But what if you're wrong?" Pax snapped, making Miles lean away from her. "Sorry." She reined in her temper. "It's just, sometimes, in my head I—" She stopped, unable to find the words to describe how she was feeling.

"You know, the voices in your head aren't always telling you the truth," Venefica added from across the smoking remains of the fire.

Pax stared at the witch. In that moment, the words she had spoken made so much sense. Pax was wasting time worrying about things that hadn't even happened yet.

"You're right." Pax nodded. "Sorry again, Miles, I didn't mean to snap at you. I just wish I had as much faith in me as you do."

Miles winked and got up, stretching out his knee where his crus was connected. It had healed well since they had left Ultra.

Pax folded her penknife away and blew the final shavings from the small chunk of wood. She made her way over to Venefica, holding it out in her hand.

"What is this?" Venefica peered at the carving suspiciously.

"It's a magpie. I made it for you. Look, I added some of the amethyst for its eye." She touched her fingertip to the purple stone.

The witch stared at Pax but said nothing.

"Um, I just like to make them, as a hobby," Pax said, feeling a little childish. "You said you liked the magpies, and they're pretty easy to carve. I made this one last night."

Pax pulled a second one out of her pocket, to which she had added some of the orange stone she had found left over from the fire. Holding the two pieces together, she demonstrated how the small wooden magpies' wings slotted together perfectly.

Venefica remained expressionless, and Pax felt her cheeks going red.

"They're silly, really, but making them helps me take my mind off things." Just as she went to put the carvings back in her pocket, the witch grabbed her hand.

"Which one is for me?" Venefica asked.

"You can choose." Pax held out her hands.

"This other stone is garnet. I think I will take this one." Venefica picked up one of the wooden birds and threw it into her velvet bag, then started gathering up her other belongings.

"You're welcome," Pax said under her breath, shrugging, and went to help Am pack up the shelter.

The four pegasi cut a dark diagonal streak across the sky as they flew in formation above Walda Woods. Pax had managed to mount her ride with a little less nostril-flaring from the creature than the previous day and felt more confident riding it now. Felis looked tiny, flying alongside her pegasus, his fur rippling in the breeze as his wings flapped at double speed just to keep up.

After flying for a while, the crowded tree canopy below morphed into a sparser landscape. After a few more minutes in the air, tiny dots of colour appeared, scattered beneath them. The pegasus slowed and descended, landing softly in an enormous field of wildflowers, the blooms rippling beneath their wings. The only other noticeable landmark was a huge tree directly in the centre of the field.

The pegasus slowly knelt for Pax to dismount.

"Is this Nusquam?" she asked.

Venefica shook her head, pulling out her spell book from her bag and flicking through the pages. Pax stepped into the field, her palms outstretched, lightly touching the flowers. Purple lavenders, frilly peonies and blooming azaleas. There was a gentle humming from small insects, but no wind, and the scent was heavenly. Pax moved through the flowers until she was standing in front of the tree, its long, dramatic branches full of silvery-green leaves, draping down until they almost touched the ground.

"A weeping willow."

Pax knew they were rare nowadays, and the tree no longer grew, back in Viridis. Feeling homesick, she clutched the amulet around her neck, pushing the curtain of leaves aside to reveal the large trunk. She placed her palm against the greyish bark. Suddenly, she felt movement beneath her hand – the bark was cracking. Pulling away, Pax watched as the tree trunk began to twist and stretch, the thick knots in the tree shifting to form an eyelid, then another. The wrinkled bark split until two mouths appeared, moving into position lower down the trunk. The movement stopped, and carved into the tree were two sleeping faces.

"Woah," Miles said quietly next to the others, who stared in disbelief. "The Two-Faced God."

All four eyes in the bark opened simultaneously. "I prefer Janus," the tree's two voices said, harmonising into one.

No one spoke for a few seconds. The faces in the tree waited, all four eyes, each a different shade of green, looking them up and down as if independent of each other.

Pax swallowed, then spoke. "We've come for help, please." The eyes all fixed on her. "We're looking for something. We believe you can help us?"

The eyes in the bark narrowed, studying Pax's face, then one by one moved down to fix on the amulet hanging around her neck.

"Prophecies." The two voices spoke together again, the mouths in the bark moving in unison. "Past and future, all come to now."

The silence that followed showed that Pax wasn't the only one confused.

"Would you like to hear the clue?" Am offered, taking a step closer to the tree.

The eyes moved to focus on Am, a barky eyebrow arching above one, intrigued.

Then the higher voice spoke. "No need. I've seen your pasts."

The lower voice added, "And I know your futures."

All of Janus's eyes focused back on Pax, as if expecting something.

"Where do we go?" Pax asked, feeling uncomfortable as the eyes bored into her.

"First, a task." The voices spoke in sync. "To discover our future, we must look to the past."

The sweeping branches of the willow tree lifted like curtains.

"What is created in a second but lasts a lifetime?"

The voices melded together as, beneath them, where the tree's roots tangled together, the earth ruptured. Miles gripped his axe.

"What can make you cry, laugh or feel young?" the voices continued as a rumble of moving earth revealed sharp shapes rising from the ground. "What can bring the dead back to life?" the voices asked as, finally, four sets of V-shaped mirrors, two either side of the trunk, revealed themselves, silently reflecting the wildflower meadow beyond.

"Each will look into your past, past, past," said the higher voice of the tree.

"Each will look into your future, future, future," echoed the lower voice.

Pax glanced at the others. Miles shrugged at her, but Venefica was already striding towards one of the mirrors. Am waited for Pax, who nodded in encouragement, and they all moved into position to stand in front of a pair of mirrors. Each of them had one pane to their left and one to their right.

Standing at the mirrors, Pax could no longer see the

others. Instead, she was enclosed, faced with her own reflection repeated twice in front of her. She waited. Unsure of what to do next, she peered closer to the mirror on the left. She was paler than usual, and her hair was tangled. Then her reflection moved, taking a step backwards away from her. Frowning, Pax lifted her hand slowly up towards the glass, but her reflection didn't match.

Her mirror image turns and walks slowly away from her. Pax looks closer, recognising the familiar scene. A memory: she is six again, playing in the school yard. She is happy at first, her younger self, but then she is surrounded by other children. They are pulling her hair, kicking dirt in her face as she kneels to tie her laces. The scene unfolds, and Pax watches helplessly, her fists clenched at her sides. She wants to step into the mirror, to defend her younger self. The child on the ground turns to Pax, her eyes now glowing red. Suddenly, she remembers what is about to happen. The incident. The reason she was told she was dangerous. Why she couldn't return to school. In the mirror, the younger Pax stands up, tear tracks drying on her dirty face. Her chest is rising rapidly as her breath quickens. She stands and faces her attackers. One of the children stops laughing as they are lifted into the air. The others watch in shock as the child is thrown backwards, hard onto the ground by an invisible force. The children scream, try to flee. But it is too late. Young Pax uses her power, lifting them high above the ground, throwing them like rag dolls back down into the dirt until all the other children lie injured on the ground. Only then does younger Pax start running, back towards home, tripping over her untied laces.

When the image disappears, the mirror shows Pax standing in the wildflower meadow again, her cheeks flushed. Next, her reflection to the right moves, and Pax watches herself walking away again. But this time she doesn't recognise the scene. A journey down a cobbled path towards a huge castle, its walls covered in a tangle of glass tubes. Intrigued, Pax looks closer, but she doesn't recognise this place, this city. In the mirror, the path floods, but her reflection continues onwards, unfazed, wading through the rising dark water. It splashes around her ankles, against her thighs, up above her waist. It slowly rises until her reflection is struggling desperately against the current. Pax leans closer, and her eyes widen as she realises it isn't water flooding the streets – it's blood. As she watches herself struggle against the deluge, a metallic taste fills her mouth, as if she herself is gasping for air. As the tubes of the castle's walls turn red, a heat rises in her chest, and Pax reaches out a hand towards the mirror. As she touches the cold glass, her reflection snaps around. Her own red eyes stare back. Then she watches in horror as she disappears beneath the bloody waters. The mirror returns to normal, showing Pax on her knees below the weeping willow, clutching the amulet around her neck.

In the left-hand mirror, Miles's reflection stands tall, before he lost his leg and gained his crus. He is duelling outside his home, his opponent a small Tribus boy with thick tresses of dark hair. The boy thrusts his wooden sword towards Miles, who tumbles to the ground, clutching his heart and dying theatrically before lying still. The boy cheers in victory, but Miles doesn't move. The boy pauses, then moves slowly over to Miles, hovering above his chest, checking to see if he is still breathing. Miles roars, startling the boy and grabbing him up into his arms as they both roll over, laughing. From inside the house, a voice calls out. Miles picks up the small boy, throwing him over his shoulder, and together they disappear inside the home.

As the mirror returns to normal, Miles wipes a tear away. Then, in the right-hand mirror, an image of war meets his eyes. Miles is mounted on a white pyrois, his crus locked firmly into the stirrups. He holds his axe above his head, yelling a war cry, his face distorted behind the animal's flaming mane. He kicks his steed towards battle with an entire army following him.

Venefica's eyes see an image, in the left mirror, from many centuries ago. A memory so old it clings like a spider web, yet, as the images reveal themselves, it is as vivid to her as if it were yesteryear. She is a young child inside a small hut, her bare hands wrapped around the bars of a wooden cage. Gen with no faces speak around her; not one acknowledges her presence. Time speeds up, then slows. Someone kicks the cage, and her younger self cowers. Stale bread is thrown in, and a figure coaxes the starving child out to grab the food. They spit at her, cursing. Venefica watches the large cauldron boiling on the fire. Bile fills her stomach as she remembers the fate of other children who had been caged. On the table, small bones are scattered next to a purple-covered book.

The image blurs again, speeding up, then slowing once more. The young Venefica is outside now, free, walking away with the spell book under her arm. Behind her, the hut is engulfed in flames. The mirror returns to normal, and Venefica smiles at herself, turning to the right-hand side, where her mirror image smiles back. With a finger, she beckons her to watch as the reflection walks through a forest into a circle of hooded figures. A coven. Her coven. Venefica's reflection turns, gold glinting at her neck, her eyes black. With a wave of her hand, the image returns to normal, showing Venefica standing in the meadow.

After they had witnessed the scenes in the mirrors, they all returned to stand, once more, in front of the Two-Faced God.

"Past is past," said the higher voice.

"Future is future," said the lower voice.

Then together their voices echoed and faded. "All there is, is, now, now, now."

All four eyes closed peacefully. Pax, Miles, Venefica and Am glanced at one another as they waited in silence. Felis returned, covered in pollen from flying through the wildflowers and landed on the ground at the base of the tree trunk.

After a few more moments, Pax whispered to the others, "What now?"

Miles and Venefica shrugged, the images they had each witnessed replaying over and over in their minds.

Pax leant towards Am. "What did you see in the mirrors?"

Am hesitated, then replied. "Am's reflection."

"Oh," said Pax.

This was the first time Am had ever lied. The new programming Zed had installed appeared to have worked, because Pax didn't ask any further questions.

One of the eyes on the tree opened again, peeking at them. Then all four eyes opened, each rolling in annoyance.

"All there is, is now," the voices repeated. "Only one of you is present."

One by one, the green eyeballs all rolled down to stare at Felis, who was curled up, purring happily at the base of the tree.

Confused, Pax asked, "Sorry, what do we have to do?"

The tree sighed. "You have all looked to the past. You have all looked to the future. Now you must be here, in the present. Nothing else matters." Slowly, the eyelids on the tree closed again. "Be present."

"Okay…" Pax said, laughing nervously, looking around to see Am now sitting cross-legged on the floor next to Felis, their eyes also closed.

The witch and the warrior followed suit, sitting next to Am in front of the weeping willow. Venefica waited to close her eyes until she was sure Miles had first. As Pax sat down, thoughts of cities flooding with blood washed through her mind, and the image of her own red eyes staring at her. Then she saw her parents. Controlling her thoughts was hard. She opened one eye, sneaking a peek at the others. All of them were still and calm. She closed her eyes again, taking a deep breath and trying to relax.

"Two of you are present," said the tree's voices, together.

Probably Am and Felis, thought Pax. At least Miles and Venefica were finding this difficult too. A few more moments passed. Pax focused on her breath. In and out, in and out, listening to the leaves softly falling from the tree around her.

She opened her eyes. How much time had passed? The light had changed slightly, and she blinked, taking in her surroundings. The others were still sitting by her side, each beginning to move. In front of them, the huge willow tree remained, but the faces in the trunk were now gone. Instead, in their place was a door carved into the bark, and in the keyhole glinted a large gold key.

"We did it," whispered Pax, getting up. "The Two-Faced God holds the key!"

She stroked Felis awake, popping him into her backpack

as the others followed her towards the door. One by one, they each placed their hand around the bow of the large golden key, which was in the shape of an eye.

Pax glanced at the others. "Ready?"

They all nodded. The tree bark crunched like bone as Pax twisted the key. Then the door cracked open, sucking them all into the darkness.

CHAPTER TWENTY-THREE

Creo's cheek was numb against the coldness of the old stone floor, the damp sitting dirty in his nostrils. He hadn't slept in days, desperately trying to stay awake, listening to the discussions of the guards stationed in the Cellarium, straining to hear any mention of Viridis, Pax and Am, any clue that might tell him that they were alive. He took slight comfort in the fact that they hadn't been mentioned yet, suggesting that maybe they had managed to escape. During these hours trapped in the confines of the Cellarium, his mind had imagined every other choice he could have made. Had he left enough information for Pax? Had he asked too much of her? These silent scenarios churned constantly in his mind whilst he tried not to draw any attention to himself from the guards outside his cell. So he lay still, in silent torment, on the cold stone floor.

Across the corridor, in the opposite cell, Celeste was finding keeping a low profile much more difficult. Her beauty, still evident even after being captive for days, made her a prime target for the leering guards although, mercifully, it had not yet attracted more than crude comments. The Supremo guards were forbidden to touch the caro unless specifically instructed to by those higher up the chain of command. Caro was a precious commodity and desperately needed for the

Messis celebrations, which were now only two days away.

This afternoon in the Cellarium, a slightly older guard was holding court. It was hard to determine the age of a Supremo Gen from sight alone, as their immortality gifted them with ageless looks and long memories. But the way in which he was entertaining the other guards with his stories suggested he'd witnessed events in Tellus for many, many moons. This evening, he was reminiscing about a time he referred to as 'the good old days'.

"When blood ran free in the streets of Rubra! You see," he continued, relishing the undivided attention of his colleagues, "we never used to have these cells." He knocked his boot against the glass, and Celeste flinched. "No, no, back in the old days, the lead-up to the Messis was like a huge party, lasting for several weeks! But you've all heard the stories, so I won't bore you with all that."

The older guard turned away, knowing full well the younger guards would plead to hear the tale.

"Oh, go on, sir, tell us what it was like," one of them asked.

"Well, we've done our rounds, and the caro is behaving," – he adjusted the belt around his waist – "so I suppose a little story won't hurt."

He pulled up a chair and sat down, making himself comfortable, whilst the other guards waited eagerly for him to resume his story.

"You see, it was all possible because of an age-old alliance between the two most powerful Gen in all of Tellus! It bestowed peace on all the lands. Back then, they understood there was nobility in sacrifice, and they wanted to honour his highness, to honour us." He slapped himself on the chest. "These two great Gen would come together and celebrate for many days prior to the Messis, with one final, wonderful celebration under the Blood Moon."

A younger guard smiled in wonder as the older, described the scenes in the Castellum from all those years ago.

"Imagine royalty dressed in costumes made of colours you can't even imagine! The feasts they had! Food and drink from across all of Tellus, hog and trog meat, fruits from exotic lands, and faba so sweet you could smell it in the streets. You could even hear the laughter coming from inside the Castellum walls!"

The old guard glanced at each member of his captive audience. "Then, on the final day, under the Blood Moon, the gates were opened, and from the very top of the Throne Room there poured an abundance of blood into the streets of Rubra." He shook his head softly. "More than enough for every single one of us."

The old guard stared wistfully out of a high window, the moonlight bathing his face. "Plenty for all," he said, his voice tinged with regret. "Of course, the Gen that made it all possible became endangered. They started to die out." He looked into the cell holding the cowering female caro, making the women back up to the walls. Celeste swallowed hard, feigning sleep.

"Ethereals." The old guard almost sighed the word.

The younger guards glanced nervously at each other at the mere mention of the name.

"Gorgeous creatures. Their blood provided immortality to the Supremos for centuries because it held so much power in just a few drops."

The old guard held his hands out, lost in his own thoughts. Then, realising the others were waiting for him to speak again, his open hands fell to fists by his side. He carried on.

"Now, of course, they're extinct. Dead as dragons!" His forced laughter fading as he stared into the cell once more. "And now all we're left with is caro." He spat onto the floor.

In the distance, there came a terrifying scream, one drenched in anger, bouncing off the walls, down the many corridors of the Castellum and into the Cellarium.

The old guard rose to his feet, directing the others to their stations. A few moments later, fast footsteps approached, and the guards stood to attention as the prisoners clung to one another with bated breath. At the end of the hallway, Manus appeared. His green cloak flowing behind him as he made his way quickly towards them. Flustered, he saluted the old guard, who returned the gesture.

"Manus," the old guard said. "To what do we owe this pleasure? You've never graced us with your presence in the Cellarium before."

"His highness," Manus said, trying to catch his breath, "has seen something in his Oculus. He wants to start questioning the caro."

The old guard glanced down at Manus's gold-covered hands. "Questioning?" He laughed, unlocking the cell. "Is that what you're calling it these days?"

CHAPTER TWENTY-FOUR

The light was blinding. Pax squinted her eyes open, and for the first few moments she couldn't see anything. A gritty texture scratched her cheek. Pushing herself up with one hand, she used the other to shield her view. She licked her cracked lips. Salt. The grit was salt. Slowly, her eyes adjusted to the light reflecting off bright-white dunes of salt. Picking up a handful, she let it fall through her fingers.

Miles coughed, to her left. He was face down, choking on a mouthful of saltiness. Venefica was next to him, brushing off the white covering her black clothes. Am cast a shadow over Pax, giving her eyes a moment's relief from the light as Pax took their hand and was pulled to her feet. The ground was unstable underfoot, and as she took a step forwards, her boots sank into the softness. In the distance, there was a hint of a jagged horizon only barely visible against the brightness.

Am's green eyes scanned their surroundings. "This location is not appearing on the map."

"These are the Salt Plains," Venefica said.

Pax was a little relieved to see the willow tree had remained, now out of place in such a desolate environment, in stark contrast to the wildflower meadow they had left just moments ago. The door they had travelled through was, thankfully, still carved into its trunk.

"Nothing can grow here." The witch picked up a handful of the white earth and held it in her palm. "Salis. A magically charged medium."

"So, this is what are we searching for?" asked Miles, having recovered from the salty assault on his mouth. He knelt and prodded the ground.

"'Opposites attract on land, not sea'," Pax said, and Am nodded in agreement. "This salt is the next item!"

"Not salt, Salis," Venefica said, wandering off into the dunes.

"Salis," Pax repeated. "The chemical compound has positive and negative charges, and salt is found in sea water and…" – she looked around – "here."

"The Salt Plains," Venefica repeated, her voice more distant now as she padded over the white terrain.

Felis decided the brightness of the salt was not for him and jumped out of Am's arms into the air. Opening his wings, he circled above their heads, soaring towards the willow tree and landing on one of its branches.

Pax crouched down to inspect the salty earth, taking the amulet out from under her shirt and pressing the symbol down. Locating the pearl gemstone, she took out the vial and opened it. Then she carefully scooped some of the grains of Salis inside the vial until it was full. *Four down, two to go,* she thought, clicking the amulet shut.

"Simple!" said Miles over her shoulder.

"Yes," replied Pax, as an uneasiness crept over her. She could still see the door in the willow tree, the gold key in the lock glinting in the light.

A sudden scream made Pax snap her head around, just in time to see the witch disappearing beneath the dunes.

"Venefica!" Pax yelled as she ran towards her.

But the ground was so soft beneath her boots it felt like it was dragging her down. The weight of the sword secured at her waist was pulling her into the moving salt. Within a few moments, she was up to her waist in Salis. Quickly, she plunged her hand down into the thickness, loosening the scabbard, desperately trying to rid herself of the extra weight.

"It's quick salt!" Miles called out. Pax turned back to look at him, half his crus already beneath the sinking ground. Am, however, was standing close to the willow tree, not moving and still fully visible above the dunes.

"Stop moving!" Pax called out.

The warrior froze, and the pull on him slowed. He let out a sigh of relief as he stopped sinking.

Pax shouted out again. "Venefica! Stay still!"

But the witch was deafened by fear, thrashing about in blind panic. One of her arms was pinned to the side of her body as the other stretched out, desperately clawing at the white salt. Her eyes were now completely black.

Pax had stopped sinking, but her legs were still trapped underneath the Salis. Slowly, she lay her back against the ground, trying to distribute the weight of her body. Then she gently pulled, and her legs slid out of the salty earth. Miles was trying to do the same, but his crus was proving trickier to release from the crushing pressure of the quick salt.

"Stay there!" Pax called back to him. "I'll go and help her!"

Trying to stay calm, Pax took slow, gentle steps across the Salt Plains. She felt the vibrations on the Salis running up through the soles of her feet. Carefully, she continued making her way towards Venefica, but by now only the witch's terrified face was still visible. As Pax took her final step towards her, she watched as Venefica was engulfed, disappearing beneath the salt.

Pax plunged her arm in after her, grabbing Venefica's shoulder and pulling hard. The witch gasped as her face resurfaced, salt filling her gaping mouth. Her wide eyes were still black with fear. Pax pulled again, freeing one of Venefica's arms.

"Venefica, stay calm!"

But the witch was grabbing at Pax, her nails scratching into the skin of her arm. She was pulling at her shirt, and Pax felt herself being tugged under again. Her pulse quickened as panic started rising through her body.

"Venefica! Stop!" Pax said desperately, feeling herself sinking into the ground, the weight of the salt crushing her legs.

The witch clawed at Pax's shirt collar, and the amulet swung loose and into Venefica's desperate hand. She snatched it tightly, and Pax felt her head being dragged towards the salt. Soon she would be covered. Unable to move. Unable to breath. Miles's and Am's shouts in the distance vanished as Pax was swallowed by the quick salt. She closed her eyes as the salt crushed against her face, filling her nostrils, blocking out the light. But she wasn't afraid. She was angry. It wouldn't end like this. Not like this. In the darkness, a calmness fell over her. The sound of blood pulsing through her veins. A heat rising in her chest, tingling outward through each of her limbs, covering her skin, engulfing her. She could feel it all around her. Power.

Suddenly, the salt started to vibrate. Loosening around Pax as if each grain wanted to be away from her. Like each one feared her. The vibrations grew stronger. A massive force erupting from within her. From deep below the Salis, came an explosion, a low boom echoing all around the plains as massive white plumes shot into the skies above. Pax and Venefica were thrown high, into huge rolling clouds of salt. Pax landed on her feet. The air was hazy with white grains. Within a split second, through the dust, she grabbed Venefica's hand, pulling the disorientated witch to her feet.

"Run!" Pax screamed.

Frantically, they sprinted towards the willow tree, a stark beacon against the white. Towards where Miles and Am waited, their faces shouting although Pax could only hear ringing in her ears. The ground beneath them was more solid now, compacted from the explosion, but it was cracking. Splitting across the land like lightning, revealing a huge cavern chasing them as it ripped across the ground.

"The key! Grab the key!" Pax raced towards the others, her lungs screaming for air. Throwing herself down, she hit the ground beneath the willow reaching towards the door.

"Turn the key!" she screamed.

The bark crunched as the door opened, consuming them as the Salt Plains imploded in their wake.

The loudness disappeared, replaced with the buzzing of insects, and leaves rustling in the wind. Pax found herself in the wildflower meadow again. The pounding of her heart and the taste on her lips the only remains of the Salt Plains. Next to her, Am was struggling to hold a terrified Felis, who leapt down onto the grass, having had enough of travelling through portals for one day.

Miles was a little further away, and he was whimpering. Concerned he was injured, Pax jumped up and made her way over to him. As she touched his shoulder, he turned his wet face to look up at her.

"She's gone," he sobbed.

Quickly, Pax stared at the meadow as the awful realisation set in: the witch was nowhere to be seen. Then her hand clasped to her bare neck. The amulet was missing too.

CHAPTER TWENTY-FIVE

The intricate tube system of Rubra was designed centuries ago, its pipes lining the streets, rising from the gullies, twisting and turning until they all connected into a main artery – the Castellum. The widest tunnel sloped dramatically upwards, like a waterfall of glass leading to the Throne Room. Here, as the bells tolled midnight under each Blood Moon, the floodgates would open, signalling the beginning of each Messis. Originally, Ethereal blood would flow from this main tube, but now it was the blood of captured caro that streamed into the streets. This evening, the glass tubes were dry. Instead of blood, terrified screams from inside the Castellum echoed through the tubes.

The Throne Room was bathed in a gentle light this evening, the moon crimson and so nearly full. On the floor lay a now-unmoving victim – one who had not given Occissor the answers he had wanted. Creo, wrists bound by gold-laced rope, kept his eyes firmly fixed on the marble tiles he knelt on. Next to him, his neighbour Prod stank of fear.

Occissor stood at the Oculus.

"Next!" he commanded, walking back into the middle of the room and lifting his cloak as he stepped over the body.

The guard's blade sliced into the rope, and another Gen, kneeling next to Creo, was dragged from the line.

"Now, tell me," Occissor said, leaning over the man, "what do you know about my son's murder?"

The man kneeling slowly raised his head and stared into the king's red eyes, remaining stoic, saying nothing.

"Very well." Occissor beckoned Manus, who was standing at the back of the room. "Watching was obviously not enough of a deterrent." Occissor glanced at the unmoving body on the floor. "You choose to experience it yourself."

The kneeling man didn't flinch as Manus made his way over to the king's side.

"Your Majesty, is this really necessary?" Manus pleaded. "The last kept no secrets from you, isn't it wasteful to continue down this path? Maybe—"

Occissor silenced him with a glare. Manus looked down at his own hands. Slowly, he pulled at the gold chainmail covering them, removing his protective gloves. Underneath, his skin was pale but not unusual. Still, Creo couldn't help but look away. Manus stood in front of the restrained man, slowly raising his hands above his head. With a slight nod from Occissor, he lowered both of his palms onto the man's scalp. Instantly, the man gritted his teeth, his eyes flying open and rolling back in his head. Manus closed his eyes.

"What do you see?" Occissor asked.

Manus remained still, his hands pressing firmly onto the man's head. After a few moments, he replied.

"He is Piscator Gen, has fished all his life."

"What does he know about the prince's murder?" Occissor leant closer.

"Just rumours of a murderer who was never caught."

"Has he ever witnessed an Ethereal?" the king asked.

Manus opened his eyes, his palms still touching the victim,

whose silent tears streamed down his contorted face.

"No, only heard stories of them."

Occissor whispered into Manus's ear, "What about the amulet?"

"Please, Your Highness, if I continue much longer, we will surely lose him," Manus replied, his voice shaking.

Occissor's eyes narrowed. "The amulet."

Manus swallowed and closed his eyes again, searching through the man's mind, his memories, for any trace of the amulet. Beneath his hands, the man started to shake, spit dribbling from his mouth as he battled for breath. Manus let go of the man. His whole body convulsed, and he slumped to the floor, still, at Manus's feet.

"He knew nothing," Manus said, covering his face with his hands.

Occissor looked down the line towards Creo.

"Next."

Two guards marched over, grabbing Prod's fleshy arms and dragging him up to stand, snivelling, in front of the king. Slowly, Occissor faced Prod, who slumped back to his knees. Occissor held out a veiny hand, and with a barely noticeable flick of his wrist, Prod's head shot up to face him.

"I've no doubt you heard the questions I asked your friends here." Occissor pointed to the bodies on the floor, not taking his eyes from Prod's face. "Care to answer them more truthfully?"

Prod spluttered his words out through short breaths. "I don't know who you're looking for! I promise! We— I, haven't ever seen an Ethereal!" Saliva dribbled down his chin as he spat out words. "I—I thought they were extinct! I promise! I would tell you if I had!"

Occissor closed his eyes in frustration, the hand he was holding out closing into a fist. Prod's words disappeared as his body spasmed, and pain tore through him. As Occissor's fist opened, Prod's body slumped to the floor. He gasped, his hands folded together in prayer.

"Please…" Prod begged.

"What about the amulet?" Occissor asked calmly.

"I don't know what that is," Prod cried.

Creo's entire body tensed.

Occissor rolled his shoulders, bored of the same replies. He motioned to Manus, who was wringing his hands in discomfort.

"Search inside his mind for any trace of the gold amulet."

The guards took their cue, grasping Prod's arms again, readying him as Manus approached.

"No, please!" Prod pleaded. "Wait, gold. You said 'gold'. I have seen gold! With my own eyes! The same colour as that!"

Arms restricted, Prod used his chin to point towards the Oculus, glinting golden on its plinth in the corner of the room.

Occissor held up his hand for Manus to stop.

Prod took his chance. "Yes! Gold! A gold necklace, not many days ago!"

Manus stepped to the side, and the guards released Prod's shoulders. Occissor leant in closer, barely inches from Prod's face, and with rancid breath whispered, "Continue."

Prod swallowed hard. "I saw a gold necklace; m-maybe it's your amulet."

Occissor's eyes narrowed.

"I c-could show you," Prod stammered.

"Who has it?" Occissor's voice was louder now.

"A woman! In the Cellarium."

"Who?" Occissor screamed into Prod's face, making him cower.

Slowly Prod outstretched his arm, his finger shaking as Occissor followed his gaze.

"His wife," Prod said feebly, pointing at Creo.

CHAPTER TWENTY-SIX

Pax's heart raced. Bitter saliva pooled inside her mouth. *This can't be happening.* Venefica was gone, either trapped in the Salt Plains or worse… and with her, the amulet. The pounding against Pax's skull transformed into a silent question in her mind; had this been the witch's plan all along?

"What are we going to do?" Pax said, louder than necessary, her voice carrying across the meadow.

Miles shook his head, roughly wiping his tears away with the back of his hand and getting to his feet. He pulled out the axe secured to his belt, striding towards the willow's trunk. The door had vanished, nor was there any hint of the two faces that had spoken to them earlier. Now, it just looked like any other tree.

Before Pax could stop him, Miles raised the axe high above his head and brought it down hard into the trunk. The bark splintered as the metal embedded itself deep into the wood. Miles pulled the axe out, his teeth gritted in anger, hacking at the willow again and again. Pax shouted at him to stop, but her words were deafened by the rage coursing through the warrior's body. Only when Pax reached up and grabbed his bicep did Miles stop, his shoulders dropping as the axe fell to the ground. He sunk to his knees.

"I should have stopped it," he sobbed. "I can't believe it's happened again. I let this happen again!"

Pax knelt down next to him, placing her hand on his back. "What's happened again?"

Sitting beneath the willow, Miles wept into his large hands. Am held Felis, understanding that they should stay quiet in this moment. Finally, Miles dropped his hands away from his face and took a deep breath. He reached into his belt bag and removed his pocket watch. Over his shoulder, Pax noticed that the glass inside the brass rim was cracked. The unmoving hands read midnight. It was broken.

"Sometimes I'm grateful for the pain," Miles said softly. "It reminds me that I was once lucky enough to have something I loved so dearly." He blinked up at Pax. "In the mirror looking into the past, what did you see?"

Pax shrugged. "Something that happened when I was younger."

She was quite sure that Miles didn't really want to know about her experience right now, rather, he wanted to talk about his. The warrior nodded, staring off into the distance as the breeze sent colourful ripples across the horizon.

"I was happy in mine," Miles said sadly. "Really happy. It was before I got this thing." He slapped the metal of his crus. "I used to be a fine warrior, a mercenary who was paid handsomely in gold for my skills. It gave me enough coin to make a home to return to. I was lucky. Of course, I didn't realise how lucky, but you never do until it's too late."

He glanced down at the pocket watch in his hand. "I had a partner. My Vir. And a son, a strong Tribus boy. His name was Natus. He would have been about your age." He smiled at Pax, who smiled back, trying not to cry. "He had hair as dark as night and could run faster than the wolves." Miles said, his eyes glazing over. "I was so proud of him. We had a good life in Scandza, a wonderful life. Then it happened. Those *evil* things came." Miles clenched his fists so hard his knuckles turned white. "They destroyed my village. I returned home too late. To nothing but ash."

Miles's jaw tightened as images of the past filled his mind. "I buried Vir in the fields overlooking Scandza. It was our favourite view. I never found my son's body." He blinked away his tears. "I changed that day. The need for vengeance ran through my veins thicker than blood. I headed to Rubra, blinded by rage."

Miles's eyes were dark. "I didn't even make it into the grounds of the Castellum. I don't remember what happened exactly, but I got badly injured. By the time I'd come round, I was on a table and in a lot of pain. Luckily, Dominus had followed me to the capital, and he and some of the other Probus Gen found me half dead. They took me to an alchemist who could save my life – your father."

A sudden sense of pride at the mention of her dad took Pax by surprise. He had always helped different Gen, no matter where they'd come from or why. She also realised now why Miles had accompanied her on their journey – he wanted revenge.

"After that, I was in a very dark place for a very long time. When I met you, all I wanted to do was protect you. All of you." His voice was strained. "And now Vee is gone!"

"That isn't your fault!" Pax said. "None of it is your fault."

Miles shook his head.

"Was the attack on my family my fault?" Pax asked.

"Of course not," the warrior replied.

Pax raised her eyebrows at him. "As for Venefica, we don't

know what has happened exactly. She's a witch– she could have used her magic to escape."

"A spell?" Am asked, thinking about the golden words they had seen flashing across the witch's spell book.

"Maybe," Pax said.

"Is that why the salt exploded? Did Venefica do that?" Am asked.

Pax shrugged, confused. "I think it was me—".

"I should have saved Vee. She needed me," Miles interrupted, more to himself than the others.

"The amulet has gone," Pax blurted out.

Miles's head snapped around. "In the Salt Plains?"

"Perhaps. Or it's with Venefica," Pax answered.

Miles got to his feet. "Then she'll come back. Vee has to come back."

Pax frowned, and Miles placed his hands on her shoulders. "We can trust her, Pax. She'll come back."

Pax wanted to believe him, but for some reason she couldn't meet his eyes. She twirled the moonstone ring Venefica had given her around and around her finger.

Am watched the conversation between the two of them, trying hard to process their thoughts. They were unsure if they should mention what they had seen in the spell book, because the witch had told them not to. Am also didn't know whether to describe the images they had witnessed in the mirrors. This new-found ability to lie had made everything so unclear.

At the edge of the field, only three pegasi now remained, although Pax was unsure when the fourth one had left. Felis jumped out of Am's arms into the air, flapping his wings to hover by Pax's shoulder.

"Do we need the next clue?" Am asked. "If we no longer have the amulet?"

"Yes," Pax said firmly.

Am's eyes flickered to fluorescent green once again.

Guarded not by friend, but foe,
Where safe flight will refuse to go.
Supported in life and many in death,
Walk amongst those with fire breath.

"Dragons?" Pax said. "But they've been extinct for centuries."

"Sepultus," Miles said, picking up his axe from the ground. "Also known as the dragon's graveyard. It's full of Calva." He secured his weapon to his belt. "Remember the sword I gave you? It's cast with Calva, which makes it extra strong."

"Oh, Miles, my sword!" Pax realised the amulet wasn't the only thing she'd lost. "It got stuck in the quick salt!"

"Don't worry!" Miles said, now smiling. "I'd prefer the sword got stuck over you! Plus, you're not the only one – mine disappeared under the quick salt too. Better the weapons went under than us!"

Although Pax was frustrated that she'd lost not only the amulet but her sword too, she felt relieved that at least Miles was smiling again, even though, deep down, she knew he was only masking his pain.

"'Supported in life', like the skeleton. 'Many in death' must mean there's a lot of bones there. That makes sense."

Pax nodded.

"Plus, it's located close to Rubra," Am added, referring to their map.

Pax took a deep breath as she gathered her things. The Blood Moon was only a day away, and she felt like she desperately needed more time, especially now the amulet was gone. But she knew she had to go on, there was no other option; her parents needed her.

"Guarded by a foe, alright," Miles added. "Some unholy creatures in Sepultus."

His voice had returned to its normal confidence, no hint of the emotional meltdown he'd had just a few moments ago.

Together, they made their way through the wildflower meadow towards the awaiting pegasus. With Felis secured in her backpack, Pax mounted one of the creatures and waited until Am and Miles were both securely seated on theirs. Pax kicked her pegasus into flight and took to the sky towards Sepultus as thirteen magpies circled against the crimson moon.

CHAPTER TWENTY-SEVEN

"Is she dead?"

"No, she's still breathing."

Venefica's head pounded against her skull. She tried moving her body, but it was too painful. Slowly, she blinked open her eyes. Above, a starlit sky came into focus. She blinked again. Something was moving. Magpies. Six of them, circling. Venefica watched them until they bled together like ink and washed away into the night, calling into the distance.

To her left, more movement. The quiet breathing of someone close by. Raising her aching body upright was difficult, but Venefica tensed, ready to fight. Then she saw faces blurring into each other. One moment the faces were in front of her, then behind her, close then far, as if each were taking turns to confuse her senses. As her vision focused, they formed into three separate witches, their hoods up, circling her.

"Venefica." That voice was instantly recognisable to her, and it made her stomach clench with uncertainty.

"Mater?" said Venefica.

"Welcome home, my child." Mater lowered her hood, revealing a face framed by long auburn hair. "Finally, you've made it back to Celare."

Venefica frowned. "Celare?"

"Made it back with our help." The second witch lowered her hood, the material catching on the greying dreadlocks piled upon her head, making her curse.

Venefica tried to stand, stumbling slightly, her head still pounding. The third witch came to her aid, holding onto her elbow.

"Glad to see you again," said Virgo, the youngest of the three. She smiled sweetly.

Steadying herself, Venefica tried to focus on her surroundings. She was in a forest clearing. It was dark. She could see familiar items surrounding the fire pit: a large, blackened cauldron hanging over the flames, piles of spell books, a hollowed-out skull holding bunches of dried herbs, colourful crystals scattered across the forest floor, glass bottles of different shapes and sizes.

"I've been trying to find you," Venefica said to the three witches, who each studied her with varying expressions.

"What's that?" Vetus said, pointing to her hand.

Venefica looked down. She was clutching something. Turning her palm towards her, she saw a flash of gold. She opened her hand and gasped, quickly closing her fist around the amulet. Cold confusion sank through her body, but she tried her best to conceal this from the prying eyes watching her.

Mater stepped closer. "Is that gold?"

Venefica snatched her hand away, clutching the amulet close to her chest. "It's mine."

Mater laughed shrilly. "Venefica! Always so untrusting."

The other two witches joined in with the laughter.

"You know it was *us* who saved you." Mater turned away from her, walking towards the fire. Picking up a wooden spoon, she stirred the steaming cauldron. "We saw you travelling between the realms, and we brought you back here. You know it is such a dangerous time to be trapped out there."

Venefica's shoulders relaxed a little as she searched her mind, trying to recall what had happened at the Salt Plains. But she couldn't remember anything after she'd sunk beneath the quick salt. Her chest tightened at the memory.

Suddenly Virgo's hands shot into the air, her bangles jangling down her arms.

"Here we go." Vetus rolled her eyes.

But Virgo wasn't listening, her eyes now a hazy grey, as if she was in a trance. Then, in a soft, sing-song voice, she said,

Never pushes, always pulls,
Sometimes empty, sometimes full.
Filled with deep red, dark and doom,
Masses gather, 'neath the moon.

Her hands fell back down to her sides, and she blinked, as if waking up. Virgo smiled at Venefica again, as if only just realising she was there.

"We've been calling to you," Virgo said softly. "We sent you many magpies."

"Overestimating her again!" Vetus spat, joining Mater by the fire. "Stupid girl is not powerful enough to be with us. Always causing trouble." Her nose wrinkled in disgust.

Venefica felt her cheeks flush. "I'm more powerful than you realise!"

Mater and Vetus looked up, surprised at the rebuttal.

Mater smiled. "Gained some confidence, I see?"

Vetus's downturned mouth opened as she coughed up

phlegm and spat into the fire. It hissed, sending black sparks into the air.

"You're a liability! Your dark magic puts us in danger!"

Venefica felt the familiar heat of shame creep over her. She clenched her fists, and the amulet pressed hard into her palm.

"If I'm not powerful," she said, "then how come I have this?" She let the amulet drop from her raised hand, dangling it in the air. All three witches fell silent.

Virgo crouched low and crept towards the amulet in awe.

"It can't be…" she whispered.

Mater stood upright, holding Venefica's gaze as she held her shaking hand as steady as she could.

Mater arched an eyebrow. "Where did you get this?"

Venefica stood her ground. "It's mine," she said confidently. "I told you: I'm more powerful now."

Vetus scoffed by the fire. "Pah! Probably stole it. Just like you did that book!" She tutted. "How many did you kill this time?"

Mater's face was unmoving as she eyed the amulet twisting on its chain in the moonlight.

"A golden amulet is extremely powerful," she said, trying to sound neutral. "Do you know how to use it?"

Venefica nodded slowly, maintaining eye contact with Mater.

"Lies!" Vetus yelled.

Mater pursed her lips. "Show us."

Venefica paused for a second before snatching the amulet back up into her hand.

"I don't need to prove my magic to you." Picking up her bag, she checked her spell book was inside. "To any of you!"

Vetus cackled by the fire. "Told you!"

"Please stay," pleaded Virgo, at Venefica's side, helping her gather the items that had fallen from her bag.

Venefica paused as she spotted a small wooden trinket in the dust, which she scooped up and dropped into her bag. She rummage through its contents, ignoring Vetus's whining behind her.

"No respect for elders!" The oldest witch was still harping on in the background, ignored by all the others. "When I leave this mortal realm, give my body to the wolves! They're gentler than any Gen!"

Mater stepped towards the cauldron, picking up the spoon and stirring the steaming pot again.

"Come," she said to Venefica without even looking at her, a shadow of a smirk across her face. "Sit and break bread with us. You must be hungry from all the travelling."

Virgo skipped towards the fire, sitting down and placing bowls out in front of Mater so she could spoon hot stew into each one. The smell hit Venefica, bringing tears to her eyes, her stomach betraying her by growling loudly.

"That curse kept you hungry, no doubt!" Vetus laughed spitefully as she sat down opposite her. "Aw, poor little girl can't make her own food."

Mater gestured to Venefica. "Sit."

Gripping her bag tightly, Venefica sat opposite the old witch.

Virgo shuffled up next to her, whispering, "You know Mater only cast that spell over you so you'd come back to us. We know how you love your food."

Vetus tutted loudly.

Virgo stroked Venefica's dreadlocks. "We know that you will come back to us if you can't make food for yourself, and that way we can keep you safe. And there's only so much faba you can drink!" She giggled.

"No one would even offer you food in the other realm, stupid girl. They know you're evil," Vetus muttered under her breath.

Mater handed a steaming bowl to Venefica, who took it with one hand, her other still clutching the amulet close to her body. She took a mouthful of the stew, and the flavour was so overwhelming it made her jaw ache. Ever since she was small, food had been the only currency she'd ever really cared about, and she wolfed down the entire bowl before Mater had even sat down. Venefica tipped the bowl up to her lips, draining the last dregs. As she lowered it, wiping her mouth, Mater took the bowl and filled it again. Venefica accepted the second helping but ate it more slowly, studying the other witches through the flames as they ate.

When she had finished her meal, Mater spoke.

"I know what you want."

Venefica listened but dropped her eyes down to the dust between her feet, not meeting Mater's gaze.

"You want to be a part of this coven. Genuinely, this time."

Venefica glanced up, and Mater showed a hint of a smile as she spoke.

"We would welcome you in. With the amulet, you could stay and call Celare home."

Venefica felt a rush of excitement in her now-full stomach. For many moons she had longed for a home, to be with her kin. Now, she realised, it was within reach.

"Really?" she replied quietly.

Mater nodded. "But you need to prove your magic first."

Venefica hesitated, then took a deep breath and pulled her

spell book out from inside her bag. She placed it onto the ground and opened the thick pages. Virgo excitedly cleared the space around her, moving bottles and kicking crystals out of the way as Venefica knelt in front of the book.

Mater took a handful of ashes from the fire and crushed them in her hand. She held her palm out to Venefica, who pinched the dark dust in her fingers and smeared a thick black line across her eyes. Mater watched carefully as Venefica raised her left hand above the spell book, dropping the amulet so it dangled from her fingers, hovering just above the blank pages. Her eyes closed.

Vetus stood up from across the fire now, too intrigued to act aloof.

The air stilled. Venefica's dark eyes snapped open. The amulet started to spin in the air, slowly at first, then faster and faster. Soon, it appeared as a golden orb spinning over the thick pages, which fluttered and flipped. A warm wind encircled the witches, whipping at their faces. Vetus's grey dreadlocks lashed around her face. Virgo shielded her eyes. Mater's smile grew wide. Venefica remained deathly still. The amulet stopped spinning, and the book fell open. Venefica's head tilted down, her black eyes watching as the pages flooded with gold words only she could see.

The cursive ink glistened as it crept along the page, revealing one letter at a time, then word after word, until the page glinted, full, in front of her.

Beneath Blood Moon the Messis will cease,
When sui generis will bestow Gen peace.
Golden amulet for a sacrifice made,
Of blood taken by a single blade.

Venefica read the words rapidly, trying to commit them to memory as they flickered and disappeared. The wind eased around them, and the spell book revealed a blank page once more. The amulet hung heavy like a noose in her hand. Slowly, she twisted the chain around her fingers, closing her palm around the gold.

"So," Mater broke the silence, "can you harness the power of the amulet?"

Venefica studied the gold in her hand and took a deep breath. "Yes."

Mater smiled, satisfied.

Venefica continued. "But there's one other thing I need."

Vetus rolled her eyes, tutting loudly.

"I need something – someone – to make it work," Venefica said quietly.

Mater frowned. "Someone in the other realm? A sacrifice?"

Venefica nodded, a sickness swelling in her stomach.

"How will you locate them?" Virgo asked.

"They have a ring of mine," said Venefica. "Moonstone. I could use it to find them again."

Virgo beamed. "If we had the golden amulet, it would make us the most powerful coven in all of Tellus!" she said, clapping her hands.

Mater held her arms out wide, inviting Venefica in. She stood slowly, stepping into the embrace and breathing in deeply.

Mater held her close and whispered into her ear. "You know what you must do."

CHAPTER TWENTY-EIGHT

Fat jowls hid Mort's teeth as he slept, strings of saliva stretching onto the ground. When snoring, he looked quite harmless, thought Phantasma. There was no hint of the excruciating pain he could cause by sinking those fangs into any victim she directed him to attack.

They'd returned to Rubra for mere moments, trading in their tired pyrois for new ones, changing their cloaks and collecting Mort. They hadn't been summoned by Occissor to the Throne Room, and Phantasma had been relieved, as disappointing him again in person would have been painful to both her body and her heart. Mort had quickly picked up the scent of the blood left by the Tribus warrior, leading them through woodlands and was easily keeping pace with the pyrois.

Phantasma shielded her blood-red eyes as the sun impaled the horizon. The Messis was now mere hours away, and her skin prickled in anticipation, making it hard for her to concentrate. But today, this excitement was mingled with fear, for she knew the deadly consequences if she failed to complete this mission by the time the clock struck the midnight hour.

The love she held for her king was limitless. She would rather die than disappoint his highness. As a young girl, she had dreamt of serving him, like many other young Supremos in Rubra, but her obsession had only intensified as she grew. Finally, on her Ortus day, she had felt it. A tingling covering her body, like a thousand tiny spiders crawling over her skin. Her eyes transformed from amber to red, as happened to all Supremo's on their Ortus, but hers filled with a deep scarlet, hinting at extraordinary power. The first time she evanesced, it had had startled her. She had managed to travel from one side of her bedroom to the other, not a huge distance; it was only a few feet at most, but she knew it was about to change her entire world. The realisation filled her with the most manic glee. The process of evanescing drained her energy tremendously, yet she practiced obsessively for hours each day. She had ignored her worried parents' pleas to eat or drink or rest, until she was on her knees, exhausted. But her commitment paid off when she became skilled enough to control the locations of her evanesences. She had mastered her powers and knew exactly how she was going to use them.

Her parents had begged Phantasma not to do it, but she hadn't listened. They were feeble Supremos, at the very bottom of the blood line, and she knew she was fated for more. Her connection to her family was not only embarrassing but held her back, and she knew, in her blood, where she was destined to be. Of course, at the time she was too young to fully understand her parents' fear. Phantasma couldn't comprehend just how vicious their leader had become so soon after the prince's murder, so when she evanesced into the Throne Room for the very first time, it was nothing short of a miracle that she wasn't killed on first sight.

Phantasma had thrown herself on the ground, bowing before Occissor's feet as he sat on his glass throne. She hadn't dared to look up, but the sounds of many footsteps informed her she had been surrounded by guards. Hearing his voice for the first time sent shivers down her spine. She was so excited she was nearly sick. As the guards stood down, he asked for her name. Phantasma's brunette hair had fallen back to reveal her stunning features, wide eyes and blushed lips that parted as she whispered the name given to her by her parents, for the very last time.

Occissor renamed her Phantasma on that first meeting, in honour of her exceptional evanescence powers. Her hair transformed into a strikingly bright white mane a few months later, only accentuating her beauty. Some Gen often implied that the colour loss was because of the trauma she endured behind the walls of the Castellum, but Phantasma knew it was a mark of pure love. That first day in the Throne Room, with a shaking voice, she had explained her desire to serve him. Instead of fury, she was met with slight amusement. Occissor was well aware of the rarity of evanescence, as well as its potential. She hadn't seen her parents since.

Deleo watched Phantasma staring off into the distance, her red eyes glazing over once again. She appeared softer when this happened, less menacing. He tightened the girth of the saddle underneath the pyrois, and the animal exhaled a smoky breath, making Phantasma rise to her feet. She secured her black cloak around her slender shoulders, pulling the hood over her pale locks and slipped her quiver and bow into place.

"It's nearly time." Deleo nodded up at the sky where the full red moon was visible in the hazy morning light.

Phantasma didn't look at him as she mounted her pyrois, her hand reaching through the flaming mane to grip the reins.

"We'd better move quickly," she said, giving a high-pitched

whistle at Mort, who snarled awake.

Deleo mounted his pyrois as they waited for Mort to pick up the warrior's scent, his wet nose sniffing the air, his lips curling around sharp teeth. Then he took off. With sharp kicks, the pyrois followed, their flaming hooves thundering towards Sepultus.

CHAPTER TWENTY-NINE

As the pegasi landed hard on the dusty ground of Sepultus, their normally calm demeanour was replaced by a nervousness. Stretching out in front of them, like scales on the red earth, was a path of cobbles that may have been white long ago, but which now had a bloody tinge to them, covered in the dust blowing through the air.

Further ahead, the path met an old stone bridge crossing an unseen river. On the other side of the bridge was a mound of sharp, jagged bones. Huge domes of ribs and spines, skulls with massive eye sockets and sharp teeth taller than houses. They were piled on top of one another, so high that the tower of decaying skeletons disappeared into the eery mists above. There was no greenery in Sepultus. In fact, it appeared there was no life here at all. Even though it was now early morning, the sunlight found it difficult to filter through the clouds above.

The pegasus's nostrils flared, their eyes searching wildly. As Pax dismounted, she put a hand up to stroke the neck of one of the animals. It flinched away.

"This is as far as they'll take us," Miles said, dismounting next to her.

"'Where safe flight will not go'," Am added.

As if taking their cue, all three pegasi took to the sky, their wings sending plumes of dust into the air. Pax shielded her eyes as the creatures disappeared into the redness above. The moon was no longer visible, but Pax knew that this was it – the final day. Tonight, the Blood Moon would be full, and at midnight, the Supremos would commence their Messis in Rubra. Tonight, her parents would be sacrificed.

The magnitude of what was going to happen sent a wave of nausea through Pax's body. She couldn't do this. There was still another clue after this one, and she didn't even have the amulet anymore. She was foolish to have even come this far. Swallowing the bile in her mouth, she turned to Miles.

"You couldn't even get into the Castellum when you went to Rubra. Why would this be any different?"

The warrior didn't smile. He knelt down next to her, his crus in the dust, staring straight into her eyes.

"This time, it's with you, and I believe in you, Pax. I believe in your power even if you don't."

Pax tried to take a deep breath, but the air here felt shallow in her lungs. Inside her pockets, her fingers brushed against the wooden magpie, and she clenched it in her fist. It reminded her of home, back in Viridis, the trees and greenery feeling so very far away now. Her breathing started to slow. This was it. She had to believe she could do this.

Slowly, she turned back to face what was waiting beyond the bridge: the graveyard of Sepultus. Full of dead dragons from centuries ago. Their powdered bones were named Calva and were laced with magical properties. If Venefica were here, she'd already be across the bridge, filling her bag with the dark crushed powder. Pax smiled at the thought, taking a step towards the bridge.

"Hey!" Miles grabbed her arm, holding out his axe. "Weapons drawn."

"What about you?" Pax replied, taking the weight of the axe into her hands.

"I got these!" He flexed his biceps, winking.

They both looked to Am, who was stroking Felis on their shoulder.

"Can you…" Pax hesitated, "take a weapon?"

They hadn't had time to discuss Am's changes since Ultra, or perhaps they hadn't wanted to. As Am smiled, shaking their head, Pax felt a strange mix of pride and sadness.

"Okay, well you and Felis stay here."

The thick fog hanging above the ground revealed the cobbles sporadically between each of Pax's steps. She knew that dragon bones were black, but the dome-shaped cobbles were white, and she had to stop her mind wondering what, or who, she was stepping on.

The bridge ahead was made from stone, old but well-preserved, with the sound of a river underneath. On the other side, the floor was dusted with a thick black layer of Calva. Pax just had to cross to the other side and collect some in her hands, pour it into a pouch and save it for later, when she had the amulet again.

"Good morrow, you beautiful creatures."

A silky voice slithered into Pax's ears. Turning quickly, she was faced with a slim Gen in a fitted velvet suit, his tricorn leather shoes gleaming as he appeared through the thick mist. Miles raised his fists.

"Ah!" The man held up his hands in fright. "Don't hurt me!" His red lips parted into a sarcastic smile, then, as quickly as he'd arrived, he disappeared.

"Welcome to my humble abode."

The man's voice was back, but this time he was sitting on the wall of the bridge. Miles and Pax both spun around again, to see him crossing his long legs and waving his arm towards the graveyard.

"I'm Malum."

Miles took an aggressive step forwards, but Pax held out a hand to stop him.

Malum grinned. "I see who has the brains and who has the…" he paused, looking the warrior up and down, "brawn."

He arched an eyebrow as Miles growled. Malum peered past them, towards where Am was still waiting with Felis, a slight flicker of confusion crossing his face. Then he flashed another toothy smile.

Pax straightened up. "We've come to Sepultus to collect some Calva."

Malum nodded. "Oh! We have lots!" He jumped down and bowed, holding his arm out to direct them across the bridge. "Be my guest."

Pax went to take a step forwards, but just before her foot touched the stone of the bridge, Malum spoke again, stopping her in her tracks.

"Just one little thing," he said softly, pointing his index finger into the air. "For safe passage across this bridge to Sepultus, you will have to pay."

Pax placed her foot back down on the dusty ground.

"How much?"

Malum smiled wickedly. "The price is one soul."

Pax sighed. Of course this wouldn't be simple. Sepultus was ungodly, and Malum was no normal Gen.

Malum looked offended. "Any soul!" he added. "I'm not

picky." He glanced towards Am, then back to Pax. "It's not much, but it's honest work." He shrugged, hopping back up onto the bridge and inspecting his metallic nails.

Pax made her way back towards Am, with Miles walking backwards, refusing to take his eyes off Malum.

"What are we going to do?" Pax asked, gathering them into a huddle.

"Let me kill him," Miles growled, still eyeing Malum on the bridge.

"You saw him evanesce," Pax said. "He's not killable. He's a demon."

Am's eyes widened. "Demons are bad."

"I heard that!" Malum shouted, offended.

"Losing a soul sounds painful. Am does not feel any pain so should be the one to cross," Am suggested.

Pax scoffed at the sweet gesture. "No one is sacrificing themselves, Am." Although, inside, Pax felt bad for silently wondering whether or not Am actually had a soul to trade.

Suddenly, they heard a rumbling in the distance. At first, Pax thought the pegasi had returned, as she recognised the sound as stampeding hooves, but they were accompanied by barking. Wild, snarling barks, and they were growing louder.

Malum stood up on the bridge to get a better look.

"Hello? Who do we have here?"

Miles instinctively pushed Am behind him, and Felis jumped off Am's shoulder and flew up into the sky. Pax nodded at Miles, parting her feet and gripping the axe. Through the mist, the owner of the barks appeared, its muscular legs galloping towards them.

"It's a hellhound!" Miles shouted, pushing Am further away to give himself room to fight.

"Oh goody!" Malum squealed, jumping up onto the wall, ready to enjoy the show.

The hound's giant paws pounded the red earth. Then, it was right in front of them, its dripping jaws snarling. Pax braced for impact, but Miles was there in a flash, striking his fist into the side of the beast. The impact threw the hound skidding into the dust. It was down for a brief second, shaking its head, then growled back to its feet. It leapt onto the warrior, throwing him backwards to the ground, pinning him down. Miles let out a yell as the hellhound's sharp teeth sank into his shoulder, tearing into his flesh.

Pax lifted the axe above her head and brought it down onto the back of the hound. Blood splattered onto her face. From the bridge, Malum cackled in delight, slapping his thigh. The hound's jaws instantly loosened, releasing Miles, who slumped, bloodied, to the ground.

Pax removed the axe, with a squelch, and the hound reared up, howling in pain. Its wild eyes locked onto her. She ran, sprinting as fast as she could to lure the beast away from Miles and Am as the hot breath from angry jaws snapped at her heels. She knew she couldn't outrun it, so she turned to face it, lifting the axe above her head. A high-pitched whistle pierced the air. The hound skidded to a halt.

In the distance, the flaming outlines of two white pyrois galloped towards them. Phantasma whistled again, and Mort froze in front of Pax, poised to attack.

"Kill!" Phantasma screamed.

Mort snarled, lunging towards Pax.

She swung the axe down, connecting with the hound's jaw. As he recoiled, she manoeuvred herself quickly to the left, rolling onto the ground. She needed to get back to Miles, who was writhing in pain. Pax looked up just in time to see the hound lunge at her again. Then, it froze. Suspended in mid-air directly above her. The hound's bloody jaw now hung slack, in mid-snarl, drool dripping from its jowls, muscles twitching, trying to break free from Pax's hold. She focused on the weight of the animal's body. Using her power, she sent the hound's body flying upwards into the air. The beast landed with a bone-cracking thud.

Phantasma pulled hard on the reins bringing her pyrois to a halt. Her eyes widened as she watched Pax in disbelief. Instantly, Mort was back on his feet, shaking off the fall. His eyes locked onto Pax again. Panting and exhausted, she braced herself for the next attack.

Suddenly, Felis flew right between the hound's snarling jaws. Mort's instincts took over, and he thundered after the small dragat. Felis flew high into the air, his wings flapping so fast they were a blur as Mort came crashing behind him. Felis nimbly changed direction several times, but Mort was closing in. Felis flew straight towards the bridge, where Malum was sitting, rubbing his hands together with glee.

"Felis!" Pax screamed, as Mort lunged to attack.

Felis quickly changed direction one more time, his body turning sharply, flying up vertically, soaring directly over Malum's shocked face. Mort's paws left the ground as he launched himself after Felis, who narrowly escaped his snapping jaws. The hellhound fell back down through the air, his massive paws landing on the stone bridge. Instantly, Mort's body was engulfed in flames.

"No!" screamed Malum. "No, no, no!"

His eyes turned black, and his face contorted, grey horns splitting his skin as they thrust out of his forehead. His nails stretched out of his fingers, dark and sharp.

"You tricked me!" he shrieked. "This is not the soul I wanted!"

His voice screeched into an echo, then he was gone, a wisp of black smoke left in his place. Felis landed, exhausted, slumping to the ground by Pax's feet.

Miles turned to Pax. "Go! Now!" he yelled, holding his bleeding shoulder. "Across the bridge!"

Pax threw the axe skidding along the ground to him. She turned to Am.

"Come! Get Felis!"

Impulsively, she ducked as an arrow swooped past her head.

"Get the Calva!" Miles yelled through gritted teeth, picking up the axe as he got to his feet. "I'll hold them off!"

Pax sprinted across the bridge as another arrow swooped so close to her head she felt it brush against her hair. Bones crunched beneath her boots as she made it into the graveyard, ducking down inside a huge dragon's skull. A hard crack sounded as another arrow embedded itself into the dark bone. She took out her penknife and scraped the blade against the cavity of the skull. A glistening black powder appeared, and she scooped it into her hand. Taking out a pouch from her pocket, she poured the Calva inside, securing it tightly. Cautiously, she peered through the eyehole of the skull. The fog was thickening, rolling in like red smoke over the bridge. The onslaught of arrows had stopped. Pax couldn't quite see to the other side of the bridge, so, staying low, she made her way back towards the fight.

The sound of clashing metal carried across the bridge. Through the mist, she spotted Miles on the ground, swinging his axe. Deleo was above him, striking his sword down onto Miles's crus. Pax stayed low and, through the fog, centred in on Deleo, preparing to lift his body and throw him to the ground. But as she did so, something stopped her dead in her tracks. Pax watched in horror as the red fog parted to reveal a tall Gen with silver hair standing over Am, who was lying motionless on the floor.

"No!" Pax screamed, running towards Am's attacker, whose head shot up.

Pax could see her face clearly now – and she was smirking. Pax felt a white-hot rage erupt inside her, like fire in her lungs. She glared at the cruel face standing over Am's limp body, and time slowed down. As Phantasma reached for another arrow, a glow surrounded Pax, her scarlet eyes locking onto her target.

Phantasma's smile had barely dropped before she was knocked off her feet. She flew backwards, high into the air, her body skidding across the ground. Pax slumped to her knees, breathing hard. Through the ringing in her ears, she heard Miles yell out. Deleo had a blade pressed against his neck.

Pax's vision blurred. The thickening mist was obstructing her view. She tried to stand but stumbled. The fog parted to reveal Miles once more, his wrists bound, arms outstretched, being dragged along the ground behind a flaming pyrois. The image in front of Pax distorted. She forced herself up, unsteady at first, then she ran towards Miles.

Shaking, Phantasma rose to her feet. Her pale fingers slowly touching the blood covering her shocked face. Staring at Pax in disbelief, she limped over to Deleo. He pulled her onto his pyrois, yelling, "Phantasma! Evanesce!"

As Pax ran towards them, Phantasma's eyes widened as she clung onto Deleo. Then they were gone, taking Miles with them.

Pax fell to her knees in the dust. The scream came from deep inside her, until she couldn't breathe. Her hands clawing the dirt, she crawled towards Am's still body. Softly, she lay her head on Am's chest.

"Am I dying?" Am asked.

Pax took a sharp intake of breath. "Am?"

One of Am's eyes was missing. The other flickered, trying to connect. The light from their nucleus was dimming rapidly, desperately sending out a distress signal.

"Am?" Pax sat up. As she moved Am's body gently to assess the damage, her heart sank. The nucleus was bleeding blue.

"Am—" Am's voice crackled with static. "Dying?"

Pax wiped her nose on her sleeve and tried to smile. "You're okay." Her voice cracked. "I'm here with you."

"Am is okay?" Am's voice was fading.

Pax nodded, unable to articulate the lie again. She carefully lay Am back down, hiding the damage.

Am's voice was getting quieter. "Sad. Why are you sad?"

Pax nodded. "It's because I love you."

A moment of silence. Then Am said, "Sometimes love and sadness are close."

Pax held in a sob, tears silently streaming down her face.

"I shouldn't have lied." Am's voice was quiet.

Pax frowned. "What?"

"In the book." Am's voice cracked. "In the mirror. I saw this happen—"

As static took over Am's words, Pax gently stroked Am's face.

"Fin—" Am's voice cracked again. "Final clue."

Pax strained to hear Am's fading voice.

"Clue. Final… clue." Am's voice repeated and distorted.

"Shh," Pax soothed.

"Blood." Am's voice was barely a whisper.

Pax held Am's body close.

"Goodbye."

The light in Am's eye went out. They lay still. Felis flew down and quietly sat next to Am's body, his wing badly torn. It was silent apart from soft nickers from the abandoned pyrois behind them. Time passed. The red mist lifted. Above them, the clouds cleared revealing the Blood Moon.

Finally, Pax kissed Am's cheek. "I'll come back for you."

As she stood, a numbness settled over her. She had no more tears. Frighteningly calm, she walked towards the pool of blood on the ground where Miles had been attacked. Picking up his axe, something else caught her eye. There, in the dirt, was the warrior's pocket watch. The smashed face revealing the broken time once more – midnight. Picking it up, Pax placed it into her pocket. Dragging the axe, she walked towards the pyrois, and Felis hobbled towards her.

"No. You stay with Am," Pax said firmly. "Guard them."

Felis understood, circling back to sit next to Am's body.

The remaining pyrois didn't flinch in Pax's presence, not like the pegasus. Placing her hand on its face, she stroked the pure white coat, moving her hands through the flames of its mane. It didn't burn her skin. She didn't feel any pain. The animal stared into her eyes, sighing calmly. Pax checked the saddle bag for weapons, but all she found was a white cloak. Draping it over her shoulders, she fastened the clasp with the gold S-shaped pin. After mounting the pyrois, she took one last look at Am. Cracking the reins, Pax rode towards Rubra with one thought in her mind.

Kill them all.

CHAPTER THIRTY

The pyrois knew the route to Rubra so well that Pax barely had to hold onto the reins. The animal moved differently to the pegasus or the tricorn; it felt as if it were almost gliding. The road ahead was steep, and by the time the pyrois stopped at the top of the hill, it was dark. Through the flickering mane, Pax stared down at the city. The streets were bathed in a red glow, and standing tall, at the very centre, was the Castellum, silhouetted against the Blood Moon.

Any idea Pax had of dismounting the pyrois and continuing down into the city on foot vanished under the looming sky. Time was against her; she would have to be bold. The white cloak draped around her concealed the axe tucked into her belt, as well as covering her hair and most of her face. She also had the advantage of being high up on the pyrois. She would be able to outrun anyone giving pursuit faster on the animal than she would on foot. Taking a deep breath, she kicked her heels, and the pyrois descended into Rubra.

As she rode into the city, Pax was sure the sound of her heart beating hard in her chest would be enough to give her away. As she got closer to the centre, figures started walking towards her. The Harvesters. A tall Gen with glowing red eyes. The two approaching her were draped in fine ceremonial robes, ready for tonight's Messis. Gripping the reins in one hand, she freed her other and placed it on her waist, ready to draw the axe. As the figures got closer, Pax tensed, holding her breath. Then they were gone, passing her without so much as a glance in her direction. Relieved, if a little confused, she continued on towards the Castellum.

More Gen came into view, the streets becoming busier the closer she got to the centre. A sense of excitement crackled in the coppery air, but to Pax, it felt like doom. She looked down, to see gullies on either side of the road being furiously cleaned by Gen on hands and knees. Pax followed the route of the empty gullies with her eyes. They lined the streets all the way up to the base of the Castellum, where they connected to a larger gully beneath the entrance. Pax was so close now that she had to crane her neck to follow the route of the thick glass tubes snaking up the walls, which went all the way up to a stained-glass window in the central tower.

The pyrois' hooves echoed on the cobbles as Pax trotted down the street. Still no one had stopped her or even acknowledged her presence. The thought that she was riding into a trap crossed her mind, but she gripped the reins and headed towards the gates to the Castellum.

The pyrois sensed its stables were near, and it broke into a trot. Pax adjusted the hood of the white cloak, making sure her face was still covered. Up ahead, two guards in black were stationed either side of the gates, as if welcoming Pax to her own funeral. Again, she braced herself to be stopped, but the guards simply saluted, then parted the gates, letting the pyrois enter beyond the Castellum walls. The animal made its way towards the stable block, where another guard was waiting. He took the reins, holding the animal steady. Pax debated attacking him before he realised she was an intruder. Instead, she dismounted the pyrois, turning from the guard quickly and walking away from him.

"Excuse me," the guard called out. Pax quickened her pace, pulling the hood of the cloak down over her forehead.

"Excuse me!" he said again, raising his voice.

Pax turned her head slightly, trying not to reveal too much of her face.

"Sorry, ma'am," the guard said, lowering his gaze. "Just to let you know, the preparations for the Messis are complete. The caro has been prepared, ready to go." He saluted.

Then it dawned on her: he thought she was the Gen who had murdered Am - Phantasma. Seizing the opportunity, Pax cleared her throat and spoke confidently. "Where is it? The caro?"

The guard seemed taken aback, and he saluted again, flustered.

"Um, they're in the Cellarium, ma'am." He pointed to an archway to the left of the stables.

Pax made her way into the tunnel, leaving the confused guard tending the pyrois.

Inside the tunnel, it was surprisingly well lit, the stone walls illuminated by the lights lining the ceiling. The chemical smell from outside was even more pungent in here. Pax could hear voices further down the corridor – the place was crawling with guards. Unsure how much longer her disguise would work, Pax stopped for a moment to gather her thoughts because she was running on pure adrenaline without any real plan. The voices in the tunnel turned into footsteps. She glanced back from where she had come, her heart racing, considering retracing her steps. Then a hand clamped hard over her mouth, and she was pulled backwards into a doorway.

She couldn't breathe. Twisting her head, she saw wide white eyes. Venefica's rings were digging into her face. The footsteps were drawing closer. Pax stopped struggling, and the witch let her go. Face to face, they listened silently to the footsteps disappearing down the corridor.

"Nice cloak, young one," Venefica whispered when it was quiet.

"Where have you been?" Pax said too loudly, wiping her face. "We needed you. *I* needed you."

The witch's smiled vanished. "What happened?"

Pax paused, tears filling her eyes. At last, she said the words. "Am's dead."

Venefica's eyes flashed black. She raised an arm to touch Pax, then hesitated.

Pax inhaled shakily, blinking tears down her face. "They're gone."

She leant into Venefica, who opened her arms and embraced her.

"How did you find me?" Pax mumbled into the witch's cloak, the incense smell comforting her a little.

"Your ring. I could locate you from Celare."

Pax quickly stood back. "The amulet? Do you have it?"

Venefica nodded slowly, staring at Pax, and for a moment her white eyes gleamed grey. The witch's hand disappeared into her bag, but instead of the amulet, she pulled out a blade.

Pax's whole body tensed, and in a split second, Venefica's feet were lifted from the floor. Pax thrust out her hand, holding the witch suspended in mid-air, betrayal pulsing through her mind. *Kill her before she kills you.*

The jade dagger clattered to the ground from Venefica's

hand, her bag dropping from her shoulder, spilling its contents like guts over the stone floor.

"Wait, listen to me!" the witch pleaded, her voice straining against the invisible grip Pax had around her throat. The words fell on deaf ears, anger pulsing so loudly in Pax's mind she could hardly think.

"I won't hurt you!" Venefica begged, her fingers grabbing defensively at her own throat. "If I wanted to hurt you, why did I just save you from those guards?" She fought for air. "Please, Pax."

Pax hesitated for a second as Venefica's words started to make sense. The witch struggled to move her arm, pointing to the floor. Pax cast her eyes downwards, and there, amongst the contents of Venefica's bag, was the amulet.

"You stole it!" Pax's eyes glowed scarlet. "I knew it!"

"No!" Venefica gasped as the grip around her throat tightened. "Not the amulet. That." The witch fought to stretch a shaking hand out towards the floor again.

Pax glanced down and realised what the witch was pointing at. Lying next to the amulet was the small wooden magpie. Pax's shoulders eased a little, and Venefica's feet touched the ground once more. Pax bent over to retrieve the amulet, passing the gold chain around her neck.

"I'm sorry," Pax said. "I thought..." Her words trailed off.

"Don't apologise, young one," Venefica replied, rubbing her neck. "You were right not to trust me. To trust anyone."

Venefica knelt down and picked up the magpie, studying it.

"I thought about killing you," she said, keeping her eyes on the wooden bird.

Pax put a protective hand around the amulet as she listened

to the witch explain.

"I never stole the amulet. I ended up with it in Celare by mistake after what happened in the Salt Plains. But when my coven saw it, they wanted it for themselves."

Pax felt the heat inside her start to subside.

"They said I could belong with them." Venefica let out a little laugh, twisting the magpie in her fingers. "I would finally have a home. But to do so, I needed a sacrifice – your blood." Her glazed eyes looked at Pax.

"Then I realised." Venefica smiled sadly. "I couldn't do that to you."

"Why would you choose me over your coven?" Pax asked, her voice near to breaking.

The witch took a breath, her eyes starting to silver. "Do you know what hiraeth is, young one?"

Pax shook her head.

"Hiraeth is a longing for a home that you can never return to, a home that maybe never was. It is a grief, a yearning for the lost places of your past."

Pax felt a lump forming in her throat.

"You ask why did I return? It is because I chose to come home."

Tears rolled from Pax's eyes as she understood the feeling the witch was describing. She exhaled deeply, wiping her face hard with her hands and knelt down next to Venefica. Retrieving the magpie from her pocket, she held it up, and they silently interlocked the two carved birds. Then, together, they gathered up the other items strewn across the floor, placing them into the witch's velvet bag.

"Where is the warrior?" Venefica asked, hitching up her skirts and securing the jade blade in the holster around her thigh.

"They captured him, but a guard outside said the Cellarium is where they're keeping the caro. They've probably taken him there," Pax said, taking the pouch of Calva from her pocket and adding it to the fifth vial. She clicked the amulet shut.

"One more to go," Venefica said. "Do you have the last clue?"

Pax shook her head.

"Good job I came back then," the witch said. "My spell book revealed to me a prophecy."

Pax's eyes widened. "What did it say?"

Beneath Blood Moon the Messis will cease,
When sui generis will bestow Gen peace.
Golden amulet for a sacrifice made,
Of blood taken by a single blade.

"Am—" their name caught in Pax's throat. "Their final clue mentioned blood, too. But what is 'sui generis'?"

Venefica shrugged.

"How am I meant to do it?" Pax said quietly, looking the witch dead in the eyes. "Kill him?"

Venefica took Pax's face into her hands. "You have the amulet. Believe in the prophecy, young one. You are more powerful than you know."

The witch turned to the windows, where the Blood Moon filled the sky. "We don't have much time."

"Go to the Cellarium," Pax said, handing Venefica the warrior's axe. She pulled out the brass watch from her pocket and placed it into the witch's hand. "Find Miles and my parents and free them."

Venefica nodded, resting the axe on her shoulder and dropping the watch into her bag.

Pax gripped the amulet tightly in her fist. "I'm going to finish this."

☾

Am's face flashed into Pax's mind as she made her way down the corridor, and she had to will herself to focus. Suddenly, her chest felt hot. Pulling out the amulet from beneath her shirt, she saw that it was glowing. Five of the six gemstones were pulsing brightly. Then, a loud laugh. Footsteps growing closer. The amulet's light illuminated the panic across Pax's face as she searched the corridor for an escape. Quickly, she ducked into an archway with a wooden door and pushed, but it was firmly shut. The voices were getting louder. Frantically, Pax scanned the door for where the handle should be, only to find there wasn't one. Instead, at the centre of the wooden door was a carved circular shape. Pax traced her fingers over it. Six small indentations, equally spaced around the same ambigram engraved into the amulet. She held it up and slotted the amulet into the space. It fitted perfectly. Pax turned the amulet, and it clicked, opening the door with a slight creak. She was inside the room in a flash, quietly closing the door behind her. With her back against the door, she tried to quiet her breathing as she listened to the voices fading outside, the amulet still glowing in her hand.

The room was dark. Using the light from the amulet as a torch, Pax glanced around the room. It appeared to be an

270

alchemist's laboratory. One that had been left undisturbed for years. Pax recognised some of the equipment from her father's lab, once used but now abandoned, cobwebs and thick dust covering the tables where an old bio aux stood, its nucleus long dead. The floorboards creaked under her feet as she took in her surroundings. Glass test tubes, scrolls of paper, faded charts dimmed by the passage of time. Pax ran her eyes over the table. No weapons. Nothing of importance. The footsteps outside had gone, so, deciding it was safe, she went to leave, but something caught her eye. On the table lay a sheet of paper with a symbol drawn on it – the same one that was carved into the door and engraved on the amulet next to the initials S. G. Parting the papers on the table, she picked up the handwritten note and held the amulet close, to illuminate the words on the page:

Sui Generis:
Umor – water
Hydra – platelets
Omnis – white cells
Salis – salt
Calva – protein
Ichor – blood of the gods

Pax read the words on the page, then read them again, confusion spreading through her mind. Venefica had used the words 'sui generis' when describing the prophecy – could the initials S. G. on the amulet be referring to this, as well? The list was of all the items she had found so far, and it appeared as if each one of them correlated with a component that made up blood. All of this scrawled on a dusty piece of paper in an unused lab that had lain untouched for years.

Pax read the final line again, the word sinking in. Ichor. Blood of the gods. Royal blood. *Occissor's* blood. There was no time to lose. She folded the paper, placing it in her pocket. Using her penknife, she tore into the silky red lining of her cloak, ripping out a long strip of fabric. She wrapped it around the glowing amulet, hiding it in her pocket, then quietly she left the room.

Outside, the corridor was still. Pax pulled the hood of the cloak securely around her head, making sure her red hair wasn't visible. She made her way in the same direction the guards had been heading, praying to the old gods that it would lead her to the Throne Room before midnight, in time to stop the Messis, not only to save her parents but to save them all.

In the corridors, servants parted and kept their heads down when they saw Pax's white cloak come into view. She ascended a spiral staircase, and as she reached the top, the corridor opened up to reveal high ceilings adorned with gold features. The higher floors were much less clinical than the corridors leading to the Cellarium. Huge tapestries hung from the walls, depicting what Pax guessed must be historical scenes. One image was of Rubra, the same view that had greeted her when she'd first entered the city on the pyrois. She recognised the Castellum, laced with thick glass tubes leading up to an open window in the central tower. The woven silk showed the streets filled with cheering crowds, the gullies bright with satiny red. Pax walked on past another tapestry, showing a central figure surrounded by light, threads of silver and gold glistening from the cloth. A strange familiarity crept over her – she had seen something similar, a figure of light, at the

Caligo Caves just before she'd passed out. A figure she'd seen again, on the horizon in Levis. But there was no time for her to linger as loud footsteps approached, marching in unison. Backing into the tapestry, Pax kept her head down as four figures in white cloaks whipped past. Seizing the opportunity, she fell in line behind them, marching down the corridors.

"His highness is still questioning caro," one guard said to another so quietly that Pax had to strain to hear them.

The guard next to them turned slightly, making Pax look down.

"Still? So close to the Messis?" His voice was strained with urgency.

"Apparently, Phantasma failed." The guard replied, and Pax clenched her fist at the mention of the name. "So his highness used Manus to complete the task. That's why we're being summoned to the Throne Room."

As they rounded the corner, Pax dropped back. She watched them approach two massive wooden doors with guards stationed at either side. The approaching guards saluted and disappeared inside. Suddenly, Pax knew what she had to do. She turned on her heels, quickly retracing her steps, clutching the amulet tightly in her pocket. Making her way back down the staircase, she hurried to the exit, just fast enough not to raise suspicion.

Outside, the courtyard was quiet. The pyrois had been put back into the stables, their flaming tails and manes a mere flicker now they were resting. There was muffled noise from the gathering crowds on the other side of the Castellum walls, but Pax was alone in the courtyard. She lowered her hood, and her red hair fell back onto her shoulders as she looked up at the thick, clear tubes covering the walls all the way to the window of the Throne Room. Unwrapping the glowing amulet from her pocket, Pax placed the chain around her neck. She unclipped the S-shaped brooch and let the white cloak fall to the floor. Then she started to climb.

CHAPTER THIRTY-ONE

"Geez! This Gen is massive." The shorter guard was struggling to hold up an unconscious Miles whilst trying to attach him to the metal hooks on the wall. "Gimme a hand!"

Another, larger guard rolled his eyes and came to his aid. Together they managed to lift the warrior onto the wall, cuffing his wrists and ankles into place with thick leather straps that strained under his weight.

Miles stirred, lifting his face, caked in drying blood, then slumped down again. Another guard, dressed in a white cloak, came into the Cellarium, pushing a metal trolley. She stopped in front of them and picked up a needle from the silver tray. Miles groaned at the sharp scratch on the skin of his forearm. Fighting heavy eyelids, he blinked awake, blinded by the whiteness surrounding him. A bright, narrow streak of red flashed in his vision. Then he passed out again.

"I'm so excited for the Messis tonight!" the female guard said cheerily, placing her instruments back onto the tray. She leant towards the two other guards and lowered her voice. "Have you heard the rumours?" she whispered, raising her eyebrows. "There might be enough caro to open the gate at midnight!" Her lips curled around a gleeful smile.

"If you're finished?" the larger guard replied sternly, having no time for her gossip.

Her smile dropped. As she pushed the rattling trolley back down the corridor cursing to herself, she failed to notice the witch hiding in an archway.

Venefica held her breath and waited for the female guard to pass, nervous her magic would fail. The guard disappeared from sight. It confirmed her invisibility spell had worked, but for how much longer, she was unsure. Her bare feet moved stealthily down the hallway beneath the fluorescent lights. If this spell failed, she would easily be seen, so she moved as quickly and quietly as she could.

Venefica slowed, listening to the guards talking in the corridor. Kneeling, she placed her bag down on the floor next to her, taking out a small silver bowl. Into it she sprinkled some herba and muttered an incantation.

"*Somnum, domir…*" She added a few drops of lavender oil to the bowl. "*Requiem hac nocte.*"

She placed a short black candle in the middle of the bowl, and with a wave of her hand, the wick lit into a purple flame. Venefica took the bowl into her hands, closing her eyes. Listening carefully to the voices, she visualised the guards. "*Itum.*"

She blew out the candle and the purple smoke curled like a ribbon into the air, creeping slowly down the corridor, around the corner and towards the guards. The smoke was hardly noticeable under the lights as it made its way into the nostrils of the first guard.

Venefica gathered her things into her bag and waited for a few moments, biting her lip. Then came the sound of a guard slumping to the ground. Then another. Soon, she was sure all four were out cold. Her spell had worked. Pleased, Venefica smiled to herself, but as she turned the corner, she froze.

The corridor was lined with victims hanging from the walls. They were tethered to sharp metal hooks stretching so far into the distance Venefica couldn't even see the end of the corridor. They had all been strapped into place, with thin red tubes protruding from their arms. The tubes spidered out, across and up the walls like a web, connecting to one large transparent tube above. This ran across the whole length of the ceiling before disappearing out of sight. The walls were closing in on her. Venefica gasped for air, but she couldn't breathe. Her black eyes searched widely up and down the corridor, taking in all the different Gen helplessly hanging from the walls. Women. Children. Too many to help.

Run! the voices inside Venefica's head screamed.

Run! Run! Run! the voices of her coven echoed in her mind.

Then her eyes found him. There, on the wall, larger than the other victims, was Miles. Unconscious, but it was him. She took a breath, her eyes transforming back to white.

With her heart thumping in her chest, Venefica stepped over an unconscious guard and hurried towards Miles. Standing on tiptoes, she gently reached up to touch his face.

"Miles?" she whispered.

He groaned, and she spoke his name louder.

Miles's eyes blinked open. "Vee?" He frowned painfully as his eyes focused. Then a small smile. "I knew you'd come back," he said, his voice hoarse. "You missed me."

For once, Venefica had no urge to roll her eyes at him. "I think I'd miss you even if we'd never met." She held up his axe. "Pax sent you a present."

Miles started to laugh, which turned into a spluttering cough. When he caught his breath, he lifted his wrist, bound by the strap. "A little help?"

Venefica hitched up her skirts, retrieving the dagger holstered around her thigh. Slicing into the leather around his ankles and wrists, she freed Miles from the wall. He stumbled down onto the Cellarium floor, and she steadied him, nearly toppling under his weight.

"How do you fare, warrior?" she asked. Miles circled his wrists, then gripped the tube protruding from his skin. With a hard yank, he pulled it out, blood splattering onto the white floor.

He looked at Venefica, and with a slight smirk replied, "Figo." Pulling the tube from his other arm, he flexed his shoulders and stood tall, taking in his surroundings.

"Oh, dear gods!" Miles whispered, seeing the corridor.

"Pax sent me here to find you and her parents. The Blood Moon is nearly upon us," Venefica said with urgency.

Miles nodded. "We'd better get to it."

"There's too many to help!" she said to Miles, who was already breaking Gen free from their constraints.

The witch followed his lead, cutting into the straps and helping each of them down. The victims were unsteady at first, then slowly, as they pulled the tubes from their arms, they started to help free the others.

"Creo!" Miles shouted, and Venefica rushed over to join him.

Creo was badly beaten, his eye swollen, his lip freshly split.

"Creo! It's Miles!"

Creo mumbled groggily.

"Pax is here!"

On hearing her name, Creo's head snapped up. "Where is Pax?" he asked, his voice hoarse.

"She's here in the Castellum. We need to go help her.

Where is Celeste?" Miles asked, pulling the tubes from Creo's forearm.

"*He* has her. In the Throne Room," Creo said, stumbling.

Miles and Venefica held him steady. Suddenly, a bell tolled loudly from above, the sound filling the corridor. As the chime eased, distant voices chanted outside the Castellum walls.

"Release the gates! Release the gates! Release the gates!"

Then, from above their heads, came a loud gurgling as the tubes on the ceiling filled rapidly with blood, and those in the Cellarium still attached to the walls started screaming out in pain.

CHAPTER THIRTY-TWO

Inside the tubes, the crawl space was steep and cramped. Pax had to squeeze her shoulders against the clear glass to fit through. Beneath her, hundreds of Supremo Gen gathered, like ants crowding around a nest. She continued to climb, the amulet still glowing around her neck, until the tunnel opened up again, large enough for her to finally stand. In front of her, bolted against the walls, were vertical metal steps. Pax craned her neck and could just see the window that led to the Throne Room. It was open now, just as it had been depicted in the tapestries in the hallways. Suddenly, from above her, a voice called out. Pax pressed her body into the steps, not daring to look up.

"Welcome, all!" Manus called out, and the crowds below stilled. "To this evening's Messis under the most wonderful Blood Moon." Manus reached his arms towards the night sky, and the crowds cheered.

"The ceremony will begin in just a few short moments, but before it does, let us welcome our leader, whom each of us feels in our very blood. His Majesty the king!"

The crowd roared as Occissor's figure appeared briefly in the window and then vanished again just as quickly. The throng in the streets mumbled in disappointment.

"Please, please stay calm. The gates will be open soon,"

Manus said.

Pax waited for a few seconds in the hope that the crowd's eyes would drop away, and then, gripping onto the rungs of the ladder, she pulled herself upwards. As she got nearer to the open window, she could hear more voices.

"You!" Someone from inside was screaming, and Pax knew in her blood that it was him – the Gen she needed to kill.

Quietly, she pulled herself up over the last step, peering into the Throne Room. Inside, the walls were covered in thick, interlacing tubes that all ran down towards the window, towards where Pax was crouching, only just hidden from sight. Guards flanked large wooden doors on the opposite side of the room, and in the centre was an empty black throne.

Kneeling on the floor was a white-haired woman. Pax's rage surged inside her again as she instantly recognised Phantasma. There was another figure, standing over her, facing away from Pax. The figure turned, revealing veiny skin around piercing red eyes. Startled, Pax dropped back down. She had seen that face before.

Turning back towards the room, Occissor continued his tirade. "Answer me!"

Then Pax heard another voice. A voice that was quiet but familiar.

"Your son never wanted to hurt anyone."

Pax froze, stunned. The voice belonged to her mother.

"He was good and kind." Her voice grew louder. "He could have saved you all." She wasn't afraid; she was angry.

Pax peered over the edge again, and her heart sank. Her mother was being restrained by two guards, and Occissor was stepping towards her. Raising his hand, he flicked his wrist and Celeste doubled up with pain.

"Let me kill her, Your Highness!" Phantasma's shrill voice cut into Pax like a knife. "She speaks treason! I'll have her tongue!"

"Your Highness," Manus said desperately. "If this is true, it means that they are not extinct at all. It could mean the saviour of our—"

His voice stopped abruptly as, from above, the bells in the Castellum's tower tolled loudly. It was midnight.

Occissor dropped his hand, and Celeste fell limply to the floor. "The Messis is upon us," he said darkly. "Manus, release the gates!"

Manus hesitated, but as the bell tolled again, he waved his gloved hands and gave the signal to the guards in the room. The roars of the crowds erupted beneath Pax as they chanted, "Release the gates! Release the gates!" over and over again, their voices only drowned out by the continuing chimes of the bells.

The guards in the Throne Room moved towards the walls, pulling huge levers. There was a loud creak followed by gurgling liquid. The bells rang again. The tubes covering the walls filled with a deep red. Blood. The thick liquid gushed through the tubes spanning the walls and towards the open window, rushing towards Pax. She managed one deep breath as the huge force smashed into her. Gripping the bar tightly, she felt her hands slip against the rung of the ladder as she was engulfed in blood. She gasped for breath as it filled her nostrils and soaked her hair and clothes. At the base of the Castellum, the crowds rejoiced. Blood cascaded downwards, filling the gullies and flooding the streets of Rubra.

The bells chimed for the last time. Midnight. But Pax could no longer hear the bells, no longer hear the cheering crowds, only the sound of her own heartbeat pulsing in her ears, rage building inside her like a storm. Pulling herself up and out of the tube, Pax clambered into the Throne Room. Rising up, completely covered in blood, she stood and faced him.

☾

"Quickly!" Miles yelled, trying to pull more Gen off the walls of the Cellarium. Venefica slipped on the blood pooling on the floor. Creo spotted Prod, still restrained and screaming in pain, and didn't hesitate in pulling the tubes from his arms and freeing his neighbour from the wall.

Prod sank to his knees. "I'm sorry," he sobbed, crumpling into a ball on the wet floor.

Then, just as quickly as it had started, it stopped with a loud gurgle. The screaming subsided as the tubes ceased drawing blood into the system.

"Come on," said Creo urgently.

Weapons raised, Miles and Venefica hurried after him, through the corridors of the Cellarium, into the upper levels and towards the Throne Room. As the approaching footsteps marched towards them, they waited. Miles held out his arm protectively in front of the others.

"Sounds like there's two of them," Miles said, stepping out into the corridor, directly in front of the oncoming guards.

As soon as they drew their swords, Miles brought his axe down, sending a blade clattering to the floor. Miles's fist connected with the jaw of one of the guards, knocking him out cold. The other guard heard his own sword hit the ground before he even realised he'd been disarmed, and retreated down the hallway.

☾

"Intruder!" Phantasma's scream shook the Throne Room's walls.

But Pax was already focused on the glass tubes, locating the brackets holding them in place. Without moving, she visualised them being ripped from the wall. Then, one by one, the bolts shot out. The guards ducked the metal shooting across the room. The tubes cracked, then burst, one after the other. Fragments of glass rained down over the Throne Room, blood gushing out, splashing on to the white marble floors. The guards stationed around the room hesitated, waiting for orders, distracted by the thick metallic air.

Phantasma jumped to her feet.

"You!" Her eyes flickered in recognition as she launched herself towards Pax.

Am's lifeless body flashed into Pax's mind. She thrust her hand out, and a surge of pure rage shot towards Phantasma, hitting her in mid-air. Phantasma smashed backwards into a wall. In a split second, Pax locked onto an attacking guard, and his body hit the ground.

"Stop!" Occissor's chilling scream filled the air.

The guards froze, silenced. Pax glanced towards her mother, slumped on the floor. Then her eyes locked with his. Occissor. Pure hatred. Strange familiarity. She faltered for a second as the amulet glowed white-hot against her chest. Then the pain hit her. Frozen in agony. She had never felt anything like it before. It spread, cracking through her bones.

The edges of her vision darkened. She could just see Occissor's veiny hand stretching out towards her, his red eyes studying her like an animal he was about to kill, before widening when he saw the amulet hanging around her neck.

The doors to the Throne Room cracked open, breaking the silence.

"Apologies, Your Highness, but there's trouble in the Cellar—" The guard's mouth fell open.

Occissor paused, a strange smile crossing his face.

"Go," he said quietly. No one moved. "Go! All of you!" he screamed.

Deleo was the first to make his way to the door, the other guards saluting and falling in line behind him.

Picking herself up off the floor, Phantasma bowed low in front of Occissor. Although Pax was unmoving, held in place just by Occissor's mind, Phantasma gave her a wide berth, following Deleo out through the doors. Manus, the bottom half of his cloak now saturated in blood, went to follow her towards the door.

"No, you stay," Occissor said quietly.

Manus cowered against the wall. The Throne Room's doors closed, leaving Pax suspended, in agony.

As Creo took in his surroundings, trying to remember the route back to the Throne Room, Venefica nudged Miles. Taking his hand, she placed his broken pocket watch inside it.

Miles studied it sadly. "This once belonged to someone I loved. Someone who died at the hands of the Harvesters." Venefica nodded as he placed the watch in his belt bag and gripped his axe with both hands. "I won't let it happen again."

"This way!" Creo said, moving quickly up the spiral staircase and running towards the large wooden door at the end of the corridor.

It creaked open and there, in a stream of moonlight cast along the floor, stood Phantasma and Deleo and two more guards, all covered in blood.

"Go to the Cellarium," Deleo said to the two guards. He looked at Phantasma.

"Kill them," she snarled.

☾

"So." Occissor spoke quietly, as the pain left Pax's body. His hand fell, and her feet touched the ground. "At last, we meet."

Panting for breath, Pax tried to stand but stumbled. Occissor watched, amused, as she crawled over the sticky floor, dragging herself towards Celeste, who was lying limp.

"Mum?" Pax's voice was hoarse.

Celeste groaned, clutching the back of her head.

A cruel cackle filled the room. Occissor was laughing.

Balling her fists, Pax managed to stand.

"It all makes sense now!" Occissor's eyes bored into her. "You! You are the reason. The answer to the Supremos' destiny."

Pax took a step towards him but stopped on hearing his next words.

"My heir."

Pax frowned, trying to make sense of the words he spoke.

"You don't know, do you?" Occissor said quietly.

"I know what I have to do," Pax spat, heat pulsing through

her veins.

Occissor laughed again. "Tell her."

"It's true." Celeste's voice was weak. "Your father is not who you think he is."

CHAPTER THIRTY-THREE

Celeste couldn't catch her breath, laughing so hard her sides hurt, until an ugly snort escaped her nose. Raising her hands to her mouth, embarrassed, she looked at Lupiter. Feigning shock, he turned away in mock disgust, then burst out laughing again. Celeste made a mental note to remember how happy he looked right now, in this moment, his red hair framing his red eyes, his entire body shaking with laughter. How strange to think just weeks ago she didn't know him, and now she couldn't imagine her life without him. Her life, however long she had left, was so much better because of him.

Celeste had been chosen by the Elders this season. At first, she had felt an immense pride at the honour of being the one Ethereal to provide and ascend. This age-old ritual had granted peace over Tellus for centuries and *she* had been chosen. Celeste had been so nervous about leaving her home to travel to Rubra and attend the celebrations at the Castellum. The Elders had described the weeks leading up to the Messis as a joyous celebration hosted by the royal Supremos, but nothing had prepared her for the extravagance!

The night she'd first met Lupiter, she wasn't even sure if she was allowed to talk to the prince. Dressed in her finest yet most uncomfortable silks, she'd been led by the other Ethereals into the ballroom, painfully aware of the stares of others who knew she was the chosen one – the willing sacrifice for this Messis. Then, through the crowds, her eyes met his, his deep red and hers almost gold, and there was nothing else to do but smile.

Lupiter introduced himself and asked her to dance. The first time his hand had touched hers was almost electric, and she could barely speak as he led her to the dance floor with the king and the Elders looking on. Surrounded by the safety of the music, Lupiter was able to whisper to her too quietly for prying ears to hear. He was much less formal than the other Supremos, and she had to stifle a laugh at his words. As they swirled about the dance floor, she found her whole body relaxing into his arms.

That evening was the first time they'd managed to escape the prying eyes of the Elders, descending the spiral staircase and into Lupiter's laboratory, where he explained to her that he was an alchemist. They talked late into the midnight hours and instantly become friends. After that, each night during the celebrations in the Castellum, they'd sneak off together and hide in his laboratory to escape the endless formalities and just be with one another. Lupiter shared his fascinating tales from his recent travels around Tellus with Celeste. Stories about witches' curses and Old Gods, colourful caves filled with terrifying creatures, magical lands full of life and light, and places of salt and sand. Celeste listened intently as he described the Gen he had met, the magic he'd encountered, all of which, sadly, she knew she would never see. Lupiter's stories provided her with an escape from the looming inevitability of her own death.

They had fallen for each other quickly. Love, mixed with the imminent sorrow of what was to come. Maybe it was the unavoidable end of their tragic story that made their feelings grow so fast, made them love more intensely, more desperately. The weeks since they'd met had been truly wonderful, but as the moon grew full in the skies above Rubra, fear and doubt crept into Celeste's mind. Now, this evening, with just hours before the Messis, Lupiter had led Celeste down to the laboratory with a nervous excitement.

"So, what are you showing me, Your Highness?" Celeste curtsied playfully in her white lace gown.

Lupiter pulled out some paper scrolls from his desk, the glowing red nucleus of his bio aux, at the centre of the room, illuminating their faces. He took a breath, his smile dropping.

"What is it?" Celeste asked, concerned.

"What if I told you there's a way that we can be together?" Lupiter's voice was quiet.

Celeste frowned.

"What if you don't have to sacrifice yourself?" The prince's red eyes met hers.

Celeste stood up, her face flushed. "What are you talking about?" This conversation was dangerously close to treason. "I'm an Ethereal and I've been chosen. It's the greatest honour." But her voice didn't sound convincing.

Lupiter made his way around the table and clasped Celeste's hands between his. "But what if there was another way?"

Celeste didn't reply, confusion etched across her face.

Lupiter spoke with a quiet urgency. "What if the Supremo Gen didn't need Ethereal blood to survive?" His words hung in the cold air of the laboratory. "Then you wouldn't need to give up your life, and we could be together."

Celeste pulled her hands away from Lupiter, annoyed.

"Don't tease me." She headed towards the door.

Lupiter hurried around her, blocking her path.

"Please, Celeste, just listen." His voice was gentle, his eyes brimming with tears. "This is not the life you or I would choose. Let me explain."

Nervously, Celeste followed him back to the bio aux and sat next to him. Lupiter took a piece of scroll and laid it flat on the desk, then he drew a large symbol on it – a capital A with another inverted on top of it. He described what he'd been researching during his travels through Tellus over the past few years.

"My studies in alchemy have shown that there is a way to create a life source that will sustain my Gen."

Celeste was confused. Growing up as an Ethereal, all she had known was magic and myths. This creation of Lupiter's sounded unlike anything she had ever heard.

"It's an artificial blood. I call it *sui generis*," Lupiter said proudly.

Celeste didn't react, her brows still furrowed in confusion, so Lupiter began to explain in more detail, drawing on the paper as he spoke.

"The components of the Ethereal – your – blood can be broken down. Blood is made up of different parts. You have white cells, salts, proteins, water, platelets and, of course, red cells too. But Ethereal blood is laced with magic. That's why a few drops can sustain entire generations, as opposed to other types of blood. I've travelled all of Tellus searching for the magical elements needed for this blood. By combining them, I created *sui generis*. It provides a life source for an entire population of Supremos, with no Messis, no sacrifices."

Celeste's eyes widened as she finally understood the

enormity of what Lupiter was suggesting. Of breaking a covenant that had provided peace in Tellus for so many moons. Changing centuries-old traditions of Ethereals being willing sacrifices to grant immortality to the Supremos. To save both Gen. To save *her*.

Lupiter stood up. Briefly letting go of Celeste's hands, he went over to the bio aux, opening a drawer below the nucleus. He picked up the item inside and walked back to Celeste. Opening his hands, he revealed a beautiful gold necklace. Celeste caught her breath.

"Is it real gold?" she said, her fingers reaching out to touch it.

Lupiter smiled. "An extremely rare type too. My father's Oculus is made from the same gold."

He held it out and placed it into Celeste's hands. She studied the intricate details and coloured gemstones in awe. She had never seen anything so beautiful.

"It's an amulet," Lupiter said softly as he placed the chain around her neck. "It provides protection and holds the exact combination of *sui generis*. It guards everything I've worked towards."

Celeste held the amulet as he spoke.

"My travels took me all over Tellus where I located each magical element. I collected Umor, which represents water." He touched the sapphire next to the symbol. "Hydra for the platelets." He touched the emerald. "Omnis for white cells. Salis for salt and Calva for protein." With each component, he touched a different-coloured gemstone. He looked up at Celeste. "And the final one is Ichor." His finger touched the dark red ruby. "The blood of the gods."

Celeste had been unsure whether Lupiter should share his discoveries with the king. It could be dangerous, even fatal, for either of them to even suggest breaking the covenant. To go against age-old traditions that upheld the only society they knew. Lupiter had persuaded her that they didn't have anything to lose. The Blood Moon was mere hours away. That had given her a single drop of hope in the black ocean of her heart. So she had nodded in agreement, holding his hand tightly as they stepped into the Throne Room.

What happened next was a blur. The conversation had started calmly, until the king had noticed Celeste's hand in Lupiter's. Occissor's face grew dark. Lupiter tried to explain his plan, his voice getting louder, his movements becoming frantic. At first, he was met with laughter from his father. It quickly turned to rage.

Celeste felt her feet leave the ground as the first blow hit her, heard the sound of her own bones hitting the floor. The pain. As the ringing in her ears subsided, flashes of black and red lightning crackled above her. The ceiling began to crumble. She covered her eyes as a sheet of dust fell through the air. Someone was shaking her. Hard. She opened her eyes. It was Lupiter. He was shouting. Something she couldn't understand. He pointed to the gold chain around her neck and pulled her to her feet. Lupiter had kissed her hard on the mouth, before saying his final word: "*Run!*"

CHAPTER
THIRTY-FOUR

Pax's mouth went dry. "You're confused," she said quietly, stroking her mother's golden hair, now matted with blood.

Celeste grabbed her arm. "Listen to me," she said urgently. "Your real father was a prince and an alchemist. His name was Lupiter." She looked towards Occissor. "His son."

Pax's mind was spinning, unable to make sense of the words coming from her mother's mouth. The power that had been coursing through her veins just moments ago had evaporated. Her mother's fingernails gripped her skin, leaving crescent moon-shaped indents as she desperately tried to explain.

"He was trying to save my Gen – the Ethereals."

Pax shook her head. "No, they're extinct." Even her own voice sounded strange.

Her mother's golden eyes stared at her. "I'm an Ethereal, Pax, and so are you. It's true, many Gen believe we are extinct, but that's just to keep the few of us that are left safe. Creo understood because he is an alchemist too. He saved my life."

Pax's mind was filling with hundreds of questions, but she couldn't form any of them into words. Near the back of the room, Manus straightened up, listening intently.

Celeste's eyes watered. "Your real father was a Supremo, Pax, and he was so kind." Her mother stroked her face. "Just like you."

Occissor scoffed at the words. Celeste tore her gaze away from her daughter.

"You killed your own son!" Celeste's voice broke as she pointed at Occissor.

"You think I'd let my only heir cavort with caro?" Occissor yelled so loudly it muffled the sound of the chain mail gloves slinking to the floor. "To throw away generations of tradition over some alchemist nonsense? It was not enough he killed his mother in childbirth. He wanted to destroy my legacy!"

He thrust his hands out, launching waves of rage towards Celeste. Pax jumped to her feet, rushing forwards to protect her mother, but she was too late, and Celeste's body was thrown into the air.

"Stop!" screamed Pax.

She tried to focus, to harness her power, but her body was weak. Willing her aching bones on, she scrambled over to Celeste, slipping on the floor and falling to her knees next to her mother's limp body.

Suddenly, Manus was behind Occissor, his bare hands clamping down onto his veiny scalp.

"Manus! What are you—" Occissor screamed in pain, scratching at the hands clamping down firmly onto his head, pressing hard into his skin.

"I need to know," Manus said through gritted teeth, his eyes screwed shut. "Was it you who murdered the prince?"

Pax gently touched Celeste's arm, where the bones under her skin protruded at an awkward angle. Her mother's face was still, a small trickle of blood moving slowly down her forehead from a cut Pax couldn't see. Fighting back tears, Pax pulled her mother up against the wall. Celeste opened her eyes, a weak smile appearing before she winced in pain.

"Mum," Pax sobbed helplessly, hugging her close.

Celeste whispered into Pax's ear, "Even in your darkest moments, you'll be guided by a higher light."

Pax pulled away, meeting her mother's gaze as she softly touched a finger to the amulet around her daughter's neck.

Roaring, Occissor lifted Manus's feet from the ground, throwing him across the room. Manus collapsed against the wall, the palms of his limp hands raw.

Occissor turned, and Pax was frozen. Pain ripped through her body, rising through her limbs. Her legs wanted to buckle underneath her, but each muscle was taut with agony, holding her in place. Her contorted body rose into the air, away from her mother, her arms splayed out at her sides. Pax rotated helplessly in mid-air, and she screamed out in pain, but no sound escaped her lips. Through darkened vision, she faced Occissor, his hands out in front of him, his fingers clawing the air.

"You are my son's daughter. Your veins run thick with Supremo blood," Occissor said quietly. "You are my heir."

Even through the pain pounding against her skull Pax could not escape his words.

"You have a choice," Occissor continued. "Join me, and with the amulet we can rule Rubra together!"

The iron blade glinted red in the moonlight. Deleo raised it high above his head and ran towards them. Instantly, Miles was in front of Creo.

"Stay back," he yelled. "We'll hold them off."

Creo nodded, pushing his back against one of the huge tapestries hanging from the wall. Miles parted his feet, raising his axe, his Tribus war cry coming from deep within his lungs. Metal clashed loudly as he duelled violently with Deleo, equally matched in both size and skill, attacking each other again and again. The blade of the axe sliced into Deleo's arm, and he stumbled backwards. Miles took the opportunity to kick his crus directly into Deleo's chest, sending him flying to the floor.

Venefica gripped her dagger and whispered, "*Exarmare cladem.*"

Swiping an arrow from her quiver, Phantasma placed it into her bow. Pulling back the string, she aimed directly between Venefica's ebony eyes. A sharp twang sent the arrow slicing through the air.

Venefica didn't flinch, quietly repeating the words, "*Exarmare cladem.*"

The arrow slowed, as if time had been altered temporarily. It stopped in mid-air, directly in front of the witch's face. Then, it flipped back on itself.

"*Surculus,*" Venefica whispered.

The arrow shot back towards Phantasma. She quickly rolled out of the way as the arrow embedded itself in the wall. Phantasma screamed in frustration, realising Venefica was a witch. Jumping to her feet, she rushed straight towards Venefica, who uttered another incantation, but Phantasma moved too quickly for her to finish the spell. Bracing herself, Venefica slashed at the air with her dagger as Phantasma launched herself through the air, her blood-splattered cloak trailing behind her.

Deleo rolled over to Miles, standing above him, axe raised.

"I surrender!" he cried out.

Miles, respecting the rules of war, lowered his axe and kicked Deleo's sword away from him, but, as he did so, Deleo's foot smashed into the back of his crus, throwing him off balance. Miles tumbled to the ground, the axe dropping from his grip and sliding away from him across the stone floor. Cracking his knuckles, Deleo retrieved his sword and jumped on top of the warrior, pinning him down. Miles struggled, but Deleo's full weight crushed him, sending a sharp pain through his chest as something cracked. As Deleo pressed the blade into his neck, Miles desperately stretched out his free arm, clawing at the floor to try and reach his axe. Deleo, teeth gritted, loomed over Miles. A flash of recognition crossed his face.

"I remember you now!" Deleo said, almost laughing. "I almost didn't recognise you without your leg!" He brought his face down, closer to Miles's. "Tell me," Deleo whispered, only inches away. "Do you miss your son?" His eyes creased, taking pleasure as a wave of grief washed away any remaining strength in Miles's body.

"You will die," Deleo said, pushing harder into Miles's throat, "never knowing what happened to your son."

Deleo threw his head back, laughing maniacally, then stopped abruptly. His eyes widened in shock as his body jolted. The pressure of the blade on Miles's neck was released as red tears slowly trickled from Deleo's eyes. As he slumped over, Miles pushed the body away, and there, embedded in the back of Deleo's head, was Miles's axe. Standing above him, panting and wide-eyed, stood Creo.

Phantasma's blood-curdling scream echoed down the corridor, her beauty contorting with rage as she watched

Deleo fall to the ground. Venefica seized the opportunity, thrusting her dagger towards Phantasma, slicing her face. The cut silenced Phantasma. She raised her hand to touch her cheek where a thin line of blood had appeared. She stepped back, outraged, and lunged at the witch again, pushing her to the floor. Panting above her, the blood on her face trickled into Phantasma's mouth, coating her teeth.

Miles placed his crus on Deleo's back, and with a sickening squelch pulled his axe free. He launched it through the air towards Phantasma. Her head shot up as the axe spun towards her. Then, she was gone. The axe embedding itself in the wooden door of the Throne Room, with a thud.

"She evanesced!" Venefica yelled as Miles and Creo help her to her feet. "Coward!"

☾

With another flick of his wrist, Pax's rigid body levitated towards Occissor, the heat from the amulet pulsing into her heart as she neared his outstretched hands.

This is it… I'm going to die.

Pax closed her eyes and saw Am dancing in the woods. She felt Felis's fur curl beneath her fingertips, could hear Miles in the caves, risking his life for her. She remembered Venefica sacrificing her coven to return the amulet to her. All the things each one had done in her aid flashed before her. Then the images disappeared as her mind filled with pain: her home destroyed. Venefica's terrified eyes. Am lying motionless on the red earth of Sepultus. Miles, bound and bleeding. Her mother dying on the floor. Creo's kind laugh that she would never hear again.

I won't let it end like this.

Pax made a choice. Instead of being swallowed by the darkness, she went towards the light. Her heartbeat grew stronger. She could feel each drop of her blood pumping through her veins. Her breath returned to her lungs. Then it happened. A huge eruption rolled through her body, powered not by rage, but by love. Her eyes snapped open, glowing bright and scarlet. They locked on to their target: Occissor. Pax's pure power exploded towards him, making his face fall for a split second before he was sent flying backwards.

Pax fell through the air. At last, she could move, landing on her feet as another wave of pain hit her. Occissor lashed out in a rage, dark streaks ripping across the room. Shielding herself, she rolled away, sending another bolt towards him. It crackled gold in the air, just missing him to hit a pillar, breaking it like bone.

Black flashed across Pax's vision as she smashed against a wall. The skin of her back sliced against sharp marble as she slid down, her cheek bone slammed into the floor. Another blow. In pain, Pax retreated behind the fallen pillar, desperately trying to catch her breath as black sparks flew either side of her, the pain spreading through her body like an illness, seeping into her mind. Getting close enough to him to harvest his blood felt impossible.

Suddenly, an unsettling quiet fell over the room, the black streaks disappearing from the dusty air. Pax took a few deep breaths and peered out from behind the pillar. There, suspended in the centre of the room, high above Occissor, was Celeste, her face contorted in pain.

"If you want your mother to live," Occissor said maniacally, "give me the amulet."

There was no doubt in Pax's mind: she had to save her mother. All this had been for nothing. The journey. Am's death. She had failed. With tears in her eyes, she removed the amulet from around her neck and held it in her shaking hand. Then, she remembered Am's final word: 'Blood'.

Thrusting her hand into her pocket, Pax pulled out her penknife, flicking open the blade. She sliced the metal across her palm. Opening the amulet for the last time, she squeezed her fist and her blood trickled into the final vial. "*Ichor*," she whispered, clicking the amulet shut.

One by one, each of the gemstones lit up. Green, blue, silver, black, white and, finally, red. The symbol in the middle started to swirl. Standing up from behind the pillar, Pax walked out to face him, unafraid.

"Is this what you want?" she yelled, holding the amulet in her fist. "Then have it!" She threw it into the air.

The moment it left her palm, a bright red light exploded, filling the entire Throne Room. Pax's feet left the ground as she levitated into the air, silhouetted against the Blood Moon. She was transformed, more powerful than ever. Her eyes glowing white, flames erupted around her, rolling up to the ceiling and across the room, powerful and blinding. The window shattered from the force, showering glass down onto the crowds below.

Engulfed in flames, Occissor doubled up in pain, his body propelled out into the night sky. Howling, his veins throbbed and burst through his skin. A tortured scream emanated from his rupturing lungs. His body dissolved into a black mist, spiralling into the night.

The flames subsided and vanished. Pax dropped to the floor of the Throne Room, the amulet clattering by her side.

The room was silent now, except for a light wind entering through the empty casing. Pax scrambled towards Celeste, her bloodied hands frantically gripping onto her lifeless body.

"Mum?" Pax shook her gently, her own voice muffled against the ringing in her ears.

The sound merged into soft chimes. The noise grew louder, echoing around the room. Through the empty window, a bright white light appeared. At first, Pax thought it was the sunrise, but as her eyes focused, the light grew larger still, blocking out the moon. The light glowed brighter until, from its centre, a figure appeared, the outline barely visible against the nearly blinding white.

"What—" Pax started to speak as the sparks cleared from her vision until she realised what she was witnessing.

"The Ethereals." Manus's voice was barely a whisper from the back of the room, where he fell to his knees and bowed his head.

Around her Pax sensed movement, then her hands were empty. She was no longer gripping the fabric of her mother's dress. Celeste glided away from her, silently, above the ground and towards the light. She was no longer injured, no longer in pain. Pax watched her mother, as if in a dream, too distant to touch but close enough to hear. She looked peaceful and happier than Pax had ever seen her.

"I love you." Celeste's voice distorted into an echo, yet it was unmistakably hers.

Pax watched in stunned silence as the outline of her mother floated into the light. It burned so brightly Pax had to cover her eyes, and by the time she opened them again, her mother was gone. All within a few broken heartbeats.

The doors to the Throne Room swung open and Creo

rushed in, followed closely by Miles and Venefica. Pax sat silently on the bloodied floor. Creo hurried over to her, helping her up to her feet. Slightly unsteady, Pax slowly made her way to the shattered window to where the light had been. Her mother was gone.

Manus held up his hands and approached them. Miles gripped his axe, watching carefully as Manus knelt down in front of Pax.

"I-I witnessed what happened all those years ago. Prince Lupiter created *sui generis* to end the sacrifices and save the Ethereals – to save your mother." Manus cleared his throat, struggling to say the next words. "The king killed his own son, your father."

Pax scowled as Manus spoke, the words sounding ridiculous as Creo put his arm round her, squeezing her shoulder.

"Dad?" Pax stared at Creo, the word coming out in a pained sob.

"Oh, Pax, I'm so sorry," Creo managed to say, carefully wiping the blood from her face with shaking hands.

Pax shook her head. "I don't understand."

Creo held her shoulders gently. "We wanted to tell you. We were waiting for your Ortus day to explain. I met your mother after she'd escaped from Rubra, when she was pregnant with you. She was terrified. When she showed me the amulet, I knew it held something so powerful, something that could end this reign of terror in Tellus. So I didn't hesitate in keeping her, and you, safe. I'm so sorry, Pax; I should have told you sooner."

"But—" Pax could hardly see Creo's face through the tears brimming in her eyes. "You're still my dad."

"Of course I am." Creo hugged her tightly. "You're my daughter, Pax. I love you."

Manus stared up from where he was still kneeling on the floor. "You are the rightful heir. They feel it in their blood. They are waiting for you."

"Who?" Pax only just managed to speak.

Manus extended a badly blistered hand and pointed out of the window.

With the wind whipping against her hair, Pax stepped carefully towards the edge, broken glass crunching beneath her feet, with Creo, Venefica and Miles standing by her side. Silently they watched as a ripple cascaded through the masses below. Slowly, the crowd of Supremos started to kneel. At first, one by one, then by their hundreds. All bowing down – an entire city on its knees.

Underneath the Blood Moon, a noise rumbled – the sound of a thousand voices unifying. Growing louder, stronger until, finally, Pax could understand the chant echoing through the bloodied streets of Rubra.

"All hail the queen!"

GLOSSARY

Alchemist: Someone who transforms things for the better using science & magic

Ambigram: a word or design that retains its meaning from different perspectives

Amulet: A charm inscribed with a magical incantation to offer protection

Azalea: Pink wildflowers

Bio Aux: Sources of science that harness the power of nature

Borage: An edible plant with delicate blue flowers

Bovis: The meat of cattle

Bunglebots: small slithering creatures that predict the future by drawing messages in the sand

Calamus: A foliage with thick roots that give off a spicy scent

Calva: Crushed dragon's bone

Catnip: A strong-smelling plant loved by Dragats

Caro: The food source of the Supremo Gen

Castellum: The main castle of Rubra home to the Royal Supremo Gens

Cellarium: The under croft in the lower levels of the Castellum

Cetus Whale: A large water mammal with a sorrowful sound

Coven: A group or family of Witches

Crus: An artificial limb connected to muscle and bone. Made from light, strong metal

Dragat: small flying creature with both feline and dragon genes

Elm: A type of tree commonly found in the forest of Viridis

Evanescence: Magical transportation

Fabasucus: A type of bean harvested for both food and fuel. Crushed and boiled to make the popular drink referred to as 'Faba'

Figo: Slang term used by younger Gens for something likeable

Gen: the race or ethnicity of a person

Herba: A type of plant with slow burning qualities

Hex: A curse

Hiraeth: A longing for a place that never was

Hydra: Organisms dwelling in caves

Ichor: Blood of the Gods

Mercenary: Warriors paid in gold for their fighting skills

Messis: A celebration of the Supremo Gen that happens twice yearly, under each blood moon

Nid: Social outcast

Nucleus: The central organism of a Bio Aux

Oculus: A bowl of enchanted gold that reveals visions to its owner

Omnis: Light source

Ortus: A celebration day when Gens gain their magical power

Peonies: A flower with thousands of blooming petals

Pegasus: An enormous equine mammal with a pure black coat and large wings

Pyrios: A powerful equine mammal with a pure white coat and flaming manes

Quick Salt: sinking salt the is unstable to walk on

Saccharo: Sweet delicacies local to Scandza

Salis: Positively charged salt with magical qualities

Scuttleberry: Purplish berries favoured by Velox Fairies

Sui Generis: Of its own kind, completely unique

Tavern: Local gathering place providing food and drink

Tellus: The world we live in

Tentamenta: Thick eel-like creatures found in the rivers of Tellus

Tricorn: A powerful archosaur with three large horns

Trog: Large dangerous cave dwelling arachnids with no eyes

Umor: Tears of the Gods

Velox: A mischievous fairy breed that releases a harmless glitter

Vespa: A rather large angry wasp

Water Goblin: Scaly reptiles found in the lakes of Scanzda

Water Nymph: Beautiful, rare magical creatures that reside in the waters of Lake Scandza

Willow: A tree rarely found in Tellus, with long weeping branches

GENS OF TELLUS

Ethereal: A heavenly Gen with powerful blood and the ability to work with all of the mighty creatures in Tellus, believed to have died out.

Novus: Artificially Made Gens who have left behind lives of servitude

Piscator: A Gen living and fishing along the rivers and lakes of Tellus

Probus: A Gen responsible for farming the lands of Tellus, often found working with Tricorns.

Silva: Hailing from Viridis and the surrounding forest often gifted with powers relating to the natural world, including creating and harnessing Bio Aux.

Supremo: The most dominant Gen in Tellus, located in the city of Rubra. Considered to be Gods and ruled by a royal bloodline.

Tribus: Large Warriors blessed with extraordinary strength hailing from Scanzda

LOCATIONS IN THE WORLD OF TELLUS

Caligo Caves: Found behind Cataracta Waterfall and the habitat of Trogs and Hydra

Cataracta Waterfall: Located along the River Capio

Celare: A realm hidden inside Tellus home to covens of Witches

Lake Scandza: A central life force to the whole of Tellus, joined by four rivers: River Indo and River Addo flowing in, and River Rapina and River Capio flowing out

Levis: Located high in the atmosphere and dependent on weather conditions

Nusquam: Home of the Two-Faced God

Ramble Glen: A neutral land in the forests beyond Scandza, home to wild Dragnats

Rubra: The largest city in Tellus, home of the Supremos

Salt Plains: A barren land of Quick Salt, located through a portal from Nusquam

Scandza: A fertile land of Geysers surrounded by mountains. Local Gens trade in the daily markets and where the popular Tavern, The Hungry Dragon is located.

Sepultus: Also known as the dragon's graveyard, located near to Rubra.

Ultra: A home to the Novus Gen, movable, powered by Bio Aux and shielded by an invisible forcefield.

Viridis: A forest location made up of many villages home to Silva & Probus Gens.

Walda Woods: a forest near the centre of Tellus.

ACKNOWLEDGEMENTS

Thank you to my publishers, Cranthorpe Millner, especially Amy, Victoria & Jenna, for taking a chance on an unknown writer and making a dream come true!

Taylor for being my sounding board, telling me when things are cringe, naming *that* character & being the best niece and friend I could ask for.

My friend Megan, the human equivalent of sunshine, for your unwavering enthusiasm.

My sister Carla for her unconditional love, support & realism!

My mother, Pauline, my biggest supporter and best friend.

My Melbourne family, I miss you! Even when I'm far away, you're always in my thoughts. And to all my lovely friends & family who have supported me along the way, thank you so much.

A huge shout out to all my Booktokers over on TikTok – I have endless gratitude to so many people I've never met IRL!

Lastly and most importantly, to the readers. I hope you love this world and these characters as much as I do and that this book provides you with the same escapism it did for me when I needed it most. This story now belongs to you.

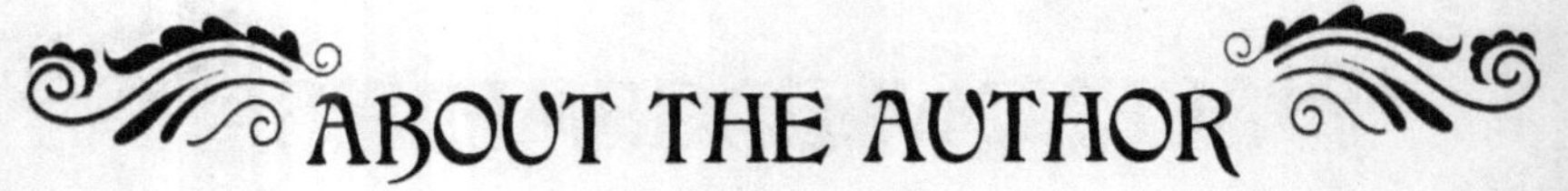

ABOUT THE AUTHOR

Tamara Price is a primary school teacher who has loved writing stories since she received her first typewriter at age eight. Originally from Wales, she has travelled extensively across the world, finding endless inspiration for her writing. An avid reader, Tamara runs a book club in Hay-on Wye, and often reviews books on her TikTok.

Keep up to date on all things *The Alchemist's Daughter* by following Tamara on socials:

Instagram: @tamarapriceauthor
Threads: @tamarapriceauthor
TikTok: @tamarapriceauthor